Also by Dominique Sylvain in English translation

The Dark Angel
Shadows and Sun

DIRTY WAR

Dominique Sylvain

Translated from the French by
Nick Caistor

MACLEHOSE PRESS
QUERCUS · LONDON

First published in the French language as *Guerre Sale*
by Éditions Viviane Hamy, Paris, in 2011
First published in Great Britain in 2015 by MacLehose Press
This paperback edition published in 2016 by

MacLehose Press
an imprint of Quercus Editions Ltd
Carmelite House
50 Victoria Embankment
London EC4Y 0DZ

An Hachette UK Company

This book is supported by the Institut français (Royaume-Uni)
as Part of the Burgess Programme
(www.frenchbooknews.com)

INSTITUT
FRANÇAIS

Designed Columbus by Patty Rennie
Typeset by Jouve (UK), Milton Keynes
Printed and bound in Great Britain by Clays Ltd, St Ives plc

TO FRANK

HE PRESENTED HIS SON TO THE MEN OF
WAR, RECOMMENDING HIM AS HIS
SUCCESSOR AND HEIR

Demetrios

You're arriving on the next train. I'm waiting on the platform for you with all the villagers.

Don't tell me you're surprised. Did you think I was going to forget you? No chance. If I'm here, it's because of you.

Even the young tearaways, the junkies who love a fight, are quiet, ranged along the fence. They know your reputation: a tough guy you only cross if you're feeling very lucky. They told me so when I shared their weed. Can you imagine? A policeman smoking with tearaways, you'd have had a field day with a story like that.

It's a shame you're dead, otherwise you could have written it.

Respectful for once, the junkies say nothing, avoid throwing their tales of sorcery in our faces. Not even they believe them. They know you were killed for a reason that has nothing to do with the devil. They've come because they want to find out more. You know what I think? I agree with them.

Every conversation revolves around you. I'm the only one who can hear you, who can tell you what's on my mind. I used to leave talking with the dead to the old gossips, but today it's different, a door has opened in my spirit. A shame I already know the legend you're telling me. It's the weed, it makes me go round and round like a donkey, your nonsense rattling round my brain:

> *This is the story of a caliph who sees his vizier running towards him in panic.*
> *He has met Death at the marketplace. A tall thin woman wearing a red scarf*

looked at him strangely, freezing his blood. He begs the caliph to lend him his best horse so that he can flee as far away as possible, to Samarkand. The caliph values his vizier, and so permits him to saddle up the horse and ride away like the wind: he is hoping to reach Samarkand before nightfall.

Your train arrives. The carriages creak, come to a standstill. The passengers from Kinshasa find it impossible to set foot on this platform laden with sorrow. The station master begs the crowd to stand back. The junkies join in, they insult the "stupid sheep", tell them to clear a path.

The men from the funeral parlour push you into the sunlight. Your cousins and I grab the handles on your coffin. On our shoulders, you seem far lighter than I had imagined. Some women weep. You're pleased at these signs of physical grief, the gnashing of pearly white teeth, aren't you? I'm sure you are, don't try to tell me a story. Or rather, go on with the one you were telling me. I know it by heart, but it's good to hear your voice, and I'm sure that in the end I'll understand what you're trying to say to me:

Concerned, the caliph dons a disguise, heads for the market, and searches for Death. He sees her; she fits his vizier's description exactly: tall, skinny, her face partly hidden beneath a red veil, slipping among the crowds unnoticed. The caliph goes up to her. Death bows to him.

"I have a question for you," says the caliph in a low voice.

"I'm listening."

"My first vizier is still youthful and full of health. He is efficient, probably honest. Why did you scare him this morning at the market?"

We lay the coffin in the jeep pulled up in front of the station. As tradition dictates, a palm-tree leaf has been draped across the windscreen. I see Papa Wonda and his musicians. Your favourite singer has come with his mother, the country's greatest wailer, in a splendid white robe. Her face is solemn, as befits this solemn day. The village headman circles round her: how can he address such a great lady? Madame Wonda is going to weep for you: do you realise the honour you are being paid? The last time I heard her wailing was at a minister's funeral. What a privilege, my friend!

The jeep travels at walking pace to your parents' house. We follow it, our shoes white with dust. At first light, the April rain was lashing the roofs; since then, the weather has been on your side. The grey was wiped away, the earth dried out, the light has taken on the transparency of a perfect day. You are parading through a brand-new world, brother; I wish I could lend you my eyes to see it with.

The cortège arrives. We carry you into the old house. The blades of the ceiling fans stir the atmosphere, heavy with the smell of stew and rice. The women have been cooking all night; I helped them, so I know what I'm talking about, even though I was drunk. I had made a detour via old Naomi's store. Naomi no longer has any teeth, but there's nothing wrong with her mind: she wanted to sell me her shop. It was her palm wine that interested me. The colour of pale moss on a rough stone, with a hint of acidity: I thought I had forgotten the taste.

We lay you down on a mat. The village headman makes a speech. He tries to cover all your achievements, gets muddled up in his anecdotes. A junkie laughs, digs his friends in the side. Everybody is relieved when the speechifying is done and Madame Wonda spreads her arms and starts to weep. Her assistants pour their warm rivers of tears on your memory as though they had known you for a thousand years. One of the young mourners is beautiful: I wish I could lend you my skin so that you could brush against hers.

I move from one group to another, listening. You are praised to the skies, you are their hero. Killed for freedom. I don't agree, but take care not to get involved. Instead, I listen to you finishing your silly story:

Surprised, Death replies:

"Caliph, I did not mean to frighten him. Your vizier and I bumped into each other in the crowd. I didn't give him a threatening look, I was simply astonished."

"Why were you astonished?"

"Because I didn't expect to see him here . . . I have an appointment with him tomorrow night in Samarkand . . ."

Samarkand, Samarkand. Forget Samarkand, Norbert. Are you trying to tell me that the vizier is an idiot? But you're the one who had no sense, my friend. You should have fled without demanding your share. In recent years, several of your colleagues have died, and the river of blood isn't about to dry up. Yet destiny had given you a warning. How many men are that lucky? Tell me how many, go on. Just give me a figure. You don't reply. I can understand that. That figure is the zero of the infinite. You should have died in the first attack, if those hooded bastards had done their job. You want me to tell you a good story? Then shut up and listen.

You had no chance, but a god offered you one. A god, not a skinny old hag. He must have been as drunk on wine and weed as I was, because he muddled things up. Those guys had failed once, but they were sure to be back. The god whispered to you to flee from there. You didn't have to make any detour to Samarkand, Kinshasa or Timbuktu. But you got the scripts confused. You told him that if you were going to die, it might just as well happen at home. You were hoping you would see the red scarf again without trembling.

You're not a hero, you're vain. Here's your sister. Myriam can't understand it any more than I can. She wanted you to take the first plane out of here. She told you so, but you wouldn't listen. It was written, so what was the point?

That won't do.

In fact, you know about as much as that baby your neighbour is carrying on her back. No more than him.

"Aren't you eating, Toussaint?"

"Thanks, but I'm not hungry."

"You ought to eat something; you spent the night drinking . . ."

Your sister is right, of course. Myriam is always right. But you couldn't care less, Norbert Konata, the greatest journalist of Congo-Kinshasa and the whole of Africa put together. It seems Papa Wonda couldn't care less either, because his music drowns out Myriam and her advice. His sing-song voice hypnotises the mourners. Soon some of the women start to move gently, their robes swaying. They are not dancing, not really, although they would like to. Perhaps that would be the best way to say farewell to you. Such a shame you're dead, friend, oh yes, a real shame. Otherwise you could have danced with them to Papa Wonda. But I'm going to tell you the truth. Even though his band is incredibly good, they cannot wake the dead, asleep in their fine coffins or buried in the cracked earth. That's the way it goes.

Yes, the dead sleep deeply, Toussaint my friend, and yet they also set off afar in the hope that . . .

You talk and talk, Norbert, but you say nothing. Who did you upset? What powerful man did you make dance in your frying pan of words?

If I were you, I'd use that damned Papa Wonda and steal his voice. Instead of his "past which will blossom anew" and his "friendship that will never die", I would sing of violence. I would sing of the faces hidden in hoods, their methods and reasons. I would name names. And here you are telling me that Destiny had an appointment with you that you had no way of refusing?

I'm not one to swallow your legends.

You too will have an appointment there one day, Toussaint . . .

A load of crap.

You too one day . . .

And now, if you won't give me a face or a name, for God's sake, Norbert Konata, the greatest journalist of Congo-Kinshasa and the whole of Africa put together, just shut up, will you? . . .

1 PIERRE-LAGRAVÈRE DEPARTMENTAL PARK, COLOMBES

Nose pressed against the windscreen, foot to the floor, Sébastien Ménard managed to read the sign through the liquid wall. He plunged down the slip-road off the A86. Sacha Duguin ordered him to slow down. The lieutenant allowed himself a sly smile. With his three-day beard and tousled hair, Ménard was a dandy straight out of the Politics faculty, a young smartass who had seen too many crime series on television.

Emmanuelle Carle was playing her Zen master role, hands stuffed in the sadness of her perennial beige coat. It was as if no upheaval of sky or man could impinge on her, and yet Sacha Duguin felt that the slightest sign of irritation on his part was taken down in an invisible notebook she would not hesitate to produce deliberately at the right moment. *If the general grows angry, his authority can easily be shaken.* Captain Carle could have written Sun Tzu's *The Art of War* for him.

Stoical beneath the stormy sky, two gendarmes stood guard in front of the building with the Olympic pool. Ménard responded airily to their military salute and swung the Renault in next to the Crime Scene Unit's van. Opening her door first, Carle strode quickly towards the building. *In a military campaign, be as swift as the wind.*

Ménard was already fishing his notebook and pen out of his jacket and beginning his note-taking. Vehicles, topography, architecture at the scene, timetables and organisation, remote surveillance, security patrols, meteorological conditions – nothing escaped the stickler for procedure on the Duguin team. His responsibility was to fold the world into tiny pieces; something that suited his obsessive nature perfectly. Origami as the response to disorder.

Squalls of wind were making the entrance-porch door shake, but the smell had penetrated the walls with the force of a biblical plague. Charred flesh and melted rubber. Chalky-faced, dressed in overalls, two men were answering the gendarme captain's questions. He cast an eye over Carle and Sacha, puzzled by a question of rank when he saw that the junior officer was ten years or so older than her boss. Sacha put an end to the suspense:

"Commandant Sacha Duguin, *Brigade Criminelle*. Can you fill us in?"

The body had been found by the cleaners – the two men here, beside the main pool. A briefcase stuffed with documents, a raincoat with a wallet containing 400 euros and I.D. papers. These revealed that the dead man was Florian Vidal, aged 32, address Rue de Vaugirard, in the 6th arrondissement of Paris. This was more or less the information Sacha had been given earlier that morning on the telephone. In the intervening period, he had checked on the victim: a business lawyer, a man on the up. So he was a V.I.P., and the local gendarmes had called in the B.C.

The gendarme held out a sealed package containing the victim's identity card. Sacha studied the features of a fair-haired man with a prominent nose and powerful neck. Bushy eyebrows, light, deep-set eyes, square jawed. An interesting mugshot.

"Given the state he's in now, it's hard to imagine it's the same man," said the gendarme, after a quick glance in Ménard's direction.

Sacha could guess what he was thinking: that youngster is going to puke his guts up when he sees the body. He doesn't know Ménard and the powers of his little notebook.

The two men from the cleaning company repeated their story for the new arrivals. Alerted by the smell, they had ventured as far as the Olympic pool and had discovered a black heap under the diving board. At first they had thought it was a refuse bag that "some kids had set on fire for fun". When they got closer, they realised it was a man's body. And were able to confirm that he must have suffered a horror nobody would have wished on their worst enemy.

Sacha and his team followed the gendarme captain to the changing rooms, where they put on polypropylene suits and vinyl gloves. In this white-tiled environment, Sacha glanced at his colleagues: the woman's saturnine face, the man's smile from Mars. Their Michelin-man garb only increased the sense of an encounter of the third kind, with decidedly hostile aliens.

"Any sign of a break-in?" asked Carle.

"The porch at the back of the building. The padlock has been sawn off."

Sacha surveyed some muddy parallel grooves on the ground, and a footprint marked by the crime scene people's yellow flags. He imagined someone pulling along his doped victim, his heels scraping the tiles. A continuous line. No sign of a struggle. Later, the same man left the same way, all alone.

A trough of muddy water separated the changing rooms from the pools. Someone had laid a plank across it as a bridge. On the far side, the traces were still visible, but fainter. Perched up on the diving board, a technician was taking photos. His colleague was sweeping the bluish waters of the pool with a net on the end of a long pole. Two other men were checking for possible fingerprints and D.N.A.

samples. Sacha wished them luck: crime scenes rarely came in such Olympic proportions.

Sacha knew that as he drew near the body he was entering a zone of horrific cruelty. He had realised this from the first telephone call: you had to be an absolute sadist to set a man on fire right next to a swimming pool, making it obvious there was no chance for him to save himself by jumping off the diving board. The victim was lying in the foetal position. He was handcuffed behind his back, and the cuffs were chained to one of the board's supports. The poor guy had been burned alive with a flaming tyre round his neck.

"Shit, that's original!" Ménard said, kneeling beside the corpse.

The gendarme captain exchanged looks with Duguin. If he was suggesting that a good kick up the backside was in order, he wasn't wrong. But Sacha overlooked this typical outburst from the lieutenant and approached the body himself.

The head, neck, and the top of the shoulders were charred and shrivelled. It reminded him of a Giacometti sculpture. Dried out, despairing. The rubber of the tyre had melted with the flesh to form a sticky tar. The eyes were nothing more than dark holes; the mouth an oven of gaping terror. The man must have screamed until his lungs burst. But in a covered pool in the middle of a deserted park, who could hear him? Ménard went over to the glass wall giving on to bushes and trees whipped by the storm. A footpath snaked its way through it, with two lamp-posts that distance turned into small twigs. The deluge dissuaded any possible joggers or walkers. The night had the same effect.

According to the pathologist with the crime scene team, death had occurred about six hours earlier. Three o'clock in the morning then. The killer must have known the cleaners would not arrive before half past six. One part of the equation was missing: the time he got here.

If he had drugged his prisoner, he must have waited for him to come round. And he could have toyed with him for a long time before setting him alight. It was up to Ménard to find any witnesses. A homeless person camping out, a night-worker, a providential insomniac. Not a very promising prospect. The park was a narrow strip between the River Seine and the motorway; there were sports complexes and a few industrial units close by, but no houses.

An empty petrol can had been found. It was probably used to sprinkle over the tyre. The dead man's chest and limbs were much less damaged than the rest. There were traces of blood around the wrists. The poor guy must have struggled like a lunatic.

To judge by the parts that had been spared, he was well-built. And definitely well-off. Tailored suit, expensive shoes, a Cartier watch considered as equally unimportant as the 400 euros in the wallet.

"Are we sure he is Vidal?" asked Sacha.

"Positive," the pathologist said. "My colleague compared the victim's fingerprints with those on the contents of the briefcase."

"I called the lawyer's secretary," the gendarme added. "Her boss had a meeting at eight o'clock this morning. She hadn't seen him since the previous day, and so spoke to his wife, Nadine Vidal. She said her husband left home in Rue de Vaugirard the previous evening. By the way, who is going to tell his widow? You or us, Commandant?"

Sacha replied that he would do it, then went over to Carle. She was surveying the contents of the crocodile-skin attaché-case: expensive pen, a bunch of keys, another single key on a Porsche ring, a packet of nicotine patches, a plastic case full of business cards. She handed him one: *Florian Vidal, Legal and Commercial Law, 35 Rue de Seine, 75006 Paris.* An email address, and two telephone numbers.

"No mobile or computer in such a smart briefcase?"

"Apparently not, boss."

He undid his jacket and slipped the card into the inside pocket. He turned towards the body. Ménard was not entirely wide of the mark. The *modus operandi* was original: it was definitely exotic. The "burning necklace" was an African invention, later used in Haiti. But where Ménard was wrong was in thinking it had never been used before in the Paris region. Sacha remembered the young man who had died a few years earlier close to the city with a flaming tyre round his neck. But that had not been a lawyer. It had been a police officer.

He knew Carle would be making the comparison. The young lieutenant's agony was branded on all their memories. Yet she was sure to keep quiet about it until the right moment arrived. *All warfare is based on deception.*

Ménard was back, a smile on his lips. He was like an explorer with a knapsack weighed down with all the diamonds of Botswana and Zimbabwe.

"It's Africa in the heart of Colombes, boss. Those in the know call it Père Lebrun's Necklace. A technique that was in vogue in Haiti during the time of the *tontons macoute*. A tyre, petrol, a match, and the show is served up hot to the lovers of that kind of thing. The custom seems to have started in Soweto, where it was one of the favourite punishments dished out to robbers. Do you know the radical anti-apartheid rallying cry?"

Sacha waited patiently for him to finish. Carle was as unmoving as a menhir; the gendarme captain had the hypnotised look of a hare caught in the headlights of a runaway truck.

" . . . 'With our boxes of matches and our necklaces, we shall liberate this country.' That was one of Winnie Mandela's favourite phrases. As for the former Belgian Congo, have you heard about that? Before Zaire became the Democratic Republic of Congo, also known as Congo-Kinshasa to distinguish it from Congo-Brazzaville, or the Republic of

Congo – yes, I know, these decolonisation stories are a bit complicated – Père Lebrun's Necklace was the method of lynching reserved in Kinshasa for the last few who remained loyal to the dictator Mobutu . . ."

Duguin's mobile began to vibrate in his pocket like a faithful friend. Relieved, he stepped away from the others. Arnaud Mars' name flashed up on the screen. The big chief had an impeccable sense of timing.

"How far have you got, Sacha?"

He liked the divisionnaire's tone and easy manner. He had got on with his superior from the outset, and was sure the feeling was mutual. Mars showed his trust by giving him the most delicate cases. The Vidal affair was proof of that. Sacha gave him a brief report.

"The name Vidal means only one thing: relations between France and Africa," said Mars. "A business lawyer specialising in arms contracts. In other words, heavy stuff."

"And political too."

"Exactly. Which means we have to be careful where we tread."

"There's another problem, boss."

"I'm listening."

"Five years ago, a young police lieutenant died the same way."

"Yes, I remember. The affair caused a real stink. O.K., get on with it and we'll speak again soon. Today is back-to-back meetings for me. Clémenti is starting on an important case. Doris Nungesser has killed her son's murderer. And escaped."

"Nungesser, that very media-friendly auctioneer?"

"And the ex-wife of a chief of staff in a ministry. In other words, we're treading on eggshells there too. But that's what we're here for, isn't it? Come and have a bite to eat at home this evening. We can catch up then. Agreed?"

"Of course, chief."

Sacha returned to the group. Ménard was still speechifying for the benefit of the gendarme captain, who must have been wondering about the B.C.'s recruitment policies. Carle was talking to the man scouring the swimming pool, who had just scooped a BlackBerry from the bottom. Florian Vidal's connections had swallowed a mouthful.

"You're going to have to revive it," said Sacha. "You can dry out the S.I.M. card, can't you?"

"Impossible," the technician said.

"Why?"

"It's vanished."

Carle and the man were obviously asking themselves the same questions. Why had the killer left the phone but removed its memory? Was he throwing them a bone, only to snatch it away again? Sacha did not like to jump to conclusions, but there were two things he linked. First, the arsonist had not bothered to rob the victim of his possessions. And second, he seemed to be immediately opening a dialogue with the police. Arrogance and a taste for provocation. A mixture every bit as explosive as the petrol he had splashed over the face of his scapegoat.

"Methodical . . . and perverse," Carle muttered, as if to herself.

"Yes, we're dealing with a bastard who thinks of everything, and quickly," Sacha said. "All the more reason to do the same. You take the patrol car and make for the Forensic Institute."

She looked at him enquiringly.

"Besiege them until you get Thomas Franklin to carry out an emergency autopsy."

"Why Franklin?"

"Because he's the best."

Of course, she didn't believe a word of it. Although Franklin was a veteran pathologist, he was no better qualified than anyone else.

Sacha flashed her a smile. Carle stared at him a moment, then went to get the keys for the Renault from Ménard, and drove off without another word.

Arrive like the wind and leave like lightning . . .

2

Lola Jost was giving her cupboard a hard time. She was pulling out old boxes, rummaging inside them, then starting again on others, muttering to herself all the time. Sigmund was watching from a safe distance, now and then allowing himself an inquisitive bark. The neighbourhood analyst's dog was worried what his guardian was up to.

"Aha! Here's those damned rubber boots at last!" roared Lola, holding up her trophy. "We're going to need them to go out into that storm, aren't we, my boy?"

Fresh yaps, more plaintive this time, from the noble animal. He could sense that the unthinkable was about to happen. Lola was going to leave their comfortable little nest and launch herself into the deluge, and no man or dog could make her change her mind.

"We've been stuck in here for ages. Antoine will give me hell if I don't make you get some exercise. Besides, your spots aren't going to wash off, are they? Obviously I could make you a coat out of a plastic bag, but you wouldn't like that, would you?"

She donned the old pair of boots she had found, the raincoat and hat that her friend Ingrid Diesel had given her for her birthday, and put the lead on Sigmund, ignoring his resistance. Soon the pair of them found themselves in Rue de l'Échiquier confronting slanting squalls of rain. Lola steered a course for her favourite restaurant.

As she came in through the door of Belles, its proprietor and chef was polishing glasses. Lola took this as a sign.

"Good thinking, I could do with a glass of the house white."

Without a word of protest, Maxime Duchamp put two glasses on the counter and filled them with a *muscat* from Beaumes-de-Venise. Then he used a towel to dry off Sigmund, who licked his hand in gratitude.

"Your *muscat*'s not bad, and it's a real pleasure to see a human face again," Lola said, rubbing her lower back.

"What's wrong?"

"The same as with everyone in Paris. This damned rain all the time. On top of that, Antoine Léger has headed for the sun with his family and left me in charge of Sigmund. Before I only had my rheumatism to worry about, now I have responsibilities too. Can I have a bowl?"

"Of course, but what for?"

"Sigmund may be four-legged, but that doesn't mean he has to have his snout always in the gutter. He has to acquire some spiritual elevation . . . . Do you know what Théopile de Busarque has to say on the subject?"

"No," said an amused Maxime.

"*Wine is a cloud of knowledge that only rains on those who are in love with existence.* That's what I call a thought that's both light and profound."

Lola sloshed *muscat* into the bowl. The Dalmatian sniffed at the strange brew.

"This animal will have its doors of perception opened an inch or two before his master returns. If not, I despair of the canine race. Along with all the others."

Just at that moment, the door to the restaurant opened. Captain

Jérôme Barthélemy came in, looking grim. Catching sight of Lola did nothing to improve his mood.

"That's nice. You're scowling at me as if I was your income tax inspector."

"It's not that, boss. In fact, I was looking for you. But deep down, I'm not so sure I'm glad to have found you."

Lola Jost had not been in charge of the local police station for a long time, but her former colleague still behaved as though nothing had changed. She was and always would be his "boss". She just had to get used to it. On the other hand, the ex-commissaire couldn't follow anything of what her ex-deputy was trying to say.

"Don't make such hard work of it, my boy. Try to make sense."

"The body of a young Parisian lawyer has been found. A murder."

"Where?"

"In Colombes. The Olympic pool."

"Drowned?"

"Burned alive with petrol, and . . ."

"And?"

"He had a tyre . . . round his neck."

Lola put her glass down. For a split second that dragged out to infinity, Maxime's and Barthélemy's faces wobbled like balloons. Lola allowed herself to slide to the tiled floor. She was going to pass out, so she might as well be horizontal.

Her friends' voices came to her through a wall of dirty cotton wool as she keeled over. They were shouting her name.

*

He had called to say he was coming. She was waiting for him on the landing, mouth quavering, denial etched all over her face. A small, slender blonde woman of around thirty. Sharp features that anguish made bleary.

"You're not here about Florian, are you? . . . Nothing's happened to him, has it?"

"We found your husband in Colombes."

"Is he . . . dead?"

"Yes, he is. I'm really sorry."

She threw herself at him and started to beat his chest. He seized her hands, found some soothing words, let her sob against him while he put his arm round her. She went back inside the apartment, numb with shock; he saw a black suitcase in the entrance hall. The sitting room stank of cigarettes but had a wonderful view of the façades of the Senate and the Luxembourg Garden, blurred by the rain. Nadine Vidal's silhouette stood out against a tall window; she was still crying, her face pressed against the glass. The muffled sound of traffic from five floors below. A miniature woman in a big, empty apartment. Sacha wondered if the couple had any children.

How had her husband died? Sacha suggested she sit down. She refused, and repeated her question. He told her. When the words really hit Nadine Vidal, she rushed out into the kitchen to vomit in the sink. He tried to support her; she shrugged him off.

She got her breath back, splashed her face with water.

She agreed to sit down, lit a cigarette with trembling hands. He questioned her gently. Her husband had received a call the previous evening. He had gone out around half past seven without saying where he was going, but promising to be back before eleven. That morning his car was not in the car park.

"Do you know who called him?"

"Florian hardly ever talked to me about business."

"Really?"

"He worked for Richard Gratien."

Sacha knew Gratien by reputation. A key player in France–Africa relations, friendly with the bigwigs at the Quai d'Orsay and the Defence Ministry. A qualified lawyer with no great track record but apparently essential: a *middleman*. In the arms business.

"Was it him your husband had an appointment with this morning?"

"Yes."

"Any problems between them?"

"I don't think so."

"Was Richard Gratien involved in something sensitive?"

"All his deals are."

"Was your husband in court on a case at the moment?"

"Florian wasn't a barrister. His job was to draw up contracts in commercial exchanges, to oil the wheels."

She took a deep breath, closed her eyes an instant. Her hands were still trembling.

"Did he seem particularly tense recently?"

"No."

"Any other private calls? Unusual appointments? A spot of bother perhaps?"

She shook her head. He promised to do all he could to find her husband's killer, but she had to help.

"You don't seem to think much of Gratien."

She made no reply.

"Why is that?" insisted Sacha.

"Florian lived in his shadow. When we first met at law school . . . Florian was already working for him."

"What did he do?"

"He helped out. I think he was already involved in drawing up contracts."

"What kind of relations did they have beyond the purely professional?"

"Gratien paid for our wedding."

"Didn't your husband get on with his own family?"

"Florian and his mother no longer saw each other."

"Since when?"

"For years."

Anger in her eyes now. He gave her time to get what she had to say off her chest.

"I kept on telling him to get a life of his own. He was starting to listen to me. It was a tough decision. It's not easy to turn your back on all that money. Besides . . ."

"Besides what?"

"You can't thank someone like Gratien and just walk away."

"Why's that?"

"He's like vampire with those close to him. So you have to get as far away as possible. My idea was to start again from scratch . . ."

"Meaning . . . ?"

"To go abroad, so we could both work in an international law practice."

"You're a lawyer too?"

"A criminal lawyer with a leading Parisian firm. I've worked hard to get where I am, postponed my desire to have children . . . But this time I was ready to quit."

"Did your husband talk to Gratien about your plans?"

"No, that was between the two of us. I was the one who kept coming back to it. I thought that over time . . ."

"I saw a case in the hallway. Were you about to go away?"

"In the middle of the night, after leaving ten messages on Florian's phone, I was furious . . ."

"Tell me more."

"We both worked like mad in our own careers. We hardly saw each other. It was becoming ridiculous . . ."

"You wanted to teach him a lesson?"

"To get away for a few days without warning him, to go and stay with a female friend, pay him back in kind. I was so stupid . . ."

Tears again. He found a box of tissues and handed them to her. He spotted a crumpled scrap of something on the floor. He unfolded it: a nicotine patch. Vidal's briefcase had several in it.

"Are you sure your husband didn't come back in the night?"

"That patch is mine. When it seemed Florian was not coming back, I had a cigarette . . ."

"Did your husband know Toussaint Kidjo, a police lieutenant of African origin?"

"I don't think so."

"Kidjo died five years ago."

"What has he got to do with my husband?"

It took her some time to digest his explanation.

"Does the name really not mean anything to you?"

"No."

"Lieutenant Sébastien Ménard is the procedural expert in my team. I'd like him to be given access to your husband's personal papers. In other words, to his office on Rue de Seine."

"When?"

"As soon as possible."

"Phone your colleague. We may as well get it over with."

Sacha called Ménard and instructed him to come to Rue de Vaugirard.

"Has Richard Gratien called since the missed appointment this morning?"

"He hasn't stopped. I ended up unplugging the phone. I had no wish to . . ."

"Could you give me his personal details?"

Vidal's office looked out over an inner courtyard surrounded by centuries-old trees that absorbed the sunlight. On the marble fireplace stood several African statues: warriors with shells for eyes and skulls bristling with feathers. They looked as if they were standing guard.

"Did your husband use email?"

"Of course."

"I can't see a computer. Did he use the one at his office?"

"He had a laptop, but mostly he used his BlackBerry. His secretary, Alice Bernier, takes care of the longer mails."

Nadine Vidal tapped in the combination of a safe, took out a large, shiny address book, found an address and a mobile number and wrote them down for Sacha.

"May I?" he asked, pointing to the book.

She handed it to him. It contained hundreds of numbers written in meticulous handwriting.

Kidjo's number was not among them.

*

He met Alice Bernier at the Rue de Seine office. It took her some time to register what had happened, and then she could not hold back tears. When Sacha questioned her about the relationship between Vidal and his wife, she described them as a close-knit couple, but added that Nadine must suffer from her husband's many absences. She made no fuss about opening her diary, and showed him her boss' business timetable. Endless appointments and dinners, frequent trips to Africa. The last had been a fortnight earlier: Vidal had gone to Abidjan and Yaoundé, accompanying Gratien. No conflict or threat that she could recall.

Sacha gave her the address book and asked her to put a job description alongside each name, or to indicate the kind of relationship the young lawyer had with them. She promised to scan and send him the information as soon as possible.

Had Gratien been in touch after Vidal's disappearance? She confirmed he had called at regular intervals. He had seemed concerned: it was not like Vidal to miss an appointment. As for the nicotine patches found in her boss' briefcase, she confirmed that he had been trying to give up smoking for several months.

"And his wife?"

"They had decided to give up together."

3

The clerk made him fill in a form to take the dossier out. He chose the desk next to the window. The purple sky was spreading a lake of anthracite-coloured clouds. On the Left Bank, the roofs were welded into a silvery sheen.

Sacha had not forgotten the name: Toussaint Kidjo. Nor had he forgotten the place: Le Plessis-Robinson, to the south-west of Paris, a peaceful commune in Hauts-de-Seine department, like Colombes. That made the savagery meted out to the young lieutenant even more jarring.

For a while, the investigators had followed a possible neo-Nazi lead. But got nowhere. Kidjo had been of mixed race, a Frenchman of Congolese origin, born in Kinshasa: in the end a racial motive for the murder had been rejected. Despite a superhuman effort, the crime had never been cleared up. The last person to see Kidjo alive was someone called Aimé Bangolé, a stringer for several African newspapers and a well-known police informer.

His statement was as uncontroversial as could be. He declared that he had met Kidjo the morning of his death in their usual café, a few yards from the Saint-Louis hospital. The informer had told Kidjo about rumours concerning the burglary of an apartment in the area, owned by an African hair-stylist. She was going out with a musician, who had another life as a ganja dealer. And money problems he had hoped to solve by making his girlfriend pay. Bangolé's tip-off was a good one. It had eventually led Kidjo's colleagues to put away the musician.

One woman had moved heaven and earth to try to uncover the truth about Toussaint's death: Lola Jost. At the time, the lieutenant was working under her at the police station in the 10th arrondissement. All the leads had turned out to be dead ends, but the commissaire had been stubborn as a mule, using her officers to continue the search for months. Her superiors had reined her in, arguing she was neglecting other cases and wasting taxpayers' money chasing shadows. Then all of a sudden Lola had left, slamming the door behind her, and not before she had dispensed a few choice remarks. Her departure, a year before her official retirement, must have been a relief to more than one in the hierarchy, and a blow to quite a few others, starting with the members of her team.

Lola was not easy to forget. Sacha had grown close to the ex-commissaire, and in particular to her best friend, the American Ingrid Diesel. That was a short but intense episode he thought he had relegated to a remote corner of his memory now that he was so busy in his new post. Who would have thought that Ingrid and Lola would come barging into his life again? He wasn't convinced this was good news.

He returned to his reading.

A municipal employee had discovered Toussaint's body in an abandoned mechanical engineering factory one October day that was as rainy as today was, so bad in fact it had been impossible to take any clear prints of car tyres. No I.D. papers, service Smith & Wesson missing, its holster found close by. It was only through dental records that the lieutenant had been identified. The lab had discovered a powerful sedative in his blood. Kidjo had been drugged, abducted, tortured and then killed with the same ferocity as he had witnessed at Colombes. The tyre round his neck had been doused with petrol, just as in the more recent murder.

One notable difference: the degree of torture inflicted before death. In Vidal's case, this seemed to have been purely mental. Kidjo though had been found half naked, chest and arms cut with a Stanley knife, and burnt with a blowtorch. Not to mention the mutilated fingers. If he had possessed information that interested his executioners, no trace had been found in the cases he was working on that could justify such ruthlessness.

Sacha reread the autopsy report signed by Thomas Franklin. He knew Carle would obey his orders to the letter, and eventually succeed in having Franklin conduct the autopsy on Vidal.

The best way of gaining time to compare the two homicides.

Recognising Carle's voice, Sacha interrupted his note-taking. She could not see him as she spoke to the desk clerk at reception: she wanted the Kidjo dossier. Sacha stood up to meet her, tucking the dossier under his arm. She hid her surprise. They walked in silence to his office. Mars' door was open; the divisionnaire was busy with Serge Clémenti, a commissaire Sacha thought highly of and got on well with. The two men were discussing the Nungesser case.

Sacha offered Carle a seat, placed the dossier on his desk, and went over to the window. Five floors below, the Seine was furiously churning greenish waves; the rain was so heavy it almost blotted out the looming mass of the Châtelet. Go on, explode like the storm, Carle, let's get it over with . . . or rather, let's start finally to work together. That was why he had kept the link with the Kidjo affair to himself: to get her to understand that even if he was the last to arrive in the B.C., he wasn't the worst.

In her big dirty beige coat she looked as huge and immovable as a boulder.

"Well?"

He pushed the Kidjo dossier towards her.

"Franklin will carry out the autopsy on Vidal tomorrow, boss. I did as you asked."

Beyond reproach, this officer Carle.

"And you've guessed why I wanted Franklin."

"He did the same for Kidjo."

Finally.

"The dossier's yours. But you can save time. I got the essential bits out of it. Photocopy my notes. There are plenty of points in common. Similar *modus operandi*, with a large dose of sadism, both isolated places, a few kilometres outside Paris, same time of year. Both victims in their thirties, both in professions related to the law. One born in Africa, the other devoting most of his professional life to it. But one thing is missing."

"Whether or not they knew each other."

"Correct. I want you to find Aimé Bangolé for me. One of Kidjo's informers. At the time, he was a freelance journalist and lived on Avenue de Clichy."

"I was thinking of questioning the Vidal widow with you. And then the secretary."

"I've done that already. Ménard is still with the widow."

She must have been thinking: instead of asking me to meet Nadine Vidal and Alice Bernier, I'm sent off to chase some miserable informer. He gave her a summary of what he had learned at Rue de Vaugirard.

"Nadine Vidal was pole-axed when she heard of her husband's death. But something isn't right."

He gave her the details. Angry at her husband's lateness, she wants to pay him back in kind, packs a suitcase, but finally decides not to leave. She is so anxious she takes up smoking again.

"According to his secretary, Vidal and his wife had been trying to stop for months. The lawyer was a hard worker. Nadine must have been used to him being late. So why was she so anxious she forgot about her little act of vengeance and began smoking again?"

"Because she couldn't get through to him on the phone?" suggested Carle. "Vidal was probably in the habit of calling her if he was late."

"But the secretary is adamant: Vidal was the kind of man who switched his mobile off so that he wouldn't be disturbed in his meetings. He met Gratien and their clients at any time of the day and night. Nothing unusual there for Nadine Vidal."

"You could have asked her straight out."

"I will when the time comes. Before that though, our target is Bangolé."

A shrug of the shoulders, an ironic smile: you're in charge, and I'm your humble slave.

I've got the job I've always dreamed of, and no wet blanket like you is going to put me off, his look was intended to convey in return.

"His evidence is too smooth. Find him for me. If necessary, take an inspector."

Carle picked up the dossier, and made to leave.

"You're forgetting my notes."

She turned back:

"I prefer to make my own mind up."

"Meaning?"

"All the details are important; your notes are too much of a filter. If need be, I'll finish reading the dossier tonight."

That's the first time I've been called a filter, thought Sacha as he dialled the public prosecutor's number. He filled him in on all the details of the investigation. The magistrate told him to be very careful with the press and announced that Judge Maxence would be leading the investigating team. That did not surprise Sacha. Benoît Maxence had a reputation for being extremely circumspect. Something that would not come amiss in the Vidal case.

4

From behind the window, the wine merchant was observing him. He had just parked in the store's delivery bay.

"We're expecting a delivery, monsieur . . ."

Sacha flashed his police credential, promised to be brief.

Could she be feeling a sense of *déja vu*? A police officer turning up without warning, ready to smash her existence to smithereens. Possibly in this very same store: she had already worked in the wine trade back then. Was it Lola who had interviewed her? Probably. She wasn't the sort to delegate tough tasks.

The press had not yet got wind of the Vidal affair, and so Sacha outlined the murder at Colombes. Adeline Ernaux was quick to spot the similarities.

"How can someone inflict such torture on another human being? I don't know where you get the strength to do your job."

Had she asked Toussaint Kidjo the same question when they lived together? She was wearing a wedding ring: she had made a new life for herself.

"Florian Vidal, a Paris lawyer – does the name mean anything to you?"

"Toussaint never mentioned him to me."

"Richard Gratien?"

"Who is he?"

"His employer, also a lawyer. A middleman specialising in arms trafficking."

"Doesn't mean a thing to me."

Sacha had reread the statement Kidjo's partner had made very closely. They had been living together for two years when the young policeman was murdered, but she had not been able to offer the investigators any concrete information. Just like Vidal, Kidjo kept his private and professional lives well apart. Another similarity between the two cases. Sacha remembered the very different exchanges that took place between him and his ex-wife, with whom he used to discuss his cases openly. But Béatrice was a commissaire's daughter and had grown up with the force, and so was able to put up with lonely nights and his fits of the blues when an investigation became too painful. For Adeline Ernaux, the world Toussaint Kidjo had inhabited was a different planet.

"Perhaps you could think it over?" he said, giving her one of his cards. "If you remember anything at all, give me a call. Any time."

Slipping the card into the pocket of her big black apron, she cast an eye on a customer who was prowling round the white Burgundies.

"What do you recommend?"

"What do I recommend for your investigation?" she asked, perplexed.

"No, as a wine, for a dinner where I don't know what's on the menu."

"This Côtes-du-Rhône," she said with a sigh. "It goes with everything. Do you need a receipt for your expenses?"

"No, thanks."

"Can I ask you a question?"

"Of course."

"Is the wine to create a good impression so that I'll feel like searching my memory? In other words, don't you separate your private life and your job in any way?"

"Is that how Toussaint Kidjo lived?"

"You've lost the knack of answering questions. Probably because you're the one who always asks them."

"That's quite likely. Thank you for your time."

"I would have preferred it if you had called first. No-one likes to be hit on the head by a block of concrete."

The delivery van had arrived, and was blocking the street. The blast of a horn tore the air. Within a few seconds, Rue d'Oberkampf was packed with ten or more hysterical drivers.

"I'm working, dammit!" shouted the delivery man. "Don't you give a fuck?"

"No, I'm a cop."

"Yeah, a cop who doesn't give a fuck, that makes sense."

An anarchist delivery man. Nice touch.

Sacha smiled sweetly and started the ignition. It had been a long, long time since he had allowed his fellow countrymen's "armchair rebels" act to get to him.

Karen Mars, with her irresistible smile and her ever youthful air. Sacha presented her with the Côtes-du-Rhône, she told him he shouldn't have. He was always welcome, there was no need for him to bring anything. Her bronze-tinted hair framed a velvety face overwhelmed by a pair of huge green eyes. In her simple white shirt, black masculine waistcoat and faded jeans, she looked more elegant than any great lady dressed in Chanel.

Aurélie was hiding behind her mother. The little girl flung herself at Sacha and wanted to drag him off to her bedroom to get him to listen to the latest song by some obscure American singer. Arnaud Mars' daughter had been crazy about music from a very early age, a passion her father encouraged by buying her quantities of C.D.s and taking her to concerts as often as possible. He announced proudly that she got it from her mother, a jazz pianist of Swedish origin whom he had met when he was in charge of security at the French Embassy in Stockholm.

"Leave our friend in peace, Aurélie. He's had a hard day. And if I'm not mistaken, it's not over yet," her mother said.

The commandant was regularly invited to share the family meal by the divisionnaire. It was pleasanter for Karen to have her husband at home, even if he was not completely free.

Arnaud Mars had his head deep in his files. He was sipping his favourite scotch and was soothed by a jazz tune that Sacha recognised: "Kind of Blue". The atmosphere in his study was very different from the one at headquarters. Rare books, family photos, Swedish furniture. And that glass statue he occasionally brushed with his finger when he talked. A 1930s dancer, bought at an auction in Paris. "For a disgusting amount of money, especially for a cop," he had confessed. "Karen didn't hold it against me. That's what you get when you marry an artiste . . ." The superintendent was almost twenty years older than his wife, but even though his face was lined, he was still commendably slim and boasted a mane of fair hair. At police headquarters more than a few clerks and officers of the female sex were susceptible to his raffish charm.

"You've got nothing against Miles, have you, Sacha?"

"On the contrary."

"If I had to classify the all-time greats of jazz, I'd put 'Kind of Blue' on top of the pile. Wouldn't you?"

"Yes, it's an excellent choice. And in second place, 'Autumn Leaves' by Cannonball Adderley."

"With Miles."

"The unforgettable."

The divisionnaire offered Sacha a seat. A minute later, Karen slipped a glass of wine into his hand before withdrawing, a hint of a subtle perfume hanging in the air as she left.

"How's the Nungesser affair going?"

"It's crazy. Doris Nungesser waits patiently for the guy who raped and killed her child to get out of prison. He was put away for seventeen years. She guns him down at point-blank range, in front of witnesses. She goes home without rushing, telephones the local police station to announce she has just killed her child's murderer, and that she is handing herself in. *Handing herself in*, if you please. But when our men show up at her place, she has disappeared."

"She must have changed her mind and realised that freedom is priceless."

"Clémenti is going crazy trying to lay his hands on her, and at the same time is being pestered by journalists. Seventeen years plotting your revenge: that's something that stirs interest. What about you? How far have you got?"

Sacha described the links with the Kidjo case. He was hoping to find Lola Jost. Mars remained thoughtful for a moment, then declared it was imperative to locate her as quickly as possible. The recent merger between the different branches of the intelligence services to create a central national security agency, the Direction Centrale du Renseignement Intérieur or D.C.R.I., had left him somewhat paranoid. He saw this as a real "French version of the F.B.I.", with similar resources and ambitions. The mission of these French "Feds" was not confined to the war on terrorism, counter-espionage or keeping an eye on any extremist threat, but included the protection of the country's economic interests.

"The death of a close associate of one of the key players in the France–Africa project is bound to attract their attention. But this is our investigation," the superintendent insisted. "There's no way those spooks are going to steal it from us by claiming that it's a 'defence secret'. Do you follow me?"

Not really, thought Sacha. If the case was linked to some shady business in France–Africa, surely it would be better dealt with by the big shots in the intelligence services than by the B.C.

"They have more going for them than we do, boss. And more contacts outside France. The main thing is to get a result."

"I don't agree. The main thing is to want it. And I'll prove it to you with a little magic trick."

Mars stood up and looked in his bookshelves. He unfolded a map and pointed to Africa, Central America and Scandinavia.

"These are the places where I've been in post. You can see what makes up a fellow's life. Three dots on a two-dimensional image."

His eyes were glinting. Had he been relieving the tension of recent days with too much scotch, his favourite poison? It didn't matter: Sacha enjoyed his boss' theatrical gestures.

"Our fellow spends two years here, three years there. He's stuffed his head with images, but what has he learned? What has changed his life?"

Mars had plied his trade from embassy to embassy before he finally settled in Paris. Some people called him "the buccaneer". His face bore the traces of the sun and his responsibilities. Moments like this when he dredged up his memories for whoever happened to be there, only to abandon them again abruptly, as if he had let too much slip. The difference between him and those who always stroked their superiors the right way.

"Nothing changed his life, because our fellow was just passing through. He thought he understood, but at bottom all he did was pick up a few mementos, like a tourist. My bones never stop reminding me I'm an old crock. So now I intend to make my mark. This Vidal affair has the unmistakable smell of something *big*. I want it, you understand?"

"I think so, yes."

"And do you want it too?"

"Of course."

"Sure?"

"I've wanted it ever since the gendarme captain got me out of bed. There has to be a link with the death of the young cop. And a pile of dirt along with it."

"Well, you see, I don't think I could have this kind of conversation with your deputy! Carle, or the love of straight lines and complete respect for the rules."

He smiled, like a pirate delighted to have a companion on board to go on the rampage. Sacha nodded, waiting for him to continue.

"I need you to keep an eye on Lola Jost for me. I know her well. She was a great professional in her day, and she's someone who throws herself into an investigation. But we don't want her spoiling things for us with those big feet of hers."

"I'll take care of her."

"I'm sure you will. The problem is we're doubly between the devil and the deep blue sea. Between spooks, spooks and more spooks, if you follow me."

"Totally."

This concerned the continuing existence of the Paris B.C. under the control of a police commissioner rather than being directly responsible to the Interior Minister. This new reform was intended to cover the entire country, but for now the capital had retained its previous status. They also had to take into account the Foreign Security Bureau, which was linked to the Defence Ministry and dealt with French interests abroad. If someone involved in arms trafficking with Africa had been eliminated, the case concerned all these different institutions. Sacha considered how delicate the affair he had inherited was, and although it made him a little queasy, he was determined not to let Mars down. And even more, not to let himself down. For years he had coveted a move to the B.C., the *ne plus ultra* of a police career. There was no way he was going to slip up now.

"According to my sources, more than eighty per cent of Vidal's legal practice were Gratien's clients," Mars went on. "Logically, the people who bumped off the lawyer must have done it for a reason involving them. But beware of preconceptions."

"I intend to."

"Are things with Carle improving?"

"Slowly."

"One of these days she'll get used to the idea that it was you who won the promotion. I don't regret my choice: she doesn't know how to delegate, because she doesn't trust other people. She has to stick her nose in all the files and cover all the ground in order to make her mind up. It's splitting hairs, but it's a real problem. She's angry because she didn't get the job, but not for any reason beyond herself. And that makes all the difference. She'd do better to direct her anger into her work. In the meantime, I hope she isn't making life too difficult for you."

"No, I can manage."

On his arrival at B.C. eight months earlier, Sacha had very quickly formed his own team. His colleagues soon told him that Carle had been expecting a promotion for a long while, and that as far as length of service was concerned, she was the one who should have got his job. The big chief had decided otherwise, declaring that he couldn't give a damn about positive discrimination or the policy of appointing more women in the French police. He had chosen to "promote the best, quite simply". With any luck, Emmanuelle Carle's hostility would not have a negative impact on their work. Sacha had no wish to complain about her to Mars.

Carle would eventually get used to his way of doing things.

5

The next morning, Sacha arrived at headquarters before all the rest of his team. Dawn was brushing the Seine a gentle pink; it had finally stopped raining. He read the note Carle had left in a prominent place on his desk without a word. A list of the people she had talked to the day before with Inspector Stefani, together with summaries of their statements. Aimé Bangolé, Kidjo's informer, had vanished into thin air; over the past five years nobody had any news of him. Some thought he had gone back to Kinshasa. Carle had made a detour to the 10th arrondissement station to talk to the young lieutenant's former colleagues. A waste of time.

Sacha picked up his notes on the Kidjo case and reread them carefully.

Carle appeared as usual around eight-thirty. She liked to have breakfast with her children, two teenagers of fifteen and seventeen, and her husband, a French teacher at a secondary school in Montrouge, where the family lived.

"Did you read my note, boss?"

"Of course."

"I didn't miss anyone out."

"Let's just say you kept the best for last."

"You mean Lola Jost? She's nowhere to be found. I went by her place, and phoned twenty times. No luck."

Sacha snatched up his jacket and ordered Carle to follow him. In the car park he handed her the keys to the patrol car. He liked the way she drove: she was quick and adroit, and smoother than Ménard. He asked her how her family was, and could sense her stiffen.

"There's no rule against having a family and a job. I think you manage the two perfectly. I used to swap personal info with my colleagues at Place d'Italie. It helps lighten the atmosphere, don't you think?"

She turned the ignition and declared that her family was just fine, thank you. They drove in silence to Châtelet.

"As regards info, I would have preferred to be there for the Widow Vidal interview. There are nuances that two people can pick up better than one."

Her tone was neutral; her driving just as relaxed. She had a remarkable gift for turning reproaches into statements of fact.

"It's all in my notes. You wouldn't have discovered anything more. Go back and question her if you like."

"She'd take that as harassment, and she'd be right."

"That's up to you."

Her eyes never left the road. He was expecting her to finally have it out with him, but all she did was turn on the press review on *France Actu*. The presenter spoke about the loss of a huge contract for the French nuclear industry to the Koreans; the Elysée's displeasure over the closure of certain car factories by a firm that was only 15 per cent state-owned; the stabbing to death of a seventeen-year-old student in a school in the northern suburbs; a worrying rise in the unemployment rate among young graduates; and finally mentioned the Vidal affair. The journalist remarked that the Colombes murder victim was a close associate of Richard Gratien, a lawyer specialising in the arms trade who was regularly called as a witness in the EuroSecurities affair. This clearing house based in Liechtenstein was embroiled in a political and financial scandal of global proportions. Several of its executives were suspected of permitting the transfer of massive concealed bribes.

This is our investigation. There's no way those spooks are going to steal it from us by claiming it's a "defence secret". The night before, Mars had made no secret of his concern. They had to get hold of Lola Jost as quickly as possible.

When they reached Rue de l'Échiquier, Sacha dialled the number stored on his mobile. The answering machine came on: *Brevity is the sister of talent, Chekhov used to say. Please leave your message.*

"Lola, this is Sacha Duguin. I'm downstairs. Please pick up your phone and tell me the code to get in. Your sense of hospitality is as well-known as your love of quotes. Don't leave me here growing mouldy in the rain."

No reply.

"Perhaps she isn't home?"

"Do you really think she'd be out in weather like this, Carle?"

He slipped his master key in the front lock and dragged Carle with him up to the second floor. He rang the bell: a long minute went by. Finally, the ex-commissaire came to the door, draped in her disgusting claret-coloured velvet dressing gown: an unforgettable garment apparently cut from theatre curtains that made her look more than ever like a pensioned-off Valkyrie. Sacha noticed a bruise on her forehead.

She stood there without moving, staring at him as if she didn't recognise him. For a brief moment, Sacha wondered if perhaps she was ill; she was old enough to fall prey to one of the many delights modern life has in store for us.

"Come in," she said mournfully.

That's the Barthélemy effect, Sacha wagered. He was certain the captain had already alerted his former boss.

The living room matched the mood if its owner. A battlefield after a bloody engagement. Dirty crockery kept a three-quarters-empty bottle of port and a half-done jigsaw puzzle company. A few pieces had ended up on the parquet floor among old newspapers and scattered documents. The lid of the box showed that, in a cruel twist of fate, Lola had been trying to recreate a view of Kilimanjaro, before giving up that innocent and now ridiculous pastime. The Dalmatian lay amidst the debris on a corner of the rug that had mercifully been spared. He came over and pressed himself against Sacha's legs, wagging his tail. The commissaire scratched its head.

"Traitor," Lola growled to the dog.

Sacha explained to Carle that Sigmund belonged to the neighbourhood shrink. Lola had collapsed onto a battered couch and looked like a depressed giant Turkish delight ravaged by a monstrous mouth. Carle introduced herself before declaring how honoured she was to be there. She launched into a speech that could be summarised as: in the close police family, everyone knew about the legendary commissaire. If Carle wasn't being sincere, it was a good performance, especially for a woman normally so sparing with her emotions. Their hostess let the compliment slide over her with a sigh. Sacha feared the worst: a Lola overwhelmed by events, who would be of no help to them.

"And you manage to work together without wanting to strangle him?" she snapped, to Carle this time.

Thank heavens, Lola was alive and kicking. It was a rhetorical question; she had already risen to her feet and was offering round the port, a treat she apparently appreciated as much as ever. The bottle was finished by the time it was Carle's turn. Lola unearthed another one from an old-fashioned sideboard covered in an imposing collection of Post-its. She downed her drink in one, poured herself another, then went to sit down again, not forgetting to place the precious bottle beside her.

"Barthélemy didn't tell me you'd taken over the investigation," she said. "It looks as though all my phantoms have come back to haunt me at the same time. Sad season. O.K., that's enough of a moan. What do you want?"

"You to help me find a possible link between the two cases."

"That would be an unexpected bit of good luck, and I stopped believing in fairy stories more than fifty years ago."

Sacha glanced at all the scattered papers. It must be the Kidjo dossier, which Lola had kept a copy of. She had obviously dug it out and been studying it again from top to bottom.

"Did Kidjo know Vidal? Closely or from a distance?"

"Not that I'm aware of."

A moment's silence. Lola's mouth twisted bitterly. Sacha could imagine her shock when Barthélemy told her how the lawyer had been tortured. She had ended her mourning after five long years, finally accepted she had to close the Kidjo dossier unresolved. Now it seemed all her efforts had come to nothing. She bore a grudge against the whole world. And for the moment, the world has got my face on it, thought Sacha. The face of the guy who in addition had dumped her best friend.

"Tell me about Toussaint."

"You mean you haven't read the dossier?"

"I want your version."

She laughed like a troll and poured herself another glass of port, downing it with a grimace. Carle did not move a muscle. Lola's silence lasted so long it seemed as though she had forgotten they were there.

"Toussaint was a lad it was impossible not to like. A good mind, and always good-humoured; respectful, but never obsequious. He had chosen France, his father's country. He wasn't interested in politics. We sometimes discussed the situation in the Democratic Republic of Congo, but my little lieutenant did not seem particularly affected by events there. He had got used to it. His life was here. He came to France to study." A sudden sarcastic gleam in her eyes, above her glasses, which had slipped down her nose: "Don't you want to know what he studied?"

"Yes, I'd like to know."

"Law. Oh yes, Toussaint was planning to be a lawyer. He quit to join the force. If there's a link with Florian Vidal, that must be it.

Especially as they were the same generation. But I've got some bad news for you."

"What's that?"

"They didn't study at the same faculty, nor at the same time. I checked. With Barthélemy's help."

Her arms folded, she seemed to be waiting for him to add something.

"But you're looking for a link, aren't you? Otherwise you wouldn't have come sniffing around me."

"There hasn't been another similar murder since Kidjo. That would be a bit too much of a coincidence, I agree."

"That's my opinion too. And besides, in spite of everything, I've always thought you were a good cop."

In spite of everything. Sacha suppressed a smile.

"You still have the same bosses. They are jobsworths who use their little fingers to make sure their trouser creases are straight. Back in my day, they prevented me digging too deep. Why? Possibly because Toussaint had stumbled upon one of those mega-swindles between France and Africa our dear country specialises in. Nothing happens for five years. And now it starts up again. If it's the same filthy business behind all this, your bosses won't let you do your job."

"We'll see about that."

"For me, it's a done deal. And I feel sorry for you. It's not easy to swallow snakes. Still less boa constrictors."

"I don't intend to swallow anything at all."

Lola treated him to a disillusioned smile.

"Give me Aimé Bangolé's contact, Lola. Please."

"That's the only reason you came here, isn't it? You knew about his law studies, you read the dossier and reached the same conclusions. Or am I wrong?"

"You're seldom wrong, Lola."

"Well, for the informer, the answer's no."

"We have the same objective. I'm not the enemy."

"Perhaps not, but an informer is sacred. I've got my reputation to defend around here."

"You've retired . . ."

"You know what I mean."

Lola might be retired, but she had such a reputation that people in her neighbourhood didn't hesitate to call on her to sort out their problems. She and her friend Ingrid were a duo of amateur, unpaid detectives who had chalked up many successes. Riskier than Scrabble or jigsaw puzzles, but better at staving off boredom and neurosis. But this time the stakes were high, and Sacha had no intention of yielding an inch.

"Be reasonable."

"My, that's a big word! We see Bangolé together, or not at all. Take it or leave it."

"You know that if I visit your old station I can get what I want. But that would be wasting time."

"Over-optimism has killed cleverer people than you. It's your choice. I can put my coat on and follow you. Or stay here in the warm and let you struggle through the storm."

"Carle and I are efficient, rapid, and official. I don't take any civilians with me in my investigations."

"Too bad for you!" she bellowed. "I won't see you out. You're so much more efficient and rapid than me."

"That's not what I meant. As you well know, this is an ultra-sensitive political affair."

"It's exactly what you meant, and it doesn't surprise me coming from you. Other people's feelings aren't that important where you're concerned. Right, I've changed my mind. You don't seem to know the way."

Upon which she got up with surprising agility for someone of her weight and age, closed the folds of her dressing gown over her stomach, and strode to the door, her face like thunder. She motioned for them to clear out.

"Goodbye, Commissaire, and sorry for having disturbed you," Carle said, dripping respect.

"We're walking through a minefield, Lola. Think twice before you get involved. The B.C. could get the case taken away from it. Once and for all."

"Out."

"You're wrong. But I'm sure you'll see that eventually."

As they walked downstairs, Lola's voice gave them a start.

"I wish you luck. My successor is a pen-pusher with the I.Q. of a paramecium. And would you like to know who Toussaint's partner was?"

At the top of the stairs, the ex-commissaire raised an avenging finger. She took a step forward.

She's going to get her feet caught in that stupid dressing gown, thought Sacha. He raised an arm to warn her to be careful . . .

"Captain Jérôme Barthélemy. He'll be as silent as the grave. I'm going to call him right now . . ."

Somehow, the ex-commissaire got tangled up in her fateful robe. Her body soared into the air. Carle and Sacha rushed up the stairs. Lola landed heavily on her side; her head banged against the iron rail. She groaned, and passed out.

Sacha called an ambulance, which arrived after ten minutes or so. In the meantime, Lola had come round, and was cursing her throbbing neck. Carle urged her not to move. The paramedics laid her on a stretcher. As she was being taken past Sacha, Lola gripped his sleeve.

"Beautiful as a ten-ton truck as always, and just as dangerous. You've always brought me bad luck. But I repeat, either we see the informer together, or not at all."

"But Lola, they're taking you to hospital . . ."

"I'm well aware you're not sending me to the local music-hall, you dimwit. So what? I'm not dead yet. In an hour from now, it'll be over. I'll be back in business."

Sacha held back Sigmund, who was trying to climb into the ambulance.

"What should we do with the Dalmatian?" asked Carle.

"We'll leave it at Belles. It's Lola's restaurant headquarters. The owner is one of her best friends."

To add to their misery, the rain started to come sheeting down once more. Taking a welcome umbrella out of her vast coat, Carle suggested Sacha share it. A few minutes later, the two of them plus Sigmund entered the small restaurant in Passage Brady. It was only a little after ten, but a few regulars had already gathered round the enticing smell of a *blanquette de veau*. Maxime Duchamp was standing behind the counter talking to a young woman perched on a stool with her back to them. She was wearing a pair of torn jeans and a shabby airman's jacket. Sacha had already recognised the style, the lanky profile, the cropped blonde hair.

Noting the expression on Maxime's face, the person he was talking to turned round. Her mouth fell open in a round O, then snapped shut again. Sigmund rushed towards the young American, plonked his muddy paws on her lap, and demanded affection. Ingrid Diesel's face was a study in desolation.

The surprise apparition was like a kick in the guts to Sacha. He recovered quickly.

"Is there a problem with Lola?" asked Maxime, worried.

"She's fallen down the stairs. An ambulance is taking her to the Lariboisière hospital."

"Is she hurt with seriousness?" Ingrid spoke French in an anxious whisper.

Even prettier than I remembered, thought Sacha, but her French isn't getting any better. He tried to reassure her, but Ingrid didn't believe a word of it.

"Maxime told me she was all trembling on account of the lawyer's murder, and that horrible tyre business. Her past comes back to bite her, and you . . . all you do is push her down the stairs!"

"I didn't push her."

"Possibly, but it's just the same thing. You haven't changed."

She rushed to the door. Through the window, Sacha saw her running through the driving rain towards the metro. Suddenly she came to a halt and retraced her steps. She swept in and stood in front of him, dripping wet, eyes flashing.

"I forgot one thing," she said.

"What's that?"

"This is the second time Lola has passed over today."

"Passed *out*, you mean. So?"

"So that costs double," she said, giving him two hefty slaps on the cheeks before running out again.

For once, Carle was smiling.

"I see you've left an indelible mark on the neighbourhood, boss."

6

Lola escaped with nothing worse than a neck-brace, an arm in plaster (her left arm, fortunately), an interesting collection of bruises, and a lost day. She had almost broken her neck, but luck had been on her side. Would that help her regain her calm? Ingrid doubted it.

Carried away in a monologue addressed to her former colleagues, Lola's intact arm was scything through the air to the rhythm of her oratorical passion: *Insolent, arrogant creatures, coyotes capable of anything, self-righteous ingrates, young whippersnappers stuffed with pride, they're no better than the rogues they're supposed to be pursuing.* She never actually named Sacha Duguin, but Ingrid knew he had a lead role in the baroque opera Lola was performing just for her.

She helped settle her in the ancient Twingo, asked Sigmund, installed on the back seat, to contain his joy, and took the wheel. She hated driving, especially in a city as clogged up as Paris, but she made an effort because she could sense how fragile her friend was beneath the outpouring of anger. The past, so carefully stowed away, was pouring out in a landslide of stinking mud.

Although the distance between the Lariboisière hospital and Rue de l'Échiquier was very short, it became a trial of strength in traffic slowed up by the rain. They reached the Canal Saint-Martin in the midst of an armada of stressed-out drivers. By halfway down

Boulevard Magenta, the ex-commissaire was so overwhelmed she left off her opera lament devoted to worthless cops and fell into a stubborn silence. This respite allowed Sigmund to take a little nap, and Ingrid to get her breath back. She could feel the clashing vibes Lola was giving off and promised herself she would give her a relaxing massage at the first opportunity. She heaved a sigh of relief when she could finally park the Twingo in the underground car park.

"One minute."

"What's going on, Lola?"

"We're going to wait for the time switch to finish."

"But that means we'll be in the dark."

"That's the intention."

Ingrid shut the door again, switched off the dipped headlights, and turned to Lola, who smiled at her in an odd way. Was she so doped up she was seeing things?

"*Woof*!"

"Be good, Sigmund, everything is under control."

The car park was plunged into darkness. After a long minute of jet-black silence, punctuated by several canine sighs, Ingrid plucked up the courage to ask what exactly Lola's intention was.

"It was one of Toussaint's little tricks. Whenever he was confused by a difficult case, he surrounded himself with darkness. He swore it helped him think. When there was no underground car park or basement to hand, he would wear one of those face masks you pick up on planes."

"And did it work?"

"Pretty much. Toussaint was a good cop. Calm, methodical, not at all conventional. I enjoyed his eccentricities. In the States you have that expression: *Think outside the box*. But Toussaint preferred to climb into the box and shut the lid, if you follow?"

"More or less."

"Unfortunately, it doesn't work for me. Bah, what does the result matter so long as you keep the ritual?"

Ingrid could have responded: you're not really going to get mixed up in all that again, are you? Not only going back to the investigation, but trying to outsmart your colleagues? They're the ones with the resources, the experience, the legitimacy. But she knew better than to rub her companion up the wrong way, especially at a moment like this. The ex-commissaire was struggling to free herself from the car and from her memories. Ingrid snapped the headlights back on until Lola found the light switch.

They reached the apartment – cleaned and tidied thanks to Ingrid's efforts – and settled at the living-room table. In the centre lay the jigsaw puzzle box, full of the tiny pieces she had picked up from the floor. Ingrid had even found one stuck in the bottom of a glass of port. A bad sign. When Lola neglected her puzzles, she was in a desperate way. Ingrid offered to give her a massage. Lola declined the offer: she had been "messed about enough by the Gestapo at the Lariboisière". Her American friend was careful not to contradict her. Sigmund seemed to be of a similar mind. His muzzle was resting on his crossed front paws, but his eyes were alert: he appeared to be reflecting on the unfathomable fickleness of the human heart.

Lola peered with interest at the pile next to the puzzle box. Ingrid had gathered together the documents strewn all over the floor as best she could. They were official papers, probably what the French called witness statements. One thing was for sure: they brought back a past Lola ought to be leaving to those in charge now. Even if that meant Commandant Sacha Duguin and his team.

As erect as an antique statue due to the brace, Lola looked less anxious than before.

"Do you know what annoyed me most?"

"Tell me."

"That he claimed to be coming to give me the news, when what he really wanted was Toussaint's informer on a silver platter. That was out of order. But in the end . . ."

"In the end?"

"If I were him, I'd do the same. A cop has to be wily, or he gets nowhere. He's stubborn. He wants to justify his promotion. And he'll do the best job possible. Perhaps I'll show him my magnanimous side."

"Magnanimous? That's hard to pronounce."

"Yes, it's a word that sounds as if you could chew it. It means you'll forgive someone."

"So in French you'll *magnanimer* Sacha?"

"Yes, I probably will. *Magnanimer* is a great invention, now I come to think of it."

"Doesn't the word exist?"

"No, but your charming abuse of language will remain between the two of us. I promise."

Ingrid stood behind her friend to massage her trapezius muscles whether she liked it or not. This also helped hide a fresh wave of nostalgia. When she saw Sacha in Belles, it was as though something had exploded in her brain. It was so annoying; in recent days, she had managed to spend an hour or two without him pushing his way into her thoughts. And she had lost the mania of rewriting their past conversations. He still popped up in her dreams, but his presence was becoming less irksome. In his latest guise, he was a stationary passerby on a riverbank, content to embark on a brief, philosophical dialogue and watch the waves go by.

In the restaurant the day before, this soothing dream had been shattered. She thought of the two-way slaps she had given him. She should have kept it to one. A one-way ticket, definitely with no return. In fact, overnight she had decided that a trip to some faraway place would be the best remedy. But now there was Lola with her neck-brace and her arm in a sling, her face covered in bruises. And her own agenda. She was also thinking of a journey, one that took her back to the lands of her past. Lola claimed she knew the wisest course of action would be to let Sacha do the work. But did she believe a word of what she was saying?

"Ah, you really are the best masseuse on the Canal Saint-Martin, if not the entire planet," said Lola, as Ingrid went to rejoin Sigmund on the couch.

She massaged the dog's neck and shoulders as well. He gave a low moan of pleasure. In this foul weather, his daily exercise had been reduced accordingly. Ingrid suspected him of being empathetic. He reacted to Lola's mood swings, showed his approval or his instant rejection of any newcomer. He had a definite talent for this, almost as if he had inherited an ability to read souls from his psychoanalyst owner. Even Lola, who was more Cartesian than René Descartes, had to admit he was a very special animal. Sigmund had always liked Sacha Duguin. Ingrid tried to push away this inconvenient thought, and succeeded when she saw Lola rummaging among the pile of documents relating to the Toussaint Kidjo affair. She pinched herself to make sure she wasn't dreaming. But harsh reality won out. Lola was trampling on all her good intentions.

Ingrid felt reassured when she saw her bypassing the witness statements and pulling a small book from the pile. Lola stroked the cover before leafing through it. She found the passage she was looking for, and with moist eyes announced she was going to read from a poem entitled "Breath":

Listen more often / to Things rather than Beings / Understand The Voice of Fire / Understand the Water. / Hear in the Wind / The Weeping Bush / It is the Breath of the Ancestors.

Those who are dead are never gone: / They are in the Shade that lightens / and in the shadow that darkens. / The dead are not under the Earth: / They are in the rustling Tree / they are in the wailing Wood / They are in the running Water / They are in the sleeping water / They are in the Hut, they are in the crowd: / The Dead are not dead . . .

"It's by Birago Diop, a great Senegalese poet. When Toussaint's father, Jean Texier, asked me if I'd like a keepsake of his son, I chose this book. Toussaint inherited it from his mother, who died a long time ago. I told Texier perhaps he ought to hold on to such an important family souvenir, but he insisted. He thought the collection was in good hands."

That's easy to say, thought Ingrid, not usually one to jump to conclusions. This time though, like it or not, it was as clear as day: Lola would have done better to follow her initial instinct and handed the book back to Toussaint's father. Yes, it was a beautiful gift, but a poisoned one.

7

They might not have found out who had called or sent emails to the lawyer just before his death, but they did have a fairly precise view of how he had lived his last week. Without its S.I.M. card, Vidal's Black-Berry was an empty shell, but Sacha had been able to put the old address book and the information Alice Bernier had emailed him to good effect. The team brought in to ring all the numbers had done a painstaking job: it had been established that the lawyer had played golf the previous week with the head of a chamber of commerce and a financier from Goldman Sachs, held several business meetings with African colleagues, and on the night before he died had met with two Senegalese businessmen in a nightclub on Rue la Boétie. Over the telephone, no-one had spoken of the slightest clash or sign of aggression. They all described Vidal as relaxed and professional. His last days had glided by.

Sacha was impressed. The lawyer had only set up his practice four years earlier, and yet had an address book many a political or media star would have envied. High-ranking civil servants, journalists, businessmen were listed alongside an imposing array of big noises in the police and armed forces. Vidal was friendly with a famous French footballer of African origin, as well as with several comedians and publicists. Under Richard Gratien there was a first name: Antonia, together with a mobile number. Alice Bernier had added in pencil: *Gratien's wife.*

Everyone on Duguin's team was gathered in their shared office, listening to their boss finish his update. Ménard was playing with his turquoise North American Indian bracelet, brought back the previous summer from a trip to the United States allegedly in the footsteps of de Tocqueville, along with a ghastly repertoire of stories. For once though, the young lieutenant remained silent. It was Carle who regularly interrupted Sacha with finicky questions, trying to get at the minutest details of the case.

The commandant announced his imminent meeting with Judge Armand de Sertys. He was in charge of the EuroSecurities affair, a financial scandal that had broken several years earlier and involved the politician Louis Candichard. Once a candidate for the presidency, the former minister had bitten the dust and been forced to abandon his ambitions. Richard Gratien had been called as a witness on several occasions.

Then it was Ménard's turn. As always when he had to perform, he was champing at the bit with enthusiasm. The lieutenant was made to enthrall an audience.

"Nadine Vidal has been very cooperative. I've been able to consult all the files. Gratien advises an impressive list of politicians and entrepreneurs throughout Francophone Africa. Vidal went with him everywhere, and spent almost sixty per cent of his time in Africa. For years now, the pair of them have been attending business dinners and society receptions from Yaoundé to Dakar, from Kinshasa to Libreville. Vidal's lifestyle was not to be sniffed at. A beautiful apartment in Paris. Only rare vacations, but five-star. In Bali, skiing near Vancouver, and quick getaways to New York, Cuba, or Venice. The couple own a villa in Corsica with a yacht moored there all year round. Vidal must have done a remarkable job to enjoy that sort of income, all of it duly declared to the tax authorities. That guy paid an awful lot of tax. Talking of which, he didn't just draw up the contracts for his clients' international deals, he also acted as their financial adviser. And if you want my opinion, he gave advice on all kinds of tax avoidance schemes."

"Ask the Finance Squad to examine that."

"In fact, Luce Chéreau is already looking for you. At the divisionnaire's request, she has already prepared, for your eyes only, a *very sexy little file* on Vidal. At least, that's what she called it."

Luce Chéreau's personality and eccentricities were well-known beyond the confines of the Finance Squad. A forty-something divorcee, she never missed a chance to remind Sacha she was available, and wouldn't take "no" for an answer.

The meeting lasted for more than an hour. Back in his own office, Sacha considered the picture that was emerging: Vidal was Gratien's right-hand man. This go-between in French-African affairs only worked on delicate contracts. There were no signs of any break-in either at Vidal's home in Rue de Vaugirard or in his offices on Rue de Seine. According to his wife and his secretary, he kept most of his documents on his portable computer and his BlackBerry. Was it their contents that the murderer and whoever was behind him were after?

He sensed a presence in the room, and raised his head. Thick chestnut curls, lurid make-up, figure-hugging T-shirt, black leather trousers: Luce Chéreau was observing him, file in hand.

"Mars asked me to look into Florian Vidal," she said before perching on the edge of his desk. "When I heard it was for you, I pulled all the stops out."

"Thanks, Luce."

"Gratien made Vidal. He started out as his driver. He paid for him to become a lawyer. The kid was also his tax adviser, in other words, his money-launderer. For the moment, I can't prove that. It's all so well done you can't see the joins any more. It appears Gratien has friends in high places in the Finance Ministry. Unless it's in the Interior Ministry. Or in Defence. Or in all three. But I'll carry on digging, you can be sure of that."

Sacha tried to take in all she had said. She reached a finger out to his face and stroked his right eyebrow, split in two by a small scar that was the result of a Thai boxing match that had got out of hand.

"I'd really love you to tell me one day who did that to you."

"A drug lord who was a colonel with the F.A.R.C. rebels. He attacked me with a machete in the middle of the Colombian jungle infested with tarantulas."

"I love it when you wind me up. Do you know what I'm thinking?"

"No, despite appearances, at this time of day my imagination falls asleep before me."

"Since I've just given you a summary of my report, you've no need to spend the rest of the night on it. I've got a better idea. A non-stop leg-over session! It'll be sensational!"

"You're unstoppable, Luce. I have to say I'm impressed," said Sacha, giving her a friendly pat on the shoulder.

"I start from the principle that life is short and ends badly, so why make such a fuss?"

Sacha had tucked the file under his arm and tried to recover his jacket from the back of the chair, but Luce was too quick for him. She was sniffing the material, eyes closed.

"You smell so good, Sacha."

She handed him his jacket, stressing once again that he didn't know what he was missing. He was relieved to see her cross the threshold; he left soon afterwards and went into Mars' office. Commissaire Clémenti and two of his men, Captains N'Diop and Argenson, were deep in conversation with the divisionnaire.

Clémenti had filled his group in on Doris Nungesser, who was still on the run. All the railway stations, ports and airports had been searched: she had vanished into thin air, leaving her weapon behind – a shotgun borrowed from her hunter father. Her cleaning lady said some clothes and a suitcase were missing. No money, chequebooks, or jewels had been found in her apartment. No sign of any struggle and, a worrying detail, Doris Nungesser's mother had received a phone call from her daughter just before she disappeared: she told her she loved her, asked her to forgive her, and said she wanted to leave the country.

"A woman who kills a bastard like that in cold blood, says she's going to hand herself in, and then disappears in such an . . . elegant manner is unheard of. And do you know what intrigues me most, Arnaud?" asked Clémenti, the only member of the B.C. on first name terms with their chief.

"No, but I'm interested."

Sacha had seen photos of Doris Nungesser in the press. A tall, distinguished blonde woman with a melancholy air and greeny-blue eyes. He could guess what Clémenti was driving at.

"She guns down Moutier in front of witnesses as though she were issuing a challenge. Her message is: this guy has to die, that's what matters, that's the only thing I'm living for. Then she has a change of heart. She escapes with astonishing ease. But how is all this possible if she had no idea when he was getting out? I think somebody helped her. At the last moment, and doubtless partly in spite of herself. And I don't think it was a criminal. She didn't get her gun from a dealer;

she didn't pay anyone to shoot Moutier. I don't reckon she knows anybody in the underworld."

"So, someone well connected who loved her?"

"That would be the logical conclusion. But she doesn't seem to have had any serious relationship since her son was killed. And she has been separated from her husband for a long while."

"Some ties never die," said Mars.

"I don't think René Nungesser has anything to do with it. His statement rings true."

"Well, your instinct is rarely wrong! Good luck, Serge. Good luck, gentlemen."

The three men rose to their feet. Clémenti shook Sacha's hand as he went past, then closed the padded door behind him. Mars offered Sacha the seat the commissaire had vacated.

"Do you know what I think?"

"That Clémenti doesn't really want to find her?"

"Precisely. It happens once or twice in a cop's lifetime. One feels an irresistible empathy for a murderer, one understands their motives. But Clémenti will do what he has to do. He has a lot of integrity. O.K., how far have you got?"

Sacha summarised the latest developments. Florian Vidal's personality was becoming clearer: he was a tool that the *éminence grise* of France–Africa had fashioned for his own needs. He added that the next day he was going to meet Judge Armand de Sertys and Richard Gratien, among others.

"Ah, Sertys," Mars sighed. "An unbearable poseur. He's an impostor, and a nasty one at that. Beware of him. He's one of those idealists who fight not for justice but against power. Any power. He's a dangerous ideologue, who believes he has been chosen for a purifying mission. He's always dressed in white, and loves reminding people of his humble origins. He's all the more dangerous because he's a dinosaur. So, he's going to bite. With all the rage of a species becoming extinct."

Mars was referring to the imminent change in the powers of examining magistrates like de Sertys. This was among his favourite hobby-horses. According to him, the magistrates had become a powerful caste enjoying exorbitant power. Although many of them had done their job conscientiously, some had abused their position. The Outreau child abuse scandal was a perfect example of the judicial mess caused by this imbalance.

"That little Ménard of yours would tell you that in the United States judges are elected and therefore can be held to account by their electors. Here in France, they exist by divine right. And it's high time that changed."

Sacha had no particular view on the question, but he enjoyed his boss' non-conformist attitude. He was someone who had spent most of his career abroad before heading up the B.C. His detached view of France was interesting and unusual in the force.

The two men discussed the details of the case for a while longer, then Mars clapped his hands and declared that time was up.

"I'm throwing you out. We shouldn't misuse overtime, it's a sign of a lack of organisation. Go home. That's an order."

Sacha shook his extended hand.

"Gratien is on first-name terms with the whole African aristocracy, but he's a conman, and Sertys is a crusader. It's even possible the two of them are after the same thing. If it suits them. So take care, Sacha, take care."

"I promise, boss."

He shut the padded door behind him: at this late hour, Mars liked to make discreet calls to contacts in high places. He might not have

Vidal's gold-plated address book, but he had been in post at many embassies and built up contacts that he carefully maintained. The divisionnaire was reputed to be a skilled politician despite his trenchant views; whatever else, he was a remarkable source of information for his men.

It was too late for Sacha to make for his Thai boxing club. Too bad: he'd find some other opportunity to train. The nape of his neck and his back were hurting, so he decided to walk a while before he took the metro. A free city bike brushed past him as he was waiting at a traffic light. The energetic cyclist sped off into the night. A woman in dark clothes, with short blonde hair. But her silhouette was not as supple as Ingrid's. Was Miss Diesel, alias Gabriella Tiger, still the undisputed star of the Calypso nightclub, the queen of erotic disguise?

Probably. The man who could make her give up her art had not been born.

8

Lola was too upset for Ingrid to have the heart to leave her on her own. She thought her friend was going to have a sleepless night anyway, and there was nothing to lose. So she suggested Lola went with her to Pigalle. Lola accepted, provided that Sigmund, who was bored to death with being kept indoors, went with them. There was no way he could gambol in meadows, and so it was time for him to get a change of air, even if it was at a cabaret. Timothy Harlen, Ingrid's very strict boss, did not allow animals in, but they would find a way round that.

Once they were under way, Ingrid asked the question that had been intriguing her.

"Does 'gambol' in French have anything to do with gambling?"

"No, it means you have fun shaking your body about. Seen from the outside, it can look very odd. But that doesn't matter."

Ingrid wondered if her own dances at the Calypso could be thought of as gambolling. I've been gambolling for years without knowing it, she thought, speeding through a changing light. Tonight's show was going even further in that direction. Inspired by Hallowe'en, Ingrid had brewed up a new number with the aid of Marie, her faithful, inspired costume-maker. She hoped that Timothy's clients would enjoy it, whether they were from the States or not. She knew that her adopted country had a similar custom, called Mardi Gras, but to Ingrid the two celebrations were very different: Hallowe'en had an extra dimension, a way of playing with Death, no doubt to keep it at bay. She parked the car in Rue Victor-Massé with an impeccable manoeuvre that drew an approving comment from the ex-commissaire.

"I'd forgotten how well you drive. That's interesting."

This anodyne remark boded ill. Lola was plotting something, even if she didn't admit it as yet. Ingrid would have to be vigilant, and find a way to divert the dangerous course her thoughts were taking. Another solution: a one-way ticket to Mongolia. Somewhere where doubtless she could take a gamble on gambolling in the meadows.

They made a detour via the stage door so that they would not be seen by Enrique, the Calypso's redoubtable doorman. If he had seen Sigmund, he would have immediately reported it to his boss. Enrique had a cast-iron devotion for Timothy, because he had always got him out of his scrapes thanks to his wide range of contacts. The nightclub owner treated his handpicked staff with respect, and paid promptly. He was reputed to put on the best striptease shows in Paris, and Ingrid blessed him for letting her express herself free from all restrictions. The concept she had of her second profession was very different to that of her fellow dancers. She did not take her clothes off; she was offering a sacred dance where desire was controlled to the millimetre, like a jaguar on a leash.

Her dressing room smelled of *papier d'Arménie*. Rachida, the cleaning lady who was as stubborn as she was thorough, was a devotee of all kinds of air fresheners. Ingrid opened the window on a night-time sky blurred by the rain and stared up at the moon for a few moments, secretly thanking it for being full on the evening when she was launching her disturbing new dance.

Lola was installed on a green chesterfield Ingrid had not seen before. She bet it must be a present from Timothy, who with his wife Angela was a great fan of European antiques. It looked as though her friend was enjoying the comfort of this venerable seat. She went down to the bar and came back with a bottle of port. Filling a bowl with water, she put it down for Sigmund, then slipped a C.D. into the player. Bach's cello suites played by Paul Tortelier would keep Lola's mind occupied, and soothe her at the same time. A challenge not everyone was equal to.

Somebody knocked at the door: two short knocks, followed by a long one. Timothy's signature. Ingrid called out: "One moment, please!" opened the wardrobe, and signalled to the Dalmatian to climb in. He obeyed docilely. When he saw Lola, Harlen switched to French, which he spoke perfectly despite a pronounced accent. He shook her hand warmly. He was a plain-spoken man who was a quick judge of his fellows and rarely made a mistake when he trusted a person. Lola Jost was one of the chosen ones.

"It's a real pleasure to see you again, dear Lola. You've been a stranger to us recently."

He was wearing a white dinner jacket, plain grey T-shirt and a pair of jeans. Lola had confided to Ingrid that she liked her boss' elegance, his taste for daring combinations that suited him down to the ground.

"Ingrid is of the opinion that I shouldn't go out at night at my age. She's preserving me like a pot of old jam."

"Whereas you are a glass of champagne. Speaking of which, might I offer you one?"

"No, thank you. This sixty-year-old port is just fine."

"Thank you, boss," said Ingrid. "I accept the new armchair. I had nowhere to put my guests."

"That's exactly what I thought, darling. What do you reckon to your new number?"

"I tried it out yesterday with Betsy, Marie and Enrique. They liked it. I was only sorry you had a business meeting."

"I trust their judgement. They're stricter than a Nobel prize committee. Besides, I couldn't cancel the meeting. A lunch with a friend from the *Herald Tribune.*"

Lola was following their conversation with an eager look in her eye. Ingrid studied her face for a couple of seconds, and bit her lip because she knew what was coming next.

"Timothy, do you know Richard Gratien and his young partner, Florian Vidal?"

Harlen ran his hands through his grey locks. His way of combing through his memories. Ingrid allowed herself a sigh.

"Gratien comes to the Calypso from time to time. Always with African dignitaries. The last time it was a minister from Côte d'Ivoire.

A charming man. Vidal was there too, of course. No-one can go around without their shadow, can they?"

Lola told him of the lawyer's death. Harlen took in the information without reacting. As a Vietnam vet, he had seen much worse.

"Gratien must be in a terrible state."

"Why's that?"

"He has no children. Vidal was more or less his adopted son. A lot of people labelled him the 'heir apparent'. He had started on the bottom rung of the ladder. As Mister Africa's driver."

"Mister Africa?"

"That's what my friends in the American press call Richard Gratien. Well, Mister Africa turned his driver into a rich and successful lawyer!"

"Thanks to arms trafficking," Ingrid said with a disgusted grimace.

"Someone has to do it, darling. It's no use being naive about it. Every powerful country sells weapons. It's an essential part of their G.D.P. Everyone knows it's a very special market, and commissions are part of the system. The thing is to determine whether the deals are legal or not. And whether the people getting the commissions are legally authorised to receive them."

"And does Mister Africa specialise in illegal deals?" asked Lola.

"I wish I was party to the secrets of the gods, my dear. All I know, like everyone else, is that Gratien has several times been called as a witness in the EuroSecurities affair, that international clearing house mixed up in a financial scandal. The justice system has its eye on some of his contacts."

"A clearing house sounds vaguely erotic, but I bet it's something else altogether," Ingrid said.

"That's right, darling. Officially, EuroSecurities is both a bank and a company that specialises in bond swaps. It's called a clearing house because it simplifies and guarantees international financial transfers. The problem is that its executives are accused of carrying out two kinds of parallel activities: on the one hand, transparent, regulated transactions; on the other, hidden, illegal ones. For example, neglecting to include some client accounts on EuroSecurities' books. In other words, carrying out money-laundering operations worth billions of dollars."

"Stop me if I'm wrong, Timothy, but I seem to recall the bosses of EuroSecurities are suspected of allowing hidden commissions and kickbacks in arms trading deals."

"You're not wrong, Lola. But if that involves Richard Gratien, the judges have not yet succeeded in uncovering anything that he's done wrong. His clients are arms dealers, not traffickers. No doubt he knows a lot of people's secrets, but perhaps, who knows, he's managed to keep his nose clean."

"And something tells me that a kickback had nothing to do with the dances you put on here, has it, Timothy?"

"We'll make a French citizen of you yet, my girl!" said Lola. "A kickback is the meeting of a huge wad of money with a boomerang effect. Let's say that a weapons-producing country wants to sell its sophisticated missiles and warplanes to a country that needs them. These potential clients are courted by all the arms-manufacturing countries on the planet. How to make the choice? It's possible that the vendor who can offer an extra little gift, a nice commission, will win the contract. But that's not the end of it. Part of that commission returns to square one, in other words the vendor country, and that kickback can then be used, for example, to finance a political party or an election campaign. Now you see it, now you don't."

"And that way, everyone is happy. The military and the politicians."

"Precisely, my girl. Welcome to the real world."

"I think I prefer the world of Calypso. Here at least it's obvious you have nothing to hide."

Glancing up from her magazine, Lola's eyes opened wide when she saw Ingrid's costume. A silvery wig, geisha's skin and lips, a rustling black and white costume that left no room for misinterpretation. Ingrid was disguised as a skeleton. An ultra-sexy corpse, thanks to the young American's vital statistics, but a corpse all the same. And Marie had not stinted on drawing every single one of the two hundred bones that make up the human body. The work of a professional.

"Well?" Ingrid asked her.

"Do you really think all the men straining at the leash down there have come to attend a funeral?"

"It's true, I am Death. But by emerging from my shroud, it's Life I'm setting free."

"Alright, looked at like that, why not? Well then, my sincere condolences!"

"Aren't you going to see the show?"

"No thanks. Someone has to keep Sigmund company. I think he's still annoyed at being stuffed in the wardrobe."

For music, Ingrid had chosen Michael Jackson's "Thriller", with its wolves howling in the background. Betsy had warmed up the room with a classic act of total nudity and pole dancing, twisting like a snake round a metal pole, within a confined space. Ingrid found any conversation with a stainless steel bar rather limited, and preferred to occupy the whole stage. Mathieu was announcing her as the star turn, and doing it with feeling.

"And now, ladies and gentlemen, the unique, inimitable performance of the one you've all been waiting for. The flamboyant, the irrepressible queen of Paris. I give you the one and only . . . Gabrielle Tiger!"

Betsy congratulated her on her costume. Timothy gave her a thumbs-up. Marie adjusted her wig and wished her luck.

Ingrid took a deep breath and swept on stage to loud applause. The spotlights were on her, so she couldn't see any faces, but she could sense the audience's bewilderment. For a second they were silent, paralysed. She went to the front of the stage with a swaying gait, and shouted at the top of her voice:

"HAPPY HALLOWE'EN, EVERYBODY!"

At last there was laughter, admiring whistles, and people in the audience began to applaud in a heart-warming fashion. Ingrid tore off her right sleeve, whirled it round, then threw it into the audience. A humerus and a radius bone followed. One admirer cried out GABRIELLAAA! at the top of his voice. Keeping them waiting, Ingrid spun round several times before removing her left stocking and revealing a slender, creamy-coloured thigh. A femur and a tibia flew off. The rest slipped away in a syncopated dream. A hip bone disappeared. The sacrum dissolved. The ribs capsized. The sternum evaporated. The collar bones clashed and vanished. In their place appeared a silky shoulder, a joyous curve of the back, a satin stomach, sun-kissed breasts. As she stripped away the skeleton, as she returned from the kingdom of the dead, Ingrid was filled with blood and flesh, recreated rounded contours. She had frightened them, then won them over. Always the same thing. She wanted to do them good, because she knew they desperately needed it.

As ever, she was sorry to leave the stage. She felt as if she were at one with her audience, knew it was an illusion, but didn't care. Marie was waiting, holding open the silver dressing gown with Calypso embroidered on it, a gentle but unmistakable reminder of the return to normality. Ingrid wrapped it round herself and made for her dressing room.

She was still under the spell of her show. Lola was sitting as before on the clover-coloured chesterfield, Sigmund at her feet like a sphinx guarding a gloomy goddess. The level of port in the bottle had diminished significantly. Ingrid knew that even though she hadn't moved, her elderly accomplice had ventured down a perilous path. The path of a debt she owed to deceased friends.

Those who are dead are never gone: / They are in the Shade that lightens / and in the shadow that darkens . . .

"Did your admirers run away screaming?"

"Mission accomplished, Lola. They survived."

"Unbelievable. I sometimes wonder whether you're not the high priestess of a cult that doesn't yet exist."

Ingrid removed her wig and placed it on the wooden dummy. She sat in front of the mirror and began removing her make-up. Now she had danced, everything looked better. Bring on the inevitable.

"I'm trying to think like him," Lola said. "If I were him, do you know what I'd do?"

"No."

"I would make sure I got the same pathologist as for Toussaint. Evidence disappears with time, so nothing should be left to chance."

"I'm sure you're right."

"Are you annoyed because I'm talking about Sacha?"

"It's not your fault. Nobody could have imagined that another person would die the same way as Toussaint Kidjo. Do you intend to track down Aimé Bangolé?"

"Barthélemy swears he's vanished. At the time, Bangolé had nothing to offer me. Sacha thinks he knew more than he was letting on, but that's because our dear commandant has nothing more substantial to get his teeth into."

"You could have told him you didn't know anything more."

"He irritated me."

"You want to compete with him, is that it?"

"Of course not. Can you see me chasing an informer with this neck-brace and an arm that's been through a mincer?"

"Through a mincer, that sounds dreadful. It makes me think of a heap of crushed bones."

"It would, given the show you've just put on. I can't wait for December when you turn into Mother Christmas . . . Ingrid?"

"Lola?"

"I think I'm going to do something I'm dying to do."

"Really?"

"I intend to ring Thomas Franklin, the pathologist. He's an old friend. Even if he isn't doing the autopsy himself, he'll have inside information. He owes me that at least."

"And what will you do with this inside info?"

"It's just so that I know what's going on, you see? After that, I'll leave it to the professionals. I know that."

Ingrid nodded with an almost believable air of understanding. Lola was someone who told herself stories, and even managed to convince herself they were true. Ingrid exchanged a look with the Dalmatian. Sigmund's big black eyes were a dyke struggling to hold back a sea of wisdom and compassion. This dog would love to discover an inner Mongolia, she thought, winking at him.

9

Although his window was wide open on a windy morning, Sacha woke to the customary smells of paint. Arthur had been working until a ridiculous time the night before, and had forgotten to ventilate the apartment. Taking on Ménard's cousin had been a huge mistake. The lieutenant had neglected to tell him that Arthur was an alcoholic who confused his job with a contemplative ceremony. As talkative as his cousin, he had a propensity to launch into the most unlikely topics, passing from one to another without pausing for breath; but he did the painting at the pace of a drunken slug. The decorating had begun five months earlier, and ought to have been completed before Sacha moved in. The two-roomed apartment on Rue du Petit-Musc was in a privileged location in the heart of the Marais, but the commandant felt as if he had signed a pact with a lunatic just to prove he deserved it. Arthur came and went whenever it suited him: time for him was a very relative concept. Trying to talk straight to him slid off his overalls like rain off a slate roof.

The solution was to sack him. But Sacha had wasted a lot of time trying to find a company to do the work: they were always far too busy and suggested impossible time scales. Not only that, but he had paid Arthur a hefty advance. He suspected Ménard knew exactly what he was doing when he offered his cousin's services. The lieutenant swore that Arthur had refurbished a seventeenth-century town house just off Place des Vosges and had left its owners "open-mouthed" at his work. That adjective "open-mouthed" could be taken in many ways.

Sacha opened his refrigerator to discover a supply of cans of Kronenbourg that would have delighted an entire regiment. He fished out a lonely orange juice and made himself breakfast. He ate it standing up in front of the scaffolding Arthur was using to repaint the kitchen ceiling, a challenge worthy of the Sistine Chapel. Most of the furniture was still covered in bubble-wrap, awaiting the kind attentions of the Marais Michelangelo. Sacha pushed his way through the boxes to the bathroom.

The Palace of Justice lived up to its name. Each time Sacha left the land of the police and entered that of the legal profession, he was impressed by the contrast. The tiny, nondescript offices of police headquarters, always tattered and over-crowded, gave way to a world of honey-coloured stone, marble, venerable woodwork and hushed conversations.

A cleaning lady was polishing the copper plaque that announced *Armand de Sertys*. Sacha waited until she had finished before knocking on the door. The examining magistrate came to open it. A head shorter than the commandant, he looked very neat in his white three-piece suit. The grey-striped tie went with swept-back hair, worn longer than was usual, that gave him the look of a Romantic poet. An impression instantly nullified by his steely gaze.

"Such a pleasure to meet you at last, Commandant Duguin."

His sugary tone implied that Sacha had committed the unpardonable mistake of not coming to see him the moment he had been appointed to the B.C.

"The pleasure is mine."

The two men faced each other across a desk made of a rare hardwood that was so dark it was almost black. It reminded Sacha of the one Vidal had. However, there was no African statuette to stand guard over the room. One wall was filled with old photographs: deep-sea trawlers, fishermen unloading their catch, wrecks on deserted beaches.

"My grandmother was a fisherman's daughter. She went to a school run by nuns. Punishments were terrible: on their knees in clogs for hours on end in glacial classrooms. Later on, my mother was slightly luckier; she married a ruined aristocrat. I'm the last representative of a bygone age, Duguin. And you're the exact opposite, I suppose."

Sacha said nothing, but waited for him to continue.

"It's always interesting to see a young man arrive on a case. I've been investigating the EuroSecurities affair for six years and three months now. That's as interesting and arduous as crossing Dante's Inferno. You descend from circle to circle, searching for the centre of the lies and corruption."

"And where is Richard Gratien to be found in this labyrinth?"

"On the margins, of course. He's an intelligent man. Without seeming to, he's playing his role. Like a good actor, he's protecting his friend Candichard."

Louis Candichard, former foreign minister, was at the centre of the EuroSecurities affair. Suspicions that he had been involved in the financial scandal had been enough to ruin his career. The team of magistrates Sertys was part of were trying to prove he had received secret kickbacks via the Liechtenstein-based clearing house to finance his election campaign. Now that the role of examining magistrates was itself being called into question, Sertys wanted to claim one last scalp before bowing out.

"This murder is vile," Sertys said, "but it must be said, it's come at just the right moment. Gratien has been dealt a mortal blow. Out of a desire for revenge, he could take some dangerous decisions. To betray some of his friends, for example. I'm ready to snap up any precious crumbs he may let fall. Have you questioned him?"

The question sounded like a threat. Sacha could have rephrased the magistrate's line of thought: "I hope you have waited to inform me before taking it upon yourself to meet Gratien. He's mine."

"Not yet."

The magistrate was unable to hide an expression of relief mixed with self-satisfaction. Beneath the immaculately groomed exterior beat a radioactive heart.

"He's a survivor. At seventy-two, he's known all the outstanding politicians of his time. He's seen the young tigers scale the heights of power, been privy to the secrets of the worst sharks in industry and finance, shared a table with the most significant players in the international arms trade, as well as the most disreputable traffickers. His skill, his smooth tongue, his ability to listen, his plain dealing: they've all gone to building his reputation. A shiny shop window against which dazzled suckers press their noses, without realising the filth in the back-room. Our governments have changed; Gratien has stayed the same. The indispensable middleman between our moralising democracy and certain states ruled by bellicose tyrants who are avid consumers of the most up-to-date weapons of death."

"How do you see Vidal's murder fitting into all this?"

"I see it as a consequence of him being Gratien's closest collaborator. Starting from nothing, but clever, Vidal learned good manners as rapidly as the principles of international law. Of course, there was still a touch of vulgarity beneath the veneer of sophistication he acquired thanks to Gratien. At any rate, the novice appeared to be remarkably faithful to his mentor."

"Appeared to be?"

"I never managed to get anything out of him, but if he hadn't been killed, who knows?"

"Were Gratien and he working on anything more sensitive than usual recently?"

"I've no idea. But there's an interesting rumour. All the more so because it's been going round for several years . . ."

The magistrate was building up the suspense, his manicured hands folded across his snowy-white waistcoat. Sacha copied him, and put on a polite smile.

"It's said that Gratien writes down all his transactions in notebooks, my dear boy. And don't forget, he has been around a long time."

Gratien's notebooks, or the access code to the EuroSecurities affair? The magistrate's last hurrah. Mars' words seemed to float over the vast office like leaden clouds heralding a storm. *Gratien is a conman, and Sertys is a crusader . . . it's even possible the two of them are after the same thing . . . So take care, Sacha . . .*

"It's my colleague Maxence who's in charge of the case, isn't it, Duguin?"

No "dear boy" any more, or even "Commandant", and the question was purely rhetorical. Who wasn't aware that it was Maxence who was in charge of the investigation into Vidal's death?

"That's right."

"Benoît Maxence is a remarkable man. He'll know how to handle Gratien. And now I'm sorry, Duguin, but I have an important meeting ahead of me . . ."

With this he had got to his feet. Sacha also stood up, but raised a hand to forestall the other man in a polite but resolute manner. Sertys paused, and frowned at him.

"I'd like to mention Nadine Vidal, the victim's wife, if you don't mind. She claims her husband was thinking of leaving Gratien to start a new life abroad . . ."

Sertys grunted.

"Don't tell me you imagine Gratien might have killed Vidal in a fit of pique?"

"I'm not imagining anything. For the moment I'm simply gathering information."

"Oh come on, Duguin! Nadine Vidal is a young woman from a good family who's gone astray in a marriage to somebody who was not from her background. I'm sure that was one of Gratien's bright ideas too: marrying his protégé into a good family. Money attracts money; that's his credo. And that young woman is rather fanciful: she takes what she wishes were true for reality. Vidal was living a life of luxury, thanks to his mentor. Can you see him giving up all that nice income for a romantic crisis?"

"She seemed like an intelligent woman to me."

"An intelligent woman in love. That's a difficult combination. You ought to know that."

The two men stared at each other. Had Sertys studied his curriculum? He had the reputation of leaving nothing to chance, and of boning up on his professional colleagues. Sacha decided to advance another pawn. He had the feeling the magistrate would not give him another interview for some time.

"I found an 'Antonia' in Vidal's address book."

Sacha was testing the judge, neglecting to tell him that thanks to Vidal's secretary he already knew her identity.

"If I understand correctly, you're adopting a *cherchez la femme* approach, Duguin. It's as good a one as any. But in a case that involves the trafficking of arms, do you really think it's the correct one?"

Sacha did not flinch.

"Alright," Sertys said at length, in a more conciliatory tone. "I only know of one Antonia. She happens to be Gratien's wife. A young African woman. It's true she's very beautiful, but from there to imagining her becoming involved with Vidal, that minion – no, that's impossible. That's what you're thinking, isn't it?"

"Once again, your honour, I'm not thinking of anything in particular. At least not for the moment. Thanks you for all your information."

"I was told you were stubborn, Commandant. It wasn't an exaggeration. Well, well, I've taken note of it. On the list of positive points, of course."

His tone was friendly once more. Sertys extended a firm hand, which Sacha took with the same feigned enthusiasm.

"You and I are going to blow apart this circus of the rich and powerful, my dear Duguin. And that's what matters, isn't it? It's quite possible that Vidal is merely collateral damage in a war between spooks."

"Collateral or not, he's still a victim."

"That's true, but let's not forget that when it comes to the Euro-Securities affair, it's democracy that is the chief victim, Duguin. I wish you an excellent day."

Sertys opened his door wide, then closed it smartly behind Sacha. For a moment, the commandant stood still in the long corridor where the cleaner was still busy with her baize cloth; the copper plaques gleamed in the honeyed light streaming in through the arched windows. *Sertys sees the police a cloth he can use to polish up his fame as a dispenser of justice*, he thought to himself. And he had been very clear: *the EuroSecurities affair is far bigger than anything else, so make sure you don't get in my way.* Noting yet again that Mars was a good judge of men, he started down the vast marble staircase.

A war between spooks. A very hasty judgement. Despite his refined appearance, Sertys was more emotional than cerebral. He did not stand back from things far enough. Sacha had not thought it convenient to point out to him that Vidal's execution reeked of hatred. When had spooks ever carried out their contracts with such passion? Why would a hired killer employ such a spectacular method as a burning tyre? If there were a political motive, a fake suicide, an unfortunate car accident, or heart failure thanks to a discreet poison would have been more sensible. It was something worth thinking about.

He hurried towards police headquarters.

Ménard was deep in discussion with Mars by the coffee machine. The youngster was talking and waving his arms around. The divisionnaire was listening to him with an amused look on his face. As soon as he caught sight of Sacha, he motioned to Ménard to stop and pointed him back towards the main office. Break-time over. The kid and his resentful gaze did as they were told.

"Ménard thinks he knows Africa because he's read books about it. He's no idea what he's talking about. Would you like me to give you the benefit of my moth-eaten memories?"

"I'm sure they're not that moth-eaten."

"I always used to live in the embassy quarter. Because one had to. But what I liked was to go down to the old market and the popular neighbourhoods filled with music. It would blare out from every house and every shop. All the different sounds mingled, but nobody got a headache. No such thing as cacophony under the Kinshasa sun. Everything harmonises in a world that hasn't been polluted by Cartesian logic and quartz watches. No-one arrives on time for their appointments, but everybody ends up meeting one another. That's the kind of thing that kid Ménard will never find in his damned books!"

"Do you miss your life in Africa?"

"Not my life there as such. Let's just say I miss my life abroad a little. I don't think my backside's made for a chair. Not even a boss' one. But everything comes to an end – except for a banana, which has two. That's what my African friends often used to say. How did you get on with the white clown?"

"Exactly as you thought. Sertys has his own agenda. He couldn't give a damn about Vidal; it's the ex-minister Candichard who interests him. He wants to be the saviour of democracy, and to go out with a firework display."

"I want my fireworks too. Too bad for Sertys. O.K., that's enough gabbing, we're going to the movies."

Mars dragged him into his office. He accessed the internet, and found a university website. A wide-angle view of a crowded lecture theatre, them some close-ups of students' attentive faces. On the podium, two men. The younger one, Florian Vidal. A shock of blond hair, strong features, relaxed with a winner's smile, and a lumberjack's stocky body cramped in a tailored suit. The older speaker a tanned fellow with a beard and plump-cheeked, neither tall nor strong-looking and with a receding hairline, but a slow, carefully modulated voice capable of holding his audience.

Sacha listened as he briefly touched on the joys and perils of the career of a business lawyer.

You are likely never to stand up in court, but don't forget that you will follow a very strict ethical code . . . You will be expected to show the ability to listen, a well developed sense of how things are interconnected, a well developed taste for logic, and great intellectual flexibility . . . You will be working in a world where hierarchy is not a problem and you will never be just a number . . . You will be dealing with the real players, but you will have to show the greatest discretion . . .

"I know an infallible way of measuring someone's charisma," said Mars, turning down the sound. "Take a good look at the beast. Smell his gestures. Look how he hypnotises them. He's completely caught up in what he's doing, and yet at the same time he's as slippery as an eel. Believe me, Gratien could have made a name for himself in politics."

"But he preferred the incomparable charm of working behind the scenes."

"With their golden linings. Look, I've got an equally infallible way of measuring people's human qualities."

He started the video again, then froze it on a close-up of Gratien smiling at a student asking him a question.

"What do you make of him?"

"His smile stops at his nose, and doesn't go as far as his eyes."

"Yes, some of the biggest bastards I've known looked just the same."

They watched the talk for a few seconds longer, then Mars froze the video again as it was zooming in on Gratien. He was turning towards Vidal to let him speak. He had just placed a hand on his forearm and was gazing at him affectionately. This time the smile spread across his whole face.

Vidal made an astonishing move: he flung his arm round his mentor's shoulder and launched into an accolade that appeared spontaneous:

Just now, Richard was talking about court rooms. Well, I for one almost found myself in one, but in the dock! If this man here had not dragged me out of poverty and away from the bad company I was keeping and helped me discover the best profession in the world, I don't doubt I would have turned into a petty criminal or a street dealer. I was keen for you all to know this before I began to tell you of my experience as a lawyer on a daily basis . . .

"Before you meet Gratien in the flesh, I wanted you to see him in his heyday. I reckon he's changed, Sacha. You can tell me if I'm right."

10

Undecided, Lola was staring at her telephone. Will she? Won't she? Yes, she will, she finally resolved, and dialled the number for the Forensic Institute. She asked to speak to Doctor Thomas Franklin. After a polite round of platitudes, the old fox showed he had not forgotten her working methods.

"Who would have dreamt that one day you would call me up to ask after my health, my dear Lola?"

"Life has more imagination than we do," Lola said, unable to think of anything better.

"Is that yours?"

"François Truffaut, I think."

"That fits. I find you and I are very New Wave," sniggered the pathologist. "Well, I suppose you're calling about the Vidal affair."

"I was thinking that Sacha Duguin had possibly wanted you for the autopsy."

"Alright then, put your question to him, Lola. I have a lot of respect for you, and we've been through a lot of hard work together, but I can't tell you anything. And that's definite."

"Definitely definite?"

"Irremediably definite and final and terminal. Sorry. And don't get resentful or stress out or sit stewing beside that canal of yours.

Young Duguin is one of us. He'll do what's necessary, O.K.? Trust him."

"I'd just like to point out that as far as Toussaint goes, we've still got nowhere."

"I know that."

"So do you think they'll let that kid Sacha dig deep? You can't be that green at your age."

"*They*. Who do you mean? The people who rule over us, and meet wearing masks in a dark cave after nightfall? Stop your fantasising, Lola, will you? Conspiracy theories are for crackpots."

"Do you know what Valéry Larbaud used to say? *What's terrible about stupidity is that it can look like the greatest wisdom.*"

"And do you know the one by Camus? *Stupidity never lets go.* That makes it a draw, Lola. And as I can sense that your tongue might be about to run away with you, I'm going to hang up now. Behave yourself. My best regards as ever. And I mean it."

Click.

The stubborn old goat had matched words with action. Lola swore so loudly she made Sigmund jump, then swept the puzzle box onto the floor. The pieces of Kilimanjaro did not scatter as she had been hoping, which disappointed her: she had wanted a grand gesture to calm her anger. When she looked, it turned out that Ingrid had taped the sides of the box together, anticipating some fresh drama from her volcanic friend. For an instant, Lola thought of emptying the pieces down the toilet and flushing it. She quickly gave up on the idea as being beneath her, and rushed to open the window instead. The sky was as crazy as Franklin, but she saw the opportunity to give her nerves a nice cold shower. This time she would spare Sigmund and face the unrelenting rage of the clouds on her own. Kitted out from head to toe, she plodded towards the threshold. The Dalmatian followed closely behind, leash between his teeth.

"In the past, I thought those misanthropes who preferred animals to people must be mad. If I'm not careful, you're going to make me change my mind, Sigmund."

At that precise moment, someone knocked at her door. Lola opened. Captain Barthélemy was standing dripping on her mat.

"Talking to yourself, boss?" he enquired anxiously.

"Be careful, lad. Don't you dare suggest I'm going senile. You'd be the second person to do that in less than five minutes. And my retaliation would be violent beyond belief. Besides, what you need is a good spin in the dryer. Don't you have an umbrella, for heaven's sake?"

"My colleagues think it's funny to pinch it from me."

"I knew some firemen were pyromaniacs, but this takes the biscuit. And how do you explain your presence here?"

"I wanted to make a point."

"Needlepoint?"

He wiped his forehead with his scarf, pulled a copy of the *Le Parisien* from beneath his raincoat, and held it out to Lola. Vidal's winning smile was all over the front page. The headline seemed to want to sink its teeth into the reader: YOUNG LAWYER TORTURED BY FIRE! The article described Vidal as a "pawn in the shady transactions of France–Africa". The journalist evoked Richard Gratien, "that mysterious person so indispensable and close to the circles of power in Africa", and expressed concern about "the strange similarity to the Toussaint Kidjo affair, so called because it was the name of the young police officer born in Congo-Kinshasa horribly tortured and burned to death with a flaming tyre". A box summarised the links between Paris and its former colonies.

"If it doesn't bore you, I'd like . . ."

"Nothing bores me anymore, Jérôme."

"I'd like to go over Toussaint's last movements."

Lola shrugged, handed her former assistant a towel, and went off to prepare him a camomile tea with a slug of rum in it. She served herself the same thing, straight from the bottle. Ingrid had brought this sensational drink (about 80° proof) from a Caribbean trip. After the break-up with Sacha, her American friend had gone off to forget everything for a while in the islands. Timothy Harlen had given her his blessing, and put her in touch with a friend of his in Fort-de-France.

When Ingrid had returned, her skin shone like gold, she was blonder than ever, and she was slightly less melancholy. But the sea breezes had not blown away the memory of Sacha Duguin. He was still there, like glowing embers, buried deep in Ingrid's heart.

"I'm annoyed at myself."

"Why's that, boss?"

"I was hoping to start the investigation with Ingrid. But Sacha Duguin is lurking at the next crossroads. I've seen him, and he's got even more sex appeal these days. Life stinks. You're up to your neck in work. So is Maxime. Antoine is on holiday. I can't launch myself into this all on my own because of this brace and my smashed arm. The only one left who could help is Sigmund. But you can't compare a psychoanalyst's Dalmatian with a police dog."

"You could place an advert for a part-time driver, boss. Unemployment has shot off the scale."

"Possibly, but that's not the problem."

"Which is?"

"Ingrid inspires me. She's so modest she almost seems mentally deficient, but she's brilliant at everything she does. Except when it comes to love, of course. Conclusion: now I know how exciting it is to undertake an investigation with her, I can't accept anything less. I know it's selfish of me."

"You're being frank with me, boss, and I'll be the same."

"Poor Jérôme, you're going to pieces. And you look awful. It's not good."

"It's nothing more than a lack of sleep. In fact, I didn't come here to go over Toussaint's final moments. The thing is, I might have a lead on Bangolé."

"He's supposed to be back in his mother country. And possibly even dead."

"I spent most of the night questioning an armada of taxis. My wife's livid, but it was worth it. Bangolé used to work at night, once upon a time."

"In touch with the African aristocracy in Paris, I remember. So?"

"A guy who used to drive him around told me he had taken up religion."

"Religion?"

"A sect or something of the sort."

"Krishna, Moonies, Jehovah's Witnesses, worshippers of the giant Japanese radish?"

"He didn't know. Or he was stringing me along so that I would give him some money. Here are his details. I'm sure you'll have more luck with him than me."

"Why do you think that?"

"Because Ingrid is as beautiful as one of Neptune's suns, and that encourages some people. I can sense that this guy is one of those."

"You're even scarier than me when you put your mind to it, you know that?"

"I learned from a good teacher."

"I'm still not sure."

Lola went over to her wing chair and covered her face with a rug. She could be dragging Ingrid into an exhausting if not impossible investigation that was bound sooner or later to bring them into contact with the irresistible Commandant Duguin. Or she could make a call to that same Sacha Duguin to pass on the lead from the taxi driver.

After several minutes she pulled the rug away and had another drink of the Martinique rum. Then she got a saucer out of the sink, and poured a generous amount of the divine brew into it. She waved it under Sigmund's nose. He sniffed at it, then lapped the rum up without hesitation. That animal was completely remarkable. She took a third swig from the bottle. The rum whispered that friendship was a sacred thing. And that living friends were rather more important than dead ones.

"If this rum was aquavit, I'd think I was in a Scandie thriller," she said to Barthélemy, who was paying for his late-night escapades with yawns that almost unhinged his jaw.

"Why's that?" he said, eyes half closed.

"In Scandinavian thrillers the protagonists go from one long meeting to another, and are always mulling over the problems they have. And they're a bit like you and me. On the verge of a nervous breakdown."

"I'm not close to a breakdown, I'm exhausted. Boss, have you made your mind up yet about whether to involve Ingrid?"

"Good sense tells me I should pass your info on to Sacha."

"As you wish. I'll take the opportunity to lie down for a bit," he said, stretching out on the couch.

The phone rang. Lola stared at it as if it was an intruder.

"Hello? Is that Lola?"

"No, the Princess Vanuatu. I was about to call you, Sacha . . ."

"But first you called Franklin."

"Something tells me you're annoyed with me. That's sad."

"Let's get one thing clear. I'm the one leading this investigation. It's a highly political affair. One false move and the B.C. will be pushed off the case. And if that happens, you'll be able rightly to complain that no-one will ever know who slaughtered Kidjo and Vidal."

"Well, if you want to lead, do it!"

Under the influence of the fumes of rum, Lola had just hung up on Commandant Duguin. What controls our destiny? Whatever the answer, the die was cast. Oblivious to the storm raging in Lola's heart, Barthélemy was sleeping like a log. Leaving him in Sigmund's capable paws, she headed out for the Passage du Désir.

The waiting room was deserted. The psychedelically coloured sofas faced each other in a tense stand-off that Lola had never grown accustomed to. From the massage room floated a perfume of honeysuckle, mingling with music that conjured up the sweetness of the Caribbean.

Her American friend emerged a few minutes later, followed by a smiling, relaxed client all pink in the face. Ingrid accompanied him to the front door, opened a tattered striped yellow umbrella for him, and gently pushed him out into the rain.

"What did you do to that happy mortal?" asked Lola.

"I gave him a Balinese massage and conversation. He's a trader, you understand."

"What is there to understand?"

"The whole world hates him. His compatriots hold him and those like him responsible for the financial crisis."

"The old trick of the scapegoat. Nothing new under the pouring rain. Can I talk to you?"

"Wow! That's the first time you've asked me that. But I know what you're after. Have you been drinking, Lola? You can hardly stand."

"That's the rum traders' fault. Can I sit down again?"

"That wouldn't be a bad idea."

"So you know?"

"You want me to be your Twingo driver while you question the whole of Paris to find the murderer of your ex-associate."

"I'm sorry to load this onto you."

"It's too late now. I've seen Sacha again. You've got your dragon to slay, and I've got mine."

"The dragon of a broken heart?"

"If you like. It's the only way to erase the past. When do we start?"

"Now?"

"In your state?"

"It's as good as any other. I almost have the impression I'm sniffing the meaning of life."

"I'll just put on some proper clothes and we can be off."

Lola rubbed her hands in delight as if she was at the theatre. Ingrid's costume changes were always moments of great dramatic intensity. A few minutes later, her friend resurfaced in a pair of purple and white check trousers and a greenish trench-coat probably found in Dashiell Hammett's trash can in 1937. The ensemble was topped off by a mauve polka-dot cloche hat that looked like something from a Jacques Tati film.

"What footwear is to accompany this splendid outfit?"

"My crocodile-skin cowboy boots."

"Obviously."

"Shall we?"

"I intend to ransack Paris until it surrenders. We won't stop until we die, or until we're satisfied."

Ingrid held out her open palm. Lola dropped the car keys into it. The bird of prey pressing down on her chest flew off to an unknown destination.

11

Sacha, Carle and Ménard were leaving the Forensic Institute beneath an unbelievably blue sky. The aerial metro screeched past, the waters of the Seine were a dirty yellow in the background. Sacha suggested they repair to the corner café. They could catch up over an espresso.

Franklin had offered his conclusions while the autopsy was being carried out. They confirmed Sacha's intuition. The two murders differed in their intensity: Kidjo had been tortured systematically; Vidal had not been mutilated, and the torture was psychological.

Franklin had also discovered the trace of a puncture mark on Vidal's charred throat: in all likelihood he had been put to sleep before being abducted. When he had seen this, the pathologist had recovered Kidjo's autopsy file. He had found an identical mark back then. A laboratory analysis had revealed benzodiazepine, a drug used to treat anxiety and insomnia, in the lieutenant's blood.

Carle had ordered an americano, Sacha a strong black coffee, and Ménard, true to his idea of being original, a tomato juice. With his lips stained blood-red, the dark rings under his eyes, his undertaker's suit and crumpled white shirt, to Sacha he looked every inch a vampire.

The commandant gave the others a detailed report of his visit to the judge. At night, he thought, the magistrate must dream of

Gratien's notebooks, seeing them as the key to his great obsession: Louis Candichard. "When I was studying at the Sciences-Po, Sertys came to give us a lecture," Ménard told them. "He thinks he's the bee's knees. Another reason for not letting him have his way."

Duguin was not dismayed by his lieutenant's aggressive outbursts. Properly directed, they could be useful.

"Quite a lot of people would kill their father and mother to lay their hands on those notebooks, I guess."

"Yeah, with Sertys out in front," Ménard said.

"Yet I don't see why they would set fire to a lawyer. When it comes to political skulduggery, it's best to be discreet."

He was watching Carle. She had raised her head, definitely interested in his theory. But she kept her thoughts nice and warm beneath her raincoat.

"Where have you got to with any possible witnesses at Colombes?"

"Nowhere. Nobody likes going for a walk at night in a park flooded with rain in the depths of the suburbs, boss. The gendarmes are still questioning the staff and anyone using the swimming pool. But there's nothing so far," Ménard said.

"Any C.C.T.V. footage?"

"No sign of any suspect vehicle."

"O.K., leave that to the gendarmes. Concentrate on the Africa angle. Even if the killer did it for personal reasons, we mustn't forget the political links. It may be there were some between Kidjo and the lawyer."

Carle took a call on her mobile and started a brief conversation.

"Vidal's Porsche has just been found on Boulevard Ney."

"What state is it in?"

"Untouched."

"Any witnesses?"

"At first sight, no. The boulevards are deserted at night. Apart from prostitutes and their clients."

"People not exactly known for their cooperation . . . put an inspector onto it all the same."

"Fine."

"Vidal leaves home in his own car. He has a private meeting on Boulevard Ney. He gets into the other car. The attacker drugs him and sweeps him off to Colombes. Quick and easy," Ménard summed up.

"Even quick and easy murders leave clues. We'll get there."

A doubtful pout from the Zen monk. A crazed look from the vampire. It was going to take many litres of oil to grease the wheels of this infernal duo, but Sacha did not despair. The rain had begun beating against the café window once more. He paid the bill.

Carle stood waiting stiffly under her check umbrella, collar raised, smile left for another day. Ménard ran to get the car from the Institute's parking lot.

"Are you going to see Gratien, boss?"

"Yes, and you're coming with me. Two won't be too many to corner the beast."

He wasn't expecting any reaction, and so wasn't disappointed. Carle did though offer him a corner of her umbrella. Sacha had decided to systematically forget his own, hoping this might create some sort of bond between them. Even if she wasn't friendly, Carle was well brought up.

The residence was on a par with its owner's reputation: a private house with an elegant pale stone façade only a stone's throw from the Musée d'Orsay. Even Carle seemed impressed.

Beyond the royal blue porch, an exuberant, fragrant English

garden. A black giant with an impassive, well-groomed face showed them into a marble-floored hall before slipping away. A seventeenth-century atmosphere, with futurist furniture. Soon afterwards, a woman in her thirties appeared. "Appeared" was not too strong a word: the new arrival was of a rare beauty. Milky coffee skin, green eyes, thick mane of coppery hair, cat-like features, curves in all the right places, and a languor about her that Sacha found very calming.

"Antonia Gratien. Thank you for coming. My husband will see you now."

Her voice was deeper than he had been expecting. Her outfit was as chic as her perfume: loose-fitting trousers and sweater, delicately harmonious in grey and white. They followed her through a luxury décor punctuated by contemporary paintings. One last corridor and their journey ended with the portrait of a pope who was either disfigured or on amphetamines. A Bacon, no less.

Antonia Gratien pointed to a half-open door and sashayed off. Sacha noted Carle's expression. She had registered that the physical charms of Gratien's wife had produced a definite impact on her boss' libido. A new little weakness to store in her invisible notebook? *Be extremely subtle, even to the point of formlessness. Be extremely mysterious, even to the point of soundlessness. Thereby you can be the director of the opponent's fate.*

According to the old code of politeness, a man should precede a woman when entering somewhere unknown, to protect them from the blows of fortune. But in this context, wasn't that something to be consigned to the dungeons, along with courtly love and medieval epics? His colleague was definitely the sort who had no need of a *preux chevalier*: Sacha let her cross the threshold first.

A man in a dark suit installed behind a white lacquered desk. A wall covered in photographs: Gratien standing beside his powerful African friends, a discreet smile forever on his lips.

I reckon he's changed. Mars was right. The man of the house no longer looked like the charismatic lecturer hypnotising a student audience. His beard was still more pepper than salt, but his hair had turned grey, the lines on his face had deepened. Behind the tortoise-shell glasses, his blue gaze had clouded over. At sixty-two, the *éminence grise* of the dark continent looked ten years older.

Sacha had memorised their host's C.V. Muslim mother born in Morocco; French father from a Jewish family of small traders, who had started from nothing and built up a prosperous business in public works. Six brothers and sisters. The Gratien clan lived in Morocco, then in Côte d'Ivoire, before finally settling in Cameroon. Richard, the third brother, began studying law in Yaoundé just as the country was throwing off colonial rule. At university he rubbed shoulders with the future elite in the years when the African nations were winning independence one by one. His powerful African friends presented him to their French counterparts. Little by little, the young lawyer put his knowledge of the continent at the service of France and its entrepreneurs. He gravitated towards the arms trade, a sector never affected by any crisis.

The butler reappeared to serve a peppermint tea. Gratien tapped the silent giant on his forearm:

"Thank you, Honoré, you can put the car in the garage, I shan't be going out again today."

He had picked up a set of Muslim prayer beads, an amber *misbaha*, and was twisting it between his fingers. Sacha noticed his wristwatch: identical to Vidal's. Nadine Vidal's bitter tone came back to him: *Gratien paid for our wedding.*

"I'm very grateful to you for coming, Commandant. Your minister assured me that you and your team were hard workers . . ."

His voice was slurred. Gratien was either on sedatives or had not slept for several nights. That did not stop him already trying to impress them with his important contacts.

"You were close to Florian Vidal, Monsieur Gratien."

"Yes, very."

"I suppose that in your line of work, you have quite a few enemies. Any names you'd care to mention?"

"No-one had any reason to take against Florian. He was excellent in all his dealings. Irreproachable."

His voice had trembled. Barely perceptibly, but it was there. Did the redoubtable go-between of France–Africa have a weak spot? Silence fell. Sacha could make out Carle's light breathing beside him, and the click of Gratien's nails on the amber *misbaha* beads.

"Florian Vidal left home that evening after receiving an unidentified call. His practice was devoted almost exclusively to clients of yours. It's probable that call was linked to those activities."

"Florian had no meeting that night. I've questioned everyone."

His pain was palpable. Judge Sertys' words took on a special resonance. *Gratien has been dealt a mortal blow. Out of a desire for revenge, he could take some dangerous decisions.*

What dangerous decisions was the judge talking about? He thought Vidal was collateral damage. What was really at stake?

"So your associate left home in a rush following an unexpected telephone call? That's hard to imagine in someone so well-organised."

"Yes, I can't get that out of my mind either. It's up to you to do your job and find out."

This was said without any apparent bitterness. The man who served the powerful expected to be obeyed in his turn.

"Armand de Sertys has called you in several times over the Euro-Securities affair."

"You've met Sertys?"

"Of course."

"Then you know as much as I do. I'm not in the habit of lying to justice."

"Vidal knew all your dossiers. Confidentiality is essential in your line of work. That means secrets are very valuable. And perhaps someone wanted to get them out of him."

"There was nothing in our dossiers to justify what was done to him . . ."

"A lot of people speak of Vidal as your heir."

"Meaning?"

"Was that an impression or a reality?"

"I don't understand what you're trying to say, Commandant."

"I've heard you paid for his wedding."

"If that has got any connection with what concerns us now, I fail to see it."

"If you don't intend to offer me any names from the business side, you could perhaps give me more personal leads."

"I have no children. Antonia and Honoré are my heirs. But don't go investigating them. No-one could be more loyal."

Annoyance beneath the pain. *Don't go investigating them.* A barely disguised threat?

Hatred, the desire for revenge, was simmering beneath his urbane exterior. Sacha did not have any illusions though: neither Gratien nor Nadine Vidal were ready to reveal what dossiers the young lawyer had been working on at the time of his death.

When he mentioned the Kidjo affair, the other man's fingers halted on the amber beads, then began to count them again. Sacha had hit a nerve.

"No, it doesn't mean anything to me."

"A young policeman killed the same way five years ago. Even back then, Vidal was no longer just your chauffeur."

The blue eyes hardened. Gratien was obviously displeased at having his dauphin's less than brilliant past brought up. He said he had very little time left before his next meeting. Sacha insisted.

"Excuse me, Commandant, but . . . how old are you?"

"Thirty-five, why?"

"That's very young to be a commandant. You don't seem to be aware of all the codes."

"If I've offended you, it was without meaning to."

Gratien tossed his *misbaha* on to the desk.

"I'm not easily offended, young man. Let's just say I'm a fanatic about social relations. And about getting the job done."

"Rest assured that I will do my best. That *we* will do our best. But your help is indispensable."

"Convey my respects to Mars. And tell him to expect a few telephone calls."

Gratien rang for the servant to show them out.

"You said you had some ammunition stored to help you with Gratien," Carle said on the staircase.

"Yes, and so?"

"It seems you might have been outgunned."

"Is that a reproach?"

"An observation."

"You were welcome to back me up just now."

"I've too great a sense of hierarchy to do that, boss."

She managed to serve up monstrosities on a silver platter. Good for her. Sacha was tempted to put her in her place, but these weren't the right surroundings or the right moment. He needed to concentrate, not score points in the duel she was trying to force him into.

Antonia Gratien was leafing through a fashion magazine, sitting on a cowhide chaise longue, beneath a painting that looked very much like a Dalí: a man was emerging from an egg, but in fact it was a globe, and the new-born infant was appearing between South America and Africa. A drop of blood was dripping from the tear in the map.

"Your talk didn't last long."

"You're right, madame. And that's a shame."

"You must excuse my husband. He was very close to Florian. His death has shocked him."

"And you?"

"I beg your pardon?"

"You seem so calm."

She closed the magazine, and weighed her words.

"Florian was like my little brother."

"Does the name Toussaint Kidjo mean anything to you?"

"Who is he?"

"A colleague of African origin murdered in the same way as Vidal."

"Did you ask Richard the same question?"

"Yes."

"Well then! He's the ideal person to reply."

"Apparently not."

"I'm sorry. Give him a bit of time."

"My sincere condolences, Madame Gratien."

"Thank you, Commandant Duguin."

Carle sat in the driving seat, and pulled away gently. Despite the obvious tension, Sacha was able to reflect. If Gratien had not succeeded in getting under his skin, Carle had no chance of doing so. He decided to overlook her unpleasant comments and ask her opinion. Just like that. His relaxed attitude disarmed her, and she took a while to answer.

"That guy is sick with grief. He's behaving like a father who has lost a son. Of course he knows more than he's letting on."

"And is thinking of meting out justice himself. Did you sense that as well?"

"Yes, and what's worrying is that he has the means and the connections to do it."

Sacha had the same sense of foreboding. Gratien was doped to the eyeballs, but once he came back down to earth he would start doing damage.

Sacha went back to the Finance Squad offices. Luce Chéreau looked delighted as she glanced up from her files.

"I haven't forgotten you, Sacha. Impossible. But I haven't found anything new."

"I've just come from Gratien's. Can you take a good look at his will? Apart from possible money-laundering, I want to know what inheritance plans he's made."

"In short, you're asking me to stick my nose into a public notary's business. But there's a snag."

"What's that?"

"The law only obliges notaries to open their books when it comes to money-laundering investigations. When a private matter is involved, the notary is obliged to respect professional secrecy just like a lawyer. Only the parties involved in a document drawn up by a notary or their representatives can obtain a copy. Get the picture?"

"My dear Luce, I know you're a resourceful woman. Determined, stubborn. The sort I like. You can get what you want."

"Flatterers only succeed if someone listens to them. But for you,

I'm willing to behave like an idiot. Are you free for dinner and a roll in the hay on Saturday?"

"Duty before pleasure, Luce. And it seems to me that story about a roll in the hay comes up rather often, don't you think?"

"I like running jokes, baby."

He winked at her on his way out.

"Or rather, I like *everything* about you, Sacha. Even your macho manners!"

She shouted this out loud, keen for her colleagues to catch the show. Sacha glimpsed their knowing looks, and walked out with a smile on his face.

His mobile rang just as he was reaching the lifts. Mars.

"Have you been talking to Gratien?"

"Yes. And he wasn't very cooperative."

"I've just had a call from a friend of his. A creep from the Interior Ministry who thinks that the fact he graduated from the National Administration School gives him the prerogatives of divine right."

"Gratien's made a complaint? Already?"

If the lawyer was so quick when he was on barbiturates, they could expect the worst once he'd been weaned off them.

"He didn't like your style, and demanded you be replaced."

"Is that all? Were you forced to accept?"

"Are you joking? I'm the boss here. They can all go to hell."

"Who is 'all'?"

Sacha was anticipating another theatrical outburst from Mars. He wasn't disappointed.

"I work in the civil service, but that doesn't mean I have a blind admiration for some of my colleagues. Our country is proud of its revolution, but nothing has really changed. The caste of mandarins has replaced Louis XIV's nobility, but it has the same bad habits.

They spend without counting, never question their own actions, and govern from on high. I won't be manipulated by their sort. The advantage is, they cancel each other out. I know two or three people who can get us out of this. You just have to know the score. O.K., I'm done laughing. How did you find Gratien?"

"The conqueror we saw in the video has vanished. Vidal's murder has broken him. But I sense he's the kind who can resuscitate."

"Well spotted. The proof: he's already tried to remove you from the scene."

"He didn't like the connection I made with the Kidjo affair. Not at all."

"Did he react?"

"No, but his attitude said everything. And he thought I was too young for my job."

"Excellent. We're getting to him. I think we're making progress. Did you meet Antonia?"

"Yes."

"Well? Superb, isn't she?"

"She certainly is. And very relaxed. Do you know her?"

"A little. She speaks her mind. That could be useful for you. If you stay on the right side of her, we could get our hands on information about that bastard who calls himself her husband. You'll need to play your cards skilfully."

With that he had hung up. Sacha slipped the mobile into his pocket and took the lift. *That bastard who calls himself her husband . . .* The buccaneer was up in arms against the conquistador. Ready to do battle.

12

The two women flanked the taxi under a bus shelter. Small, chubby, with sideburns too long for him, and wearing a sailor's cap, the driver was over the moon. After an awkward start, Ingrid was working like a charm. She had left her decrepit raincoat on the bench of the shelter and offered her impeccable curves to the pouring sky in an undulating dance, until the number 97 stopped the show with a impetuous blast of its horn. Like a Bollywood star stepping out of the Ganges, she had won an Olympic medal for soaking-wet T-shirts. The tight blonde curls plastered on her streaming forehead only added to her unique charm. Lola held her breath as she listened to her subtly working their witness.

"I confess to everything. Your methods are a lot more fun than those of your colleague, that cop from the 10th arrondissement. I found a book in my jalopy . . ."

"What book?"

"The one Bangolé was reading before he vanished. I was always the one who drove him round Paris, he wouldn't have anyone else. We became mates. He had a good life, the monkey! Parties of all kinds with velvety-skinned African princesses."

"Where's that book now, Dédé?"

"Wouldn't you like to know? You're the sweetest little thing around here, but it's still going to cost you a couple of smackers."

"Fifty euros each?"

"Two hundred, my child. Have I got "The Salvation Army" written on my cap?"

Lola took two banknotes out of her purse. She kept tight hold of them until Dédé produced a plastic bag for her: inside was a French thriller with a gaudily striped cover.

"Two hundred euros for that?" she said.

"There's a leaflet inside. Money back if you're not satisfied, girls: that O.K.?"

The leaflet lauded the merits of high-powered prayer with the Children of the Glorious Christ, an evangelical group based in Belleville. The invitation to a "mass of renewed hope for the children of God" was from five years earlier.

"Thousands of flyers get distributed in this city," Lola snapped. "How do I know you're not just slipping us an expensive bookmark?"

"You'll have to believe me, dear lady. I'm telling the truth. That Bangolé was a bit of a religious freak. Whenever we had five minutes to kill, we chatted about God and the angels. I like listening to the crap people talk, it keeps me sane. But towards the end, my mate was scared stiff."

"Why?"

"No idea. There were glimmers of panic in those chocolate eyes of his. Then from one day to the next, he disappeared."

Lola conceded that the tip-off was worth pursuing.

Sigmund, who had been waiting patiently in the Twingo all this time, rejoiced as soon as he saw them. They made a detour to the nearest supermarket to buy a towel. Ingrid dried herself as best she could before driving off again.

"Brilliant, your trick of a striptease with clothes on," Lola said. "I'd never have dared ask you to do anything like that."

"I couldn't care less. It felt like somebody else was getting soaked up."

"First, in French it's just *soaked*. Second, don't get started on the slippery slope of couldn't-care-less-ism. No man is worth losing your self-respect over."

"Yeah, whatever."

All they needed now was an attack of pernicious nihilism.

"*Sursum corda*, Ingrid. This investigation is for Toussaint. And for us. It's the ticket to our renaissance. Do you follow me?"

"I'm doing more than follow you because I'm the one who's driving."

"That's true. There at least you're being positive."

"I thought being positive was too American for you."

Lola gave up being the schoolmistress. Ingrid's brain was occupied with something other than Sacha: that was the main thing.

"Bah, with globalisation, everything ends up being homogenised."

"Do you French say homogenisation?"

"Yes."

"You have too many words ending in 'ion'."

"That's a matter of opinion."

They had fun with the French language all the way to Belleville. When they passed a restaurant, Les Plaisirs Celestes, Lola declared she was hungry, and demanded they back up.

"But we've only just begun the investigation."

"I need energy, Ingrid. Besides, I have fond memories of the sensational steamed dumplings here."

She sat herself at a table, a broad smile on her face, enchanted by the waltz of trolleyfuls of dishes. She treated herself to a feast of Cantonese, Pekinese and Taiwanese food, while Ingrid made do with a plate of noodles and sneaked a few crispy rolls into a paper napkin for Sigmund, who was very grateful for the thought. They drove on, and eventually parked on Rue de la Présentation.

"Yet another '-ion' word," Lola remarked. "I hope it brings us luck."

Sigmund, on the verge of a nervous breakdown in the Twingo's confined space, was invited to join the two women. On the peeling wall of a building with a dusty-looking cobbler's shop on the ground floor, a buzzer indicated "C.G.C.". The Children of the Glorious Christ might still be around. Lola rang the bell.

"Hello?" crackled a unisex voice.

"I've come about the Mass."

"What Mass?"

"I'd like to convert."

The door clicked open. Ingrid, Lola and Sigmund went into a hallway smelling of incense. The ex-commissaire's spirits rose. Ingrid put on a pair of dark glasses that covered half her face. She explained that the best way to smuggle Sigmund in was by pretending he was a guide dog.

They were greeted by a roly-poly ringleted redhead in glasses. Her yellow and black striped T-shirt made her look like a bee who had stolen all her companions' store of honey.

"I've heard wonderful things about your group," Lola said. "I'm searching for some kind of spirituality, or indeed some kind spirituality. An African journalist friend, Aimé Bangolé, was the person who mentioned you."

"I don't recognise the name," the bee said.

"Oh, that was at least five years ago. I'm a slow worker. The ways of the Lord often involve detours. I'd like to have a trial run before I join your group."

"Have a trial?"

"A Mass where everyone is in the mood. Something with a bit of life to it. Faithful who make me feel like glorifying Christ."

"Glorification, another word ending in 'ion'," muttered Ingrid before she was kicked on the shin.

"Well, there is a Mass, but it's this evening . . ."

"At what time?"

"Half past seven, in this building. And who are you . . . madame?"

"Jacqueline Martin," Lola improvised. "Spelled as it sounds. And my friend here is . . . Claude Françoise."

"Almost like the singer?"

"Yes, but she's blind from birth, so more like Stevie Wonder, her compatriot. She sings almost as well as him. You're going to be glad we came. Alright, so now you know all there is to know about us. See you this evening then. Thank you for your kindness."

Once they were out in the street again, and protected from the pouring rain by the cobbler's awning, Ingrid asked Lola how she was planning to murder time before "Operation Glorification".

"Do you have appointments?"

"No, I cancelled today's massages for you. But I have to dance tonight at the Calypso."

"That shouldn't be a problem. Let's go and *kill* time in Buttes-Chaumont Park. Sigmund needs a walk."

"Dogs aren't allowed in Paris parks, Lola."

"But perhaps guide dogs are. Besides, park attendants aren't stupid. Why would they come out in this rain? It's proof that the heavens are on our side," said Lola, clasping her hands together as though in prayer. "You know, this is the first time I've ever quivered with impatience at the idea of attending Mass."

"Why do the French say 'precipitation'?"

Lola could not follow what her friend was getting at.

"You say 'precipitation' for rainfall, but there's nothing precipitous about this endless rain. All these words ending in 'ion' are really mysterious."

"We say 'evolution' when we're talking about the change from animal to human," said Lola. "But some days I wonder whether some soft-haired primates with temperaments to match are philosophically superior to us. Everything is relative. You have to accept it."

"Yes, but all the same."

"That's how it is, Ingrid."

*

"That's how it is, sir, yes. Possibly, sir, but I can't promise anything. Yes, you're right. We'll do as we said. Call me back in an hour or two, but preferably one, alright? It's very important."

Ménard ended the call, then threw the mobile into the waste-paper basket and banged his head on the desk. Carle raised her eyes from her file, then plunged back into it. Sacha enquired what the problem was. The lieutenant replied from between clenched teeth that he "had been questioning Africa for all he was worth for a good three hours" and still couldn't get anything out of her. Their Congolese colleagues were never where you expected them to be. When finally you managed to get hold of them, they all described a wishy-washy kid no more interested in politics than in anything else. Cooperation was not a word in the Toussaint Kidjo family's vocabulary. He had no brothers or sisters, his mother was deceased, and none of his relatives seemed to want to help the police. Trying to discover a link between the lawyer and the police lieutenant "was like doing the Paris–Dakar race on a scooter". Commandant Duguin smiled as he recalled what Mars had said. *No such thing as cacophony under the Kinshasa sun. That kid Ménard will never find that in his damned books . . .*

"You studied politics. You must know Sun Tzu."

The lieutenant's face was an interesting blend of curiosity and exasperation. But exasperation was uppermost: it was clear the novice did not appreciate the methods of the master, and found it hard to conceal.

"*When an eagle breaks the body of its prey, it is because it has struck at exactly the right moment.* Patience, Ménard. And perseverance."

Carle had raised her head once again, stared at the two men, and gone back to her reading. Ménard preferred not to respond, and picked his mobile out of the basket. Sacha went out of their office to see the divisionnaire, who wanted him to meet a certain Lieutenant-Colonel Olivier Fabert: "someone from the new French version of the F.B.I. and a balls-breaker, in my humble opinion." That was not a lot to go on, but already far too much.

Sacha shook the French Fed's hand. Brown close-cropped hair, blue, cold eyes, chin with a deep cleft, the hypocritical smile of an insurance salesman.

Mars was smiling too, and was a picture of friendliness, but Sacha knew his boss well enough to be aware he could have done without this particular summit meeting. The first round, a conversation between just him and this man from the D.C.R.I., had already taken over an hour. Fabert explained that the D.C.R.I. was determined to shed light on Florian Vidal's murder, his closeness to Gratien making him a key figure in French-African relations. Fabert spoke in a dull monotone, and seemed to be using his two brain hemispheres at the same time: the first reciting the well-rehearsed lines, the second studying his adversary.

"The superintendent tells me you went to see Gratien this morning, Commandant."

"Yes, that's right."

"How did you find him?"

"Perturbed."

"Meaning?"

"Vidal was more than his secretary. Gratien sees this as something personal. On the other hand, he doesn't want to cooperate."

"You would have been better advised to inform us before you met him."

"I beg your pardon?"

"You heard me, Duguin. In future, I invite you to make contact with me before you take any initiative . . . Good, well I think we'll leave it there. The divisionnaire will keep you informed."

Sacha glanced at his boss, who gave him a discreet nod that Fabert did not notice, but which said: *Go for this idiot, you have my blessing.*

"I think we'll be doing the opposite, Fabert. *You* call *me* before you go jumping in feet first."

"Are you sure you're in a position to call the shots?"

"In what sense?"

"A commandant in the B.C. who has been involved with a strip-tease artiste, who in turn is linked to one of the witnesses in the Kidjo affair, a retired police commissaire . . . It may be that your responsible ministers see that liaison as very dubious."

"Do you always give the people you speak to a desire to punch you in the face, or am I the exception, Lieutenant-Colonel?"

"Is that a threat, Commandant?"

"Gently, you two," Mars said. "You're letting your tongues run away with you . . ."

"On the contrary," Fabert snapped back. "Duguin couldn't have been clearer. I've made a note of that. Have a good afternoon."

With these words he made his exit, a forced smile on his face.

"I'm sorry, Sacha. He caught me like a greenhorn. He came out with the usual spiel about the need for the police and the D.C.R.I. to collaborate. I had no idea he was going to try to undermine you. He claimed he wanted to meet you to put a face to a name . . ."

"I don't understand his strategy, boss."

"I reckon that beneath the bluster they're in panic mode. Gratien has notebooks that threaten to blow the whole shebang sky-high. He's wounded, and risks running amok. That means the spooks are in turmoil. And you know the sacrosanct system of the separation of powers. Everyone protects their own backs."

It was an old tradition in the security services: they were split into almost water-tight units, to control any leaks that might arise. And to avoid contamination. This method often saved their bacon. The other side of the coin was that their agents often played as soloists, in order to protect their backsides in a crisis.

"Fabert's boss is an acquaintance of mine. I'll sort it out. If need be, I'll go as far as the *responsible ministers*, as that brown-noser calls them."

Sacha stared at Mars and massaged the back of his neck. The tension had made his muscles tense.

"Continue with your investigation without a worry, O.K.? I have complete faith in you."

"Thanks, boss."

"But there's something I must mention. When I was going through your file before we appointed you, I baulked at your relationship with that American woman. A cop shacked up with a stripper isn't . . . the best recommendation."

"So you regret your decision?"

"No. Your service record speaks for itself. And also, I was your age once! Alright, now get out of here, we've wasted enough time as it is. Back to work."

"Thank you."

"Don't mention it."

Sacha walked slowly back down the corridor. He felt groggy and made a detour via the washroom to splash his face with cold water.

He was leaning over the basin, trying to analyse what had just happened, when Ménard stuck his head round the door.

"Boss, I've won a stage in the Paris–Dakar on a scooter. One brilliant idea, and the finishing line is within reach."

Ménard and his tangled metaphors.

"Tell me."

"I looked at the problem from a different angle. All Kidjo's relatives swore he had no links to the world of politics. What if that wasn't just a way of getting rid of me? What if it were true?"

"So what?"

"So, if Kidjo was never politically active, there was one of his mates who was seriously into the stuff, if you see what I mean."

"I don't, but I'm all ears."

"Toussaint Kidjo had a childhood friend, Norbert Konata. Born in the same village, a few miles outside Kinshasa. And he was a journalist. Guess what area . . ."

"Politics."

"Bingo, boss."

"And he was a journalist?"

"Double bingo, boss. He was bumped off just before the elections. Kidjo went to his funeral."

"When was that?"

"A few months before his death."

"Good. Well then, the next stage in your Paris–Dakar on a scooter is to call Jean Texier."

"Who's he?"

"Kidjo's father. A doctor who has worked for N.G.O.s all his life. He must have known Norbert Konata. Go and see him. First thing tomorrow if possible."

"Action at last! Excellent. Are you coming with me, boss?"

"We've got a slight time problem. Nothing serious, but we have to share out the work. I'm dealing with the lawyer's mother, and so is Carle."

"Have you found the mother?"

"As good as. She's never left the 20th arrondissement, where Florian Vidal was born. If the family weren't close . . ."

". . . it wasn't for any reasons of geography. Fine, I'll concentrate on Texier. See you tomorrow, boss."

Ménard and his tiresome insistence on always having the last word.

13

Sigmund was terrified by the enthusiasm of the glorious children. Ingrid could feel him trembling against her leg. The evangelicals didn't go in for half-measures. They sang in unison as if their lives depended on it, and danced with arms raised on the brink of a trance. Lola wasn't left behind. She entered into the spirit right from the start, belted out the hymns with great passion, swayed to the rhythms, thrust her good fist towards the ceiling at regular intervals, and shouted out *yeaahh* with all her might. Ingrid gave her a discreet nudge.

"You're not going a bit too far, are you? You could get us noticed."

"Do you know the nickname these evangelicals have, my beauty?"

"Absolutely not."

"The light-bulb changers. Because their arms are always stretching up to the ceiling. Besides, it's good exercise . . . you have to let yourself go. C'mon, follow me."

Ingrid sighed, then got into the mood, imitating the gestures of the great Stevie Wonder, and keeping up the tempo right to the end. One last glorification, and the group moved to a room at the back of the courtyard: time for the glorious children to fraternise in the cafeteria. Lola could not spot Bangolé anywhere, and so the couple, backed up by their trusty Dalmatian, began to question the devotees, relying on Ingrid's fake blindness to make things easier. They interrupted conversations, gently tried out the name of Bangolé. The ex-commissaire had brought the French thriller, and declared she wanted to return it to her "friend who's been lost for far too long".

"I'm beginning to wonder if our aesthete in the bus shelter wasn't taking us for a ride," Lola said almost to herself.

"I've got an idea," said Ingrid, snatching the thriller from her. She gave it to Sigmund to sniff, and bent down to explain to him all that was at stake. The dog led them straight to the buffet.

"You're spoiling him, Ingrid."

"Probably, but with reason."

"What reason?"

"Once he's eaten his fill, he's more likely to turn into a police dog. No-one can function on an empty stomach."

Ingrid offered him a generous piece of cake and a chicken sandwich dripping with mayonnaise. The Dalmatian scoffed the lot in the blink of an eye. After that, Ingrid repeated the ritual: a sniff at the thriller, plus an explanation of their mission. Sigmund pulled at his leash and led them towards the exit. Ingrid was about to admit defeat when the dog headed for the staircase. They arrived at the second floor, where Sigmund began to smell a doormat with great excitement. African music was throbbing through the door.

"Who is it?"

"You're wanted in the cafeteria."

The door opened on a man in a green tracksuit with a blue-black skin. He had put on at least ten kilos, and had let his hair and beard grow. He was wearing worn-out basketball sneakers with pink laces. The former society chronicler had lost his sheen, but Lola recognised him at once.

He shot off like a human cannonball. Ingrid threw away her dark glasses and set off in pursuit. As she reached the entrance hall, she saw him running out of the front door. He ran up Rue de la Présentation, arms scything the air to a techno-trance rhythm. Ingrid copied him. Bangolé raced into Rue Ramponeau, brought a car to a screeching halt, then headed into Boulevard Belleville, aiming for the metro. Ingrid accelerated. No flabby forty-year-old was going to shake off a girl who was a member of the SupraGym and its state-of-the-art treadmills. Two young toughs were coming in the opposite direction. A glance at Bangolé's electrified silhouette. A glance at Ingrid. The taller of the two stuck out his foot. She went sailing towards the tarmac.

"You dirty cop! Chasing my brother!" her attacker roared, giving her a kick in the ribs. "You're fucked!"

"And so are your family jewels!" Ingrid said, bounding back to her feet.

"What jewels?" scoffed the second man.

The attacker was rewarded with a Shotokan front kick accompanied by a terrifying shout, straight to the crotch. This manoeuvre left him on his knees. His friend had retreated to a safe distance. Ingrid took up the chase once more.

Bangolé rushed into the metro entrance, pushed his way past several people, and ran down the stairs. The sound of barking made Ingrid look round. Sigmund was racing in her direction. She forced her way past the protesting crowd, caught sight of Bangolé heading for the Mairie des Lilas platform, and leapt over the barrier. A pursuit along the tunnels past hypnotised passengers, a perilous descent of more crowded stairs. On the packed platform, a quick look back. Sigmund was still in the hunt.

The metallic rumble of the metro train. Bangolé was cutting his way through the crush of travellers, his arms flapping like an airplane tailfin. He gathered speed, then jumped down onto the rails a few metres in front of the approaching train. The sound of its honking klaxon, cries of terror. Bangolé made it to the far side, scrambled up onto the platform. The train heading in the opposite direction drew into the station.

With Sigmund on her heels, Ingrid turned back. She plunged up the stairs, made it to the far platform, and leapt into a carriage just as the doors were closing. No sign of Bangolé in the adjoining carriage. When the train reached Goncourt station, she raced through the compartments, and finally found the informer trying to hide under a seat. She grabbed him by the tracksuit.

"This woman is crazy, somebody get her off me!" he shouted to all and sundry.

"Police, nothing to worry about!" Ingrid shouted above Sigmund's excited barks.

"So the police employ Yanks to harass people without documents, now, do they? Is this a fresh example of globalisation? Unbelievable!" sniffed an earnest *Le Monde Diplomatique* reader.

"Perhaps they're making a film?" a secondary schoolboy said to his friend. "That cop is too hot to be real."

"The dog's not bad either," added a little girl.

While all this was going on, Ingrid was struggling with Bangolé. The tussle continued as far as République, when Sigmund decided to forget his good manners and sank his teeth into the man's ankle. Bangolé howled and let go of Ingrid. The three of them landed on the platform just as the *Le Monde Diplomatique* reader was agreeing with the school-kid that the cops didn't allow either Dalmatians or well-stacked Americans into their ranks.

"My blood ran cold," Lola managed to croak as she struggled to get her breath back, leaning against the window of the old cobbler's shop. "Sigmund ran off, and I almost found myself on the pavement with my four pins in the air and my neck-brace cracked. I was already imagining you both crushed under a passing car. Antoine Léger would never have forgiven me."

"Woof!"

"That's no excuse! Lie down now, that's enough playing at being Rin-Tin-Tin!" Then, turning to Bangolé, who was sweating like a bemused bear: "Tell me all you know about Toussaint Kidjo, and quickly."

"I already repeated the same story to you a thousand times five years ago, Commissaire."

"Ex-commissaire."

"I'd never have thought it," Bangolé said.

"If you hide for five years with the light-bulb changers, that means you must have your own light show to keep under wraps. Stop making us waste our time, and I promise to forget you for ever. The real cops are looking for you, but I'm not one of them anymore."

"That was long ago. I've forgotten the details."

"Do you think you're a goldfish?"

"What?"

"Three times round the bowl and hey presto! Everything is forgotten. Come on, Bangolé, your memory is in good shape, or you wouldn't be so scared."

Aimé Bangolé might be able to run fast, but he took his time to think this over. He needed it to reach the obvious conclusion: he might as well come clean before he found a new hiding-place, evangelical or not. Toussaint's horrible death had shaken him. If there were monsters around capable of killing a cop in such an atrocious way, it was in the best interest of that cop's informers to vanish into thin air. As for returning to his own country, no chance. Certain people were still on the lookout for him there.

Five years earlier, Toussaint Kidjo had asked him lots of questions about a fellow countryman, someone called Norbert Konata, a journalist from the Democratic Republic of Congo, who was killed near Kinshasa airport in a chase with armed men. He wanted to know if Konata had any connections in France.

"And was that a good question?"

"I know the African community in Paris like the back of my hand, but not Konata. If I didn't tell you anything at the time, it's because I didn't know anything."

"That's a matter of debate. Apart from that, did Toussaint ask you about anything else?"

"No, that was all."

"Just a minute, my friend. You were a journalist in another life, if you remember."

"I can see what you're driving at, Madame Jost. I didn't express myself properly. I knew of the existence of my colleague even though he did serious journalism and I was more into society stuff. And yes, I had read his provocative articles in the African press. But I never met Konata here or elsewhere. And nobody had mentioned him to me in Paris."

"Did Toussaint question you about Richard Gratien? And don't tell me you've never heard of Mister Africa."

All at once Bangolé's face fell. A split-second change, but Lola spotted it. Pure panic. Then he launched into a tirade that had no chance of winning an acting award: the blessed Gratien's name had never crossed their lips during any talk he had with Toussaint.

"Bangolé my friend, you smell like a wild boar at bay, and it's nothing to do with the sprint you just ran. And I myself don't have the soft heart of Bambi's mother. So, stop messing us about or I'll take you straight off to Gratien. If you have nothing on him, you have nothing to fear, do you? If you do, he'll be really pleased to see you and I'll leave the pair of you to get on with it, exchanging cookery recipes. Do you follow me?"

"It's true, Toussaint wanted info about Gratien. Who he met in Paris, where you were likely to run into him . . ."

"And did you tell him?"

"I did my best. I even gave him my invitation to a cocktail party all the V.I.P.s of France–Africa were supposed to be attending."

"Did he go?"

"I've no idea."

"What about Florian Vidal? Did he interest Toussaint?"

"Not to my knowledge. His focus was Gratien."

"Did he think Gratien had some link to Konata's death?"

"You overestimate me. I know absolutely nothing about that. And I'd pay a lot to know. The person who butchered Kidjo and Vidal is really sick."

"You think it's the same person?"

"Don't you?"

"I haven't come to any conclusions yet."

Lola looked back before clambering into the Twingo, where Ingrid and an exhausted Sigmund were already installed. On the pavement of Rue de la Présentation, beneath the yellow circle of a streetlight, the informer looked like a giant courgette left out in a storm. It was rare to see a picture of such sheer dread on a man's face. She walked back to him and advised him to put himself under the protection of Commandant Sacha Duguin.

"Your ex-colleagues have got better things to do than babysit a guy like me."

"Duguin is a pain, but he has his noble moments. You should give him a try."

"Thanks for the suggestion, but I'm not tempted."

"That's up to you."

Lola rejoined her friends. Ingrid drove their thoughtful silence to the vicinity of Père Lachaise cemetery.

"What are we doing here? Research for your skeleton show?"

"In fact, I'm just driving wherever the wind pushes me, as you say."

"Wherever the wind blows me."

"Why not. Where would you like to go, Lola?"

"Let's have a break. I want to explain my theory to you."

Her American friend raised a quizzical eyebrow before finding somewhere to park.

"Five years ago, I drew a blank because none of Toussaint's circle wanted to talk to me. I was too closely involved to ask the right questions. I stressed the witnesses out instead of reassuring them. Now we can start again from scratch. Bangolé was the first on my list. Let's go and see the others."

"Who's next?"

"Jean Texier, Toussaint's father."

"Toussaint didn't use his surname?"

"As you see."

"Didn't you find that odd?"

"No, why? Toussaint had chosen the name of his mother, Calixte

Kidjo. For a young man caught between two cultures, there was nothing odd about it."

She pulled a tattered notebook from her raincoat pocket. She had found it in an old cardboard box she had almost burnt but had changed her mind. A stroke of luck, or brilliant intuition.

Jean Texier had lived on the Rue Gutenberg, in Pré-Saint-Gervais. They had to hope he hadn't moved. Lola punched in his telephone number. She got an answering-machine, and left a message saying she would call by the next morning.

"You look disappointed."

"I'd like to have seen him this evening."

"Why so much precipitation? You've been waiting for five years, so one night won't make much difference."

"We don't have much time."

"Because of Sacha?"

"Not only him. With all the fuss the press is making, believe me, it's not just the police who are interested in the Vidal and Kidjo affairs."

14

Sacha had asked Captain Carle to go with him. A female presence would reassure Florian Vidal's mother. But now that he had met her, he realised that the presence of a woman or of a plate of rotten sushi would have had precisely the same effect on Bernadette Vidal: none whatsoever. The lady in question was propping up the filthy counter of a bar in Rue des Prairies, a stone's throw from Place Gambetta. But the name of the street and the morning light that softened the contours of the nearby buildings were deceptive: the place had nothing bucolic about it. As for Bernadette's loose tongue, that had more to do with the amount of red wine she had consumed than with any pleasure at meeting other human beings. She talked fifteen to the dozen, but Sacha had rarely heard such a litany of negative bile poured out in so short a time. The summary was irresistibly poetic.

In brief, Florian's father was a tosser who had done her a favour the day he had left her in the lurch with his brat. Nobody missed that asshole. Florian was like his drip of a father. Lazy, stupid, and a bully. Bernadette had been quick to tame him and teach him who was in charge. The cocksucker never came to see her, and she had nothing to do with him. He had sent her an announcement of his wedding to a cunt from the high whatever. It wasn't even big enough to wipe her arse on. She wouldn't go to his funeral. Her son was dead to her the day he flew the coop. End of story.

"When did you last see him?"

"I don't remember. Couldn't give a damn."

"Did a police officer come to question you about Florian, five years ago?"

"What was he like?"

"Around thirty, African in origin."

"I don't talk to negroes."

"I'm not asking who you talk to, I'm asking if he came to see you."

"Means nothing to me."

"Did you know that Richard Gratien had paid for your son's studies?"

"What the fuck is that to me?"

"Your answers could help us find Florian's murderer more quickly."

"He's the one who chose to live with those rich bastards. He got what he deserved."

"Did you ever go and ask him for money?"

An uneasy gleam came into her faded eyes. She turned to the proprietor to order another jug of wine. The commandant signalled to him not to make things worse. The bar owner went to hide behind his coffee-making machine.

"Madame Vidal? Either you answer my questions here or I'll take you to the station. Just so you know, we don't keep any red wine there."

"Who is it you're after then? The killer or me? You shouldn't confuse the two."

"You've been struggling to get by on unemployment benefit all these years. I'm guessing that a little bit extra wouldn't have hurt."

"Yeah, alright. I went to see Florian so's he could bung me a bit. It's normal, isn't it? He'd had his fair share as a kid."

"And did he give you that *bit of a bung*?"

"You're kidding: he was a real rat. Kicked me straight out. Bastard."

"Which gives you a good reason to seek revenge. Motherly love frustrated."

"Now you really are joking! It's not me, for Christ's sake!"

"You'll have to be much more cooperative for me to believe you."

She tossed back a mouthful of wine, her look of hate taking in both the bar owner and his machine. She was weighing up the pros and cons. Sacha let her calculate.

"You're a tough guy, aren't you? No respect for old ladies. O.K., so you win. The negro did come, and grilled me with his questions."

"What questions?"

"Everything I knew about Florian. What he was like as a kid.

When it was he met that guy who's always handing him dough. That Gratien guy. I had no idea, did I? That clever-dick negro with his double-barrelled questions."

"Did he mention a murdered journalist?"

"Too right he did. Another negro."

"Norbert Konata?"

"Kona what? No idea. Don't remember. Who gives a damn anyway? It all goes back a real long time. That's all I know. And now I'd like you to fuck off and leave me in peace."

"You'll only find peace once you've given your testimony properly, according to the book. You're coming with us to the station to make your statement."

"But you said . . . O.K., alright, I get it. You're all the same bastards, aren't you?"

"Careful, insulting an officer in the pursuit of his duty is a punishable offence. Don't waste words, you're going to need them."

She muttered a few more oaths, then bawled at the bar owner to put the bill on her tab. He was having none of it. Was he worried his favourite client might be inside a bit too long for the size of her debts? Cursing some more, she paid the barman, and allowed herself to be led away. She had the sense to remain silent the whole way to the headquarters on Quai des Orfèvres.

Before going into the room where Bernadette Vidal had been put to wait, Sacha turned to Carle. He realised that for once she was excited.

"Vidal might have been rolling in it now, but he was born in the gutter. Interesting, isn't it?" he said.

"We didn't waste our time talking to that saintly woman, boss."

Saint Bernadette of the Enchanted Prairies had given them two vital pieces of information. Toussaint Kidjo had been very interested in Vidal and his mentor. And thought that the murder of his journalist friend was related to the two lawyers.

"Lieutenant Kidjo must have really stirred things up in that paradise of hers," Carle said. "With his awkward questions about the death of a journalist."

"We're going to do the same to the fragrant Madame Vidal with some awkward questions of our own. She's not leaving here until she's scoured her memory."

15

Flopped on the back seat, Sigmund was snoring quietly. They left him to his siesta and went to ring Jean Texier's doorbell. Seeing the old man again after five years gave Lola a shock. Time seemed to have taken twice its usual toll on him. His wrinkled face looked gaunt, his body had shed a good ten kilos. Was it grief at losing an only son, or possibly an illness on top of that? When life chose a victim, it was not averse to piling on the agony.

"Ah, Commissaire Jost. What a pleasure! Please, do come in!"

A pleasure! There was Lola, imagining the worst, while Texier, still the true gentleman that she remembered, welcomed her into his home with pleasure after all these years. But the worst was soon confirmed, in the shape of a lanky young man with a spiky haircut, who apparently had never been taught to iron his shirts. A quick glance was enough: one-hundred-per-cent cop.

"Lieutenant Ménard and I were just talking about the terrible event. Florian Vidal was the same age as my son. It's dreadful."

A whole troop of angels passed over. The young officer took advantage of the silence to look Ingrid up and down appreciatively. Then he turned to Lola.

"And you are?"

"Toussaint's former boss."

"The famous Lola Jost, accompanied by her daughter," he said, undressing Ingrid with his eyes.

"Ingrid Diesel," she said, shaking his hand. "No relationship."

"No *relation*, we say in French, but it doesn't matter. I love your accent."

Lola was dreaming of a bucket of ice-cold water. To be tipped instantly over the crest of this little rooster.

"And the two of you are here as friends of the family, of course."

Texier had the bright idea of accompanying the young upstart to the door. When he came back, he looked troubled.

"Is there a problem?"

"I'll be frank with you, Jean. I'm retired, and my former colleagues don't like the idea of my sticking my nose into the Kidjo affair again."

"Don't you trust them?"

"They have their bosses on their backs. I'm as free as the air."

He gave her a look full of sadness. Texier had lost all hope of any-one ever finding his son's murderers. Lola recalled what he had confessed to her five years earlier: *Toussaint's got mixed up in some murky political business, Lola. We're ants compared to them.* He didn't seem to have changed his mind.

"You have to help me. Thanks to this Vidal affair, we can start again from scratch. There must be a link. You don't kill two men the same way for no reason, even five years apart."

"Lieutenant Ménard asked me if Toussaint knew Vidal. But the answer's no, Lola. At least, my son never mentioned him to me. I learned of his existence from the newspaper, like everyone else. After that, Ménard wanted to know about Norbert Konata."

Sacha was no fool, and hadn't been wasting his time.

"I've also heard that Toussaint was interested in the death of his journalist friend."

"Norbert was his best friend. When Toussaint returned from Kinshasa, something had changed in him. Back then, I didn't see the point in mentioning it to you. There didn't seem to be any immediate connection, and I thought Toussaint must have informed you . . ."

"Are you telling me that Toussaint went to his journalist friend's funeral in Africa?"

"Yes. It was in April, a few months before his death."

Lola collapsed onto the nearest chair. All those years alongside Toussaint, without ever really knowing him. She thought she had created a bond. A friendship. How could she have been so mistaken? Ingrid tapped her hand.

"Lola, are you alright?"

"I thought we told each other everything. Or almost everything. But he kept the death of his best friend from me. At the station, he claimed he had gone back to Kinshasa on holiday. *A very pleasant stay.* I can still hear him saying it."

"Toussaint was as secretive as his mother," said Texier.

"What do you know about Norbert Konata?" asked Ingrid.

He explained that Toussaint and Norbert had grown up together in a village near Kinshasa. Back when the Democratic Republic of Congo was still called Zaire, Texier had been working as a G.P. for an N.G.O. operating in the countryside. Norbert's father, a trained nurse, was his assistant. Norbert Konata had always wanted to be a journalist. He had completed his studies locally, then worked for the *Congo Globe*, a daily newspaper. He had specialised in politics.

"Norbert never shied away from asking awkward questions. Unfortunately, he's just one name on a long list of journalists killed in Africa. It's endless. Last year, a reporter and his wife, the parents of five children, were gunned down outside their home by masked men. The presenter of a Swahili news programme was attacked in the street and died in hospital. Norbert was working for an opposition newspaper. He was one of the bravest men I've ever met. And Toussaint never got over his death."

Choked with emotion, Lola didn't have the strength to utter a word. Ingrid took over.

"Do you have any press cuttings about his death?"

The old man went to fetch a box and laid it on the coffee table. He took out a cardboard folder. Ingrid found an article that had appeared in the *Congo Globe*, and read it out loud:

"*This newspaper joins with Reporters sans Frontières in condemning the death, at the age of twenty-eight, of our friend and colleague Norbert Konata. His lifeless body was found on April 3 at approximately one in the morning in a stolen car that had gone off the road on Boulevard Lumumba, fifteen kilometres from Kinshasa. The car was on its way back from Ndjili airport; its theft had been reported by its owner, a ground crew manager at the airport. Eyewitnesses report having seen the masked occupants of a grey car pursue N. Konata's vehicle, and to have heard bursts of automatic gunfire. It should be remembered that our colleague had already been the victim of a failed attack when he was covering the recent presidential elections. The military authorities in the area where N. Konata lived have opened an inquiry. This is the second killing of a journalist in eight months. The* Congo Globe *presents its sincere condolences to the family and relatives of our sadly missed and talented friend.*"

The article was accompanied by a photo of the journalist in a tan-coloured suit, smiling outside the *Congo Globe* building. While Ingrid was reading out the article, Texier had found some more photographs. Toussaint and Norbert in days of innocence and peace. A few of them showed the two friends with a pretty young woman. Some of them had writing on the back.

Texier also found a series of charcoal drawings. Portraits of Toussaint and Norbert at different ages. The artist had managed to capture their characters. Toussaint looked energetic, stocky, with a slight hint of mischief. Norbert was quieter, more thoughtful, the physique of a stable but tough liana. As the two friends grew up, their temperaments were not so clearly recognisable, but Toussaint was still the man of action, Norbert the intellectual. The drawings were signed Myriam Konata, Norbert's sister.

"Do you have her details?"

"No, Myriam moved after her brother's death. She even gave up her telephone line. I've never managed to contact her. I went back to Kinshasa two years ago, but she was nowhere to be found."

Texier agreed to lend them the photos. Ingrid asked him why Toussaint didn't use his surname. Lola protested, made excuses for her friend: to her mind, the question was indiscreet. The old man did not seem bothered, and explained that his son had called himself Toussaint Texier right up until he had decided, off his own bat, to abandon his law studies and start a career with the police. He had been twenty-four at the time.

"You didn't mind?"

"No, the idea came to him when he was choosing France. For his career. I think it was to emphasise his African origins. It was his way of keeping a balance."

Promising to keep him up to date with their findings, they said goodbye. When Sigmund saw them approaching, he started barking loudly.

"I wonder if that dog isn't losing its manners thanks to us," said Ingrid.

Antoine Léger had got the Dalmatian trained to sit in on his sessions with his clients. He of course demanded strict discretion from the dog. As a reward, he would take him for long walks all over Paris, whatever the weather.

"Sigmund is losing his manners thanks to his contacts with *you*," Lola grumbled.

"What?"

"It was a bit much of you to ask personal questions like that. I was blushing with shame."

"Make your mind up! There's no point using kid gloves if you're stirring up memories from the past."

Lola stuffed the photographs into the glove compartment, still muttering to herself. Ingrid switched on the ignition and headed for the Canal Saint-Martin. By the time they had reached their parking place, Lola had calmed down.

"I'm sorry, Ingrid. I was floored by the news that Toussaint kept things from me."

"No problem, I can understand that. But I've a question, and I want an honest answer."

"Go on, shoot."

"Are you sure you want to go on with this?"

"Absolutely. Why?"

"What if you discover things are even worse than you imagine?"

The time switch came to an end, saving Lola from the need to reply. The parking bays were plunged into darkness. Ingrid flicked off the Twingo's dipped headlights.

"What are you doing?"

"The Toussaint method, Lola. I'm putting us in the box. So that we can think. Isn't that what you wanted?"

"There's no point, switch the lights back on. To hell with the box theory. I've got a new method. What we need is a good spotlight. Even if it throws light on the worst skulduggery. Let's go and think at your place in the broad daylight."

"Why my place?"

"Because I'm sure you've got some chilled Mexican beer. I'm getting to like port too much."

"It's not even eleven."

"I'm well aware of that."

Lola opened her door and the inside car light came on. She strode over to the time switch on the wall. Ingrid thought she saw a shadow move, and flicked the headlights on. A grey cat perched on the roof of a 4x4 scuttled away so quickly that for a moment she wondered whether she had imagined the whole thing.

They were sitting opposite each other on Ingrid's psychedelic couches. Lola had a beer in her hand, Ingrid a glass of water. The ex-commissaire was going over what they had found out so far for the benefit of the latter. They had discovered that shortly before his death, Toussaint Kidjo had begun an investigation that he had kept secret from his Paris colleagues. This had started with the killing of his childhood friend, Norbert Konata, a political journalist on a newspaper opposed to the clique in government. Jean Texier had a feeling that his son had got mixed up in some dirty business linked to France–Africa's shady transactions, but had no proof. Aimé Bangolé, though, admitted that Toussaint had not only questioned him about Konata, but Gratien as well.

"We have to dig deeper into what happened to Konata."

"If that means you want to haul me off to Africa, the answer's No.

Timothy is the most understanding of bosses, but he's also a business-man. I don't want to lose my job at the Calypso."

"Who's talking about Africa? Toussaint may have investigated in the D.R.C., but it was definitely in Paris that he was looking for a lead. We need to follow his footsteps."

"So what's next?"

"Adeline Ernaux. Toussaint's fiancée. He must have talked to her about his childhood friend."

"If he had made her confidentials at the time, she would have told you, wouldn't she?"

"In French we say confidence or confession, but 'confidentials' is something you've invented, my girl. And I'm sorry, but it sounds ghastly."

"Whatever. In my country, 'confidence' means you trust someone. It's a real pig's bottom."

"No, the expression is 'a pig's ear'. Best leave bottoms out of it."

"It's very complicated."

"Not at all."

16

"They didn't leave a single brush, chief. Nothing. *Nada*. Those pigs are real barbarians from the far-off steppes. They confused your place with a town to loot and pillage. And there was I promising you I'd finish ages ago. My reputation's at stake here . . ."

Sacha was on the phone with the Michelangelo of the Marais, who had just announced in his wine-soaked voice that his equipment had been stolen. Paint-pots, bottles of white spirit, buckets and all his brushes. The thieves had been so kind as to leave the ladder behind. Ménard's cousin had just slipped out to the corner store to buy "a little fruit juice" (translation: industrial quantities of beer), and "the vandals had taken advantage of the situation to steal a workman's tools". Arthur was going to have to buy everything again, but he was sure the insurance would pay up without a murmur, wouldn't they?

Sacha stayed calm and gave the go-ahead for the repurchase of the materials. He was just wondering whether Arthur hadn't worked out a lucrative scheme to invent a non-existent robbery when Carle and Ménard entered his office. The lieutenant's beatific smile was a few megavolts brighter than ever. Carle looked like a cross between the Dalai Lama and Buster Keaton. The beginnings of cooperation he had glimpsed when they were questioning Bernadette Vidal had been reassigned to the wish-list.

The lieutenant reported back on his early-morning visit to Jean Texier. He was in luck, "the old fellow was one of those pensioners who were as awake in the head as they had been when they were doing stuff". Kidjo had gone to Kinshasa for his friend Konata's funeral. No indication as to whether he had tried to contact Gratien or Vidal. But he had learned that Konata had a sister, an artist by the name of Myriam.

"The old man didn't have her details, but I thought of another line of attack, boss."

"Do tell."

"Painters can only rarely live from their art, can't they?"

And some clients barely survive the art of certain painters, thought Sacha, nodding his head. (Any reference to cousin Arthur could wait for a more suitable occasion.)

"So I've had an idea. I guess Myriam Konata must make ends meet by teaching. In the state or private sector, or both. I suggest we telephone all the schools in Kinshasa for starters. Then in the whole of the D.R.C. if that doesn't work."

Sacha approved the battle plan. He said the three of them would work as a team, since speed was of the essence in the battle.

"Is that from Sun Tzu?"

"No, only me, sadly."

"That's what I thought. In general, Sun Tzu's tips are more on the mark. It's true though, isn't it, boss? Don't look at me like that. And talking of speed, Kidjo's former boss arrived at Texier's just as I was leaving. For a has-been, mother Jost doesn't half give herself airs. Not exactly friendly, the old cow. She wasn't happy to see a cop, in this case me, doing her job. I couldn't believe my eyes."

Sacha fought back a desire to turn the office upside down by shouting his head off. Lola was like a stun grenade. Worse still, a grenade with the pin out.

"When it comes to being stubborn, that woman is quite spectacular," he said, trying to think of a way to render her harmless once and for all.

"The adjective 'spectacular' is a better description of her chum Ingrid," added Ménard, who had suddenly gone all dreamy-eyed. "Some bombshell she is! Boom, boom! And with those big innocent eyes of hers she doesn't look stuck-up at all. I'd be happy to arrest her whenever you say the word, boss."

Sacha stared at him for a few seconds, then declared that while they were waiting for the bomb squad, it was high time they focused on Myriam Konata. He intercepted Carle's look. Almost as calm as a mountain lake, were it not for the ironic glint.

A little after eleven, Ménard hit the jackpot with his usual modesty.

"Gooaaal! I'm so good it hurts! My plan was perfect. Myriam Konata teaches at a leisure centre in Kinshasa. Her boss has just given me her mobile number."

Sacha called the number, and put the phone on speaker. He could tell Myriam was tense, on the verge of hanging up on him. It was clear her brother's murder had not exactly strengthened her belief in mankind. He succeeded in convincing her of who he was, and then of his good faith. He made her understand that there was a possibility of resolving the Kidjo affair thanks to the investigation into the lawyer Vidal's death. Unfortunately, Myriam Konata did not have much to tell him. Toussaint had taken his friend's death very badly, and had questioned a lot of people, but got nowhere.

"Did Toussaint Kidjo and your brother know a man called Richard Gratien?"

"No, the name means nothing to me."

"Vidal worked for him."

"I'm sorry, but I can't help you. Norbert wrote about political topics. That was dangerous, so he thought it better not to talk to me about it."

"Who was at your brother's burial apart from Kidjo?"

"The villagers, the members of my family, the musician Wonda and his mother, a famous wailer."

Ménard imitated a hysterical woman in tears dancing the beguine. Sacha struggled not to hit him with the telephone.

"No-one in particular worth pointing out?"

"No, not that I can think of."

Sacha pinched the bridge of his nose trying to think of what else to ask. Exasperated by Arthur, Ménard and Lola to name but three, deprived of his Thai boxing sessions for some time now, exhausted by his sleepless nights bathed in the fragrance of white spirit, he was finding it hard to concentrate.

"Ask him if anyone important *wasn't* there," suggested Carle.

Sacha put the question to Myriam.

"I was very surprised not to see Isis. Shocked even."

"Isis?"

Ménard imitated an Egyptian dancer in profile. Sacha dreamt of drowning the lieutenant in a tar-filled sarcophagus.

"Isis Renta. A woman from Kinshasa who had been engaged to my brother. Even after they split up they were very close. She came up with some lame excuse for not appearing at the burial."

Sacha took down her details. Isis Renta was a hostess with Air France, working generally on the routes between Paris and the different African capitals.

After a series of calls, they managed to track her down. She was on leave between two flights, and was due to return for the Paris–Douala service at 13.40 that day. She was not picking up the phone though. Sacha took Carle with him, leaving Ménard to try to get through to Isis, or one of her neighbours, to warn her they were on the way. The two of them ran to pick up a patrol car. Carle fixed the siren on the roof and sped off in the direction of Isis Renta's home, in Impasse de Bergame, 20th arrondissment.

17

By some miracle they found a parking place a stone's throw from the Vignes d'Oberkampf. They took a walk round the area to let Sigmund stretch his legs. Adeline Ernaux was serving a hesitant customer. Lola used the time to explain to Ingrid how Toussaint had met Adeline. A secretary at their police station was retiring, and her colleagues had asked Toussaint to buy champagne for the occasion. The policeman was bowled over by the wine merchant. In order to seduce her he had placed his own order for a dozen cases of a variety of wines.

"I've inherited them. Toussaint didn't really like wine. Whenever I open a bottle, I think of him. And when I don't too."

Adeline greeted her effusively. The two women hugged each other. Lola had not seen her since her marriage to a wine waiter from the neighbourhood. She accepted a glass of Chablis. Ingrid refused politely, and they got down to business.

"I received a visit from Commandant Duguin. He turned up without warning. Don't hold it against me, but I can't stand the sight of cops anymore."

"You can detest them all you like, sweetheart, I'm no longer part of the gang."

Adeline told them that Duguin had asked her if Toussaint had known two men involved in the arms trade, one of them being the lawyer Vidal. She had nothing to say to him. And that wasn't going to change, whatever the circumstances. Lola asked her about Konata.

"Toussaint was sad about that, and blamed himself. He had tried to persuade Norbert to leave Kinshasa and come to work in Paris. He reproached himself for not having insisted. I wanted to go with him to the funeral in his native village close to Kinshasa, but he wouldn't let me. He said it was too dangerous, that there were fanatics around with itchy trigger fingers."

"Was he hoping to do some poking around on the spot?"

"He asked Norbert's colleagues lots of questions. But it got him nowhere."

"Why didn't you mention this at the time?"

"I was convinced you knew about it."

"Toussaint kept his friend's death from me."

"Why was that?"

"That's a good question. Do you know if he carried on asking around back in Paris?"

"No. I thought the death of his friend was linked to the political situation in his own country. It had nothing to do with France."

"Think carefully. Toussaint could hardly make phone calls from the police station because he was keeping us in the dark. But you were living with him at the time, weren't you?"

"More or less. We used to get together either at his place or at mine. I do remember a silly detail . . ."

"Tell me about it."

"One day I surprised Toussaint on the phone to a woman I didn't know. I was listening behind his back, so he couldn't see me. He was begging her to meet him, for old times' sake. I made a scene.

Toussaint told me it was all above board, he simply wanted to see her to talk about his friend. Norbert and he had both been in love with her as boys. She had preferred Norbert."

"Do you know her name?"

"Isis Renta. It's so unusual I've never forgotten it. She was an air hostess, but I don't know for which airline."

Isis. Lola felt as if an electric shock had gone through her. Thanking Adeline, she left the wine cellar and got back into the car. When Ingrid caught up with her, she was rummaging in the glove compartment. She pulled out the photos Jean Texier had lent them, found the one she wanted. Three youngsters laughing under the branch of a palm tree in the teeming rain. The girl was pretty. Her hair hung in coppery, rebellious ringlets; beneath it she had a wide forehead, almond eyes, a fleshy mouth. Lola read the inscription on the back: *Isis, Toussaint and Norbert love the rainy season!*

"That's fucking great, Lola!"

"Yes, we're making progress, my girl."

"*Woof*!" Even Sigmund approved.

They installed themselves in the internet café on Rue Oberkampf. They wanted to make a list of all the airlines covering Africa and to call them one by one, until they came across the company Norbert Konata's ex-fiancée worked for. Lola had a trial run and called Bravo Air Congo. She made up a story about an emergency – a death in the Renta family. A complete failure.

"My giddy aunt, this isn't going to be easy."

"Because of the security measures in place after 9/11?"

"Well spotted. The airlines won't take any risks with the terrorist threat. They've become paranoid about giving out information regarding their staff. I don't need to tell you that, as an American."

"Let's try again. At least with the most important companies."

"*It's with water from our body that we draw water from a well*, as the Senegalese say. Alright, let's roll our sleeves up."

"Lola, there's a problem."

"What's that?"

"I have to be at the Calypso earlier than I thought."

"Don't tell me your cabaret is putting on children's matinees now."

"Timothy is organising a private party. A video artist is coming to film my show. They need me to help with the lighting. As soon as it's over, we can hunt the air hostess wherever you like."

"I don't know anyone I can nobble in the airports anymore," sighed Lola. "I used to have a few informers there, but that was another generation. It's so annoying, having to do everything yourself! Luckily there's Barthélemy. He's a bit slow, obviously . . . I'll call him, then let's head for the Calypso. It's going to end up as my second office."

"I didn't realise you had a first one."

"What have you got against my dining-room table?"

*

The door opened to reveal a young woman in a dark blue uniform, expertly made-up and impatient to leave. Marvin Gaye was singing in the background. Sacha showed her his police I.D. The air hostess bit her lip.

"I'm on duty soon."

"Yes, we know: imminent departure for Cameroon. Apart from that, do you never answer your phone?"

"I forgot to plug it in again. I often sleep during the day to recover from my night flights, and there's no way I want to be woken up by it ringing."

Moving back inside her studio, she switched off the stereo, then plugged the telephone cable back into its socket. It started to ring at once. She picked it up.

"Your colleagues have just arrived, Lieutenant Manard. Oh, I'm sorry, *Ménard*," Isis Renta said drily, then hung up. Turning to Sacha, she asked: "What's this all about?"

"The lawyer killed at Colombes. The burning tyre . . . Have you read the newspapers?"

"Yes, but I don't see . . ."

"The method used is similar to the way your friend Toussaint Kidjo was murdered. Myriam Konata told us about you, and your links with Konata."

"I still don't see the connection."

She was nervously stroking the lower part of her neck. Because she was worried about arriving late for work, or was it a different sort of anxiety?

"I know you're in a hurry, so I'll come straight to the point. Myriam can't understand why you weren't at her brother's funeral. Nor can I."

"You have no right to poke your nose into people's private business . . ."

"Wrong. I even have the right to arrest you and take you to the station here and now."

She glanced at her watch, then explained that when the funeral was taking place, a strike by ground crews at the airport had prevented her from leaving Paris for Kinshasa.

"Myriam would never believe me, but there's nothing I can do about that."

Sacha turned and whispered to Carle to ring Ménard and check.

"We'll take you to Roissy-Charles-de-Gaulle," he said to Renta. "We can talk on the way."

She grimaced resignedly at them, picked up her luggage, and followed them out. Carle drove, and the commandant and air hostess sat in the back. Ménard called back as they were going past Porte Vincennes to get onto the ring motorway. Renta's story held water. There had indeed been a strike when she said. Sacha ended the call and plied her with questions. She spoke of Kidjo and Konata as loyal and much-missed friends, and swore she only knew of Gratien and Vidal through the press. She was really sorry, she would have liked to help. The closer they got to the airport, the more relaxed she became. Logically, her earlier fear was because she was afraid of missing her flight. But Sacha never liked to trust entirely to logic.

He continued his questioning right up to the time for her to embark, and demanded her mobile telephone number. If he needed to speak to her again, this time he had to be sure he could reach her.

★

Lola was doing her best to be patient on Ingrid's green chesterfield, which was being transformed to prepare for her show. The skeleton costume was languishing in the dungeons. Ingrid alias Gabriella Tiger had turned into a creature that was hard to identify. A witch of the marshes? A mermaid with a slight radioactive problem? The secret love-child of Miss Universe with a tinned sardine? Marie had certainly not stinted on the fish scales.

The ring tone on her mobile interrupted her thoughts. Barthélemy announced that Isis Renta flew with Air France. He had even got her mobile number, thanks to a contact of his at France-Télécom. Unfortunately, the hostess was not replying.

"Roissy it is," Lola informed the thing from the swamp.

"After the show!" Ingrid said, arms akimbo and face unrecognisable under the olive foundation and fluorescent green wig.

"Who's saying otherwise? By the way, what's with the fishmonger display?"

"I'm the daughter of the waves, inspired by Shakespeare's *A Midsummer Night's Dream*."

"I wasn't far off! I'm getting good at this," Lola said.

"So, do you like it?"

Lola raised both her thumbs.

18

"Commandant, there's someone waiting to see you. She's been here some time."

Sacha thanked the secretary, took his coffee from the machine, and returned to his office.

Nadine Vidal was smoking by the half-open window. She looked pale and anxious, and the fur coat draped over her shoulders made her seem frailer. When she saw Sacha, she nervously dunked her cigarette in a plastic cup.

"I'm sorry, I know it's forbidden, but . . . I can't help myself."

"What can I do for you?"

"Give me permission to go and get some rest. A fortnight, no more, that'll be . . . sufficient. A friend of mine has a clinic in Neuilly. He said he could help me. I . . ."

"Has something happened? Have you been threatened?"

"The phone rings all the time. Journalists have laid siege to my place. It's unbearable . . ."

"I'm not going to be the one who prevents you from recovering your balance."

"Thank you, Commandant."

"Give me the address."

Her hand trembled as she wrote it down and handed it to him. He went closer, squeezed her shoulder, and shut the door.

"You're a man who can be trusted. Please, don't give this address to anyone."

He nodded, leaning back against the door.

"I think Gratien came to see you before your husband's body was found."

Was it fear that suddenly showed on her pale features, or nothing more than fatigue? She had come to confess her worries, but was still hesitating. Now that her husband was gone, she probably meant nothing to Gratien. Nothing but a source of problems.

"Let me help you, Nadine."

"I had called Gratien that evening to know if Florian was with him. He came over later that night, sick with worry."

"What did he want? Documents, wasn't it?"

"Yes, the contracts from their most recent deals . . ."

"And his famous notebooks."

"No, I'm certain Florian didn't have them in the safe."

"How can you be so sure?"

"I know what's in it. When I saw Florian wasn't coming back, I opened it."

"For what reason?"

"I was afraid he might have gone off with another woman. I was crazy. I wanted to make sure he hadn't taken his passport."

"And the passport was in the safe?"

"Yes, but there were no notebooks. Only contracts relating to Gratien and my husband's business activities."

Sacha waited for her to go on, but she remained silent. Nadine was well and truly terrified. And it wasn't only the journalists she wanted to protect herself from.

"If anything had happened, he didn't want those documents coming out in public, was that it?"

"Richard Gratien knows the safe combination. He took what he wanted."

"Was he violent with you?"

"No . . ."

"Nadine, please. I can tell you're hiding something."

"Gratien slapped me. He had guessed for some time that I was trying to persuade Florian to get away from him. He started shouting, asked me where my husband was hiding, and if I was counting on meeting up with him somewhere."

She had stopped crying, as if her supply of tears had been exhausted. But her mouth twitched as she recalled what Gratien had done to her.

"He hit me a second time, and I fell to the floor . . . He kicked me in the stomach. When he finally realised I knew no more than him, he left. Commandant, what I've just told you . . ."

"Yes?"

"I won't repeat it officially to anyone. Don't count on me giving a statement."

Yet a complaint against Gratien would have helped him a lot. It would have allowed Sacha to unsettle him and question him more effectively. At last there was a glimpse of the violence beneath the lawyer's smooth surface. He studied Nadine Vidal for a moment. She had pulled the fur coat closer, and seemed paralysed and exhausted.

She looked as fragile as the glass statue on Mars' desk. But Sacha had the feeling she would not go under. He phoned Ménard, and told him to accompany Nadine Vidal to the clinic. He stepped out to way-lay him before he reached his office.

"I don't think she's going to try to slip away from us, but check she is in fact registered there. If that's so, I want a twenty-four-hour guard on her room."

Ménard took Nadine Vidal with him without a word.

The door to their shared office was ajar. Carle was busy on a personal call, apparently to her husband. Sacha knocked and went in. She gave a rapid excuse and hung up.

A timely shaft of sunlight pierced the leaden clouds. Sacha suggested they have a drink together on Boulevard Saint-Michel. He wanted to talk to her about Nadine Vidal. Carle turned him down: she found the noise in bars deafening.

Oh, Captain Carle, you're made from the toughest hide, the sort they make leather bags from. What am I going to do with you?

*

"Can I take this big holdall?"

"But it's full of my accessories, all folded up," Ingrid said. "It's soft polyester to prevent them getting crumpled."

"Interesting."

"Marie's the one in charge of it. Be careful you don't mess up my dresser's system."

"I'll be careful," said Lola, picking up all the rustling wardrobe items and dumping them on the chesterfield. "Roissy, here we come!"

"Hey, you promised me we weren't going anywhere. No Africa, O.K.?"

"No Africa, as you wish. This holdall will come in useful in a way you'll appreciate once we get going."

They left the Calypso together with Sigmund, once again avoiding the watchful eye of Enrique the doorman. The holdall wouldn't fit into the boot of the Twingo, and so invaded the Dalmatian's territory on the back seat. Ingrid switched on the radio to help compensate, and was delighted to come across "I Feel Love" by Donna Summer. Lola complained she didn't like these repetitive songs. Her American friend pointed out that the best moments deserved being infinitely repeated.

They reached Roissy-Charles-de-Gaulle in half an hour. With infinite patience and her big polyester holdall, Lola approached a bad-tempered young man in customer service. She launched into a far-fetched story about luggage Isis Renta had left behind, and managed by a miracle and by wagering on quickly wearing down the young man's resistance to glean some information from him. She was able to reach a disappointing conclusion: the air hostess was part of the crew on a flight that had taken off hours earlier for Cameroon. She would be coming back the next day on the Douala–Paris flight that landed at 6.10 a.m. Lola accepted the situation philosophically. She offered to stand Ingrid a night in a nearby hotel: when dawn came they would be on the spot to pluck the daughter of the air.

"What if they won't accept Sigmund?"

"I have my plan," said Lola, pointing to the holdall.

While Ingrid was staring at her with a worried frown, she questioned an airport employee about the nearest hotels. He recommended the Hotel Ibis, only some three kilometres away by shuttle bus. If his information was correct, the hotel would take pets.

"You see, Ingrid, there was no cause for alarm."

"If the hotels near the airport had refused to take dogs, you were going to force poor Sigmund to hide in my holdall?"

"Of course. That animal has a sense of duty. Ten minutes in a hold-all never killed anyone. And although smoke-detectors exist, dog-detectors have yet to be invented. Three unassailable arguments. Good, let's go to bed. Tomorrow promises to be a busy day."

19

Sacha got up at five and went to his Thai boxing club. His *restaurateur* friend Rachid was there; another one who made the same detour before setting off to Rungis market for his supplies. After several rounds, Sacha felt the tension of recent days finally easing. Streaming with sweat, the two men took a break, flopped against the ropes in a corner of the ring.

"Your new responsibilities are getting to you, Sacha. Or am I wrong?"

"It won't take long before I'm up to speed."

"I'm sorry, but I don't think that's the problem. What's really going on?"

"My colleague Carle can't accept that our chief gave me the job instead of her."

"I imagine that in your line of business, problems of getting on in a team can lead to catastrophe. Am I wrong?"

"It's not that so much: I've got used to Carle."

"So the problem is?"

"The chief. I don't understand why he chose me. Carle is a pain, but she's competent. The police are an administration. And in an administration, ladders are more vertical than diagonal."

"So logically your Mars should have let you prove yourself before giving you star billing. Is that what's eating you?"

"Exactly right."

Rachid gave him a friendly pat on the shoulder, but then froze. He had obviously discovered a more appealing novelty. Sacha turned his head and saw Antonia, flanked by the silent giant Honoré, in grey peaked cap and uniform. Not exactly appropriate dress for a sports hall reeking of sweat. But Gratien's wife's outfit clashed even more. A flowing black sleeveless trouser suit with a plunging neckline. The giant was holding a fur jerkin with a red leather collar, ready to save his mistress from the slightest shiver. In his huge paws, the jerkin looked like a small animal run over on a country road.

"How are you, Commandant?"

That amazingly deep voice of hers, and a graceful wave of a hand adorned with rings. Rachid muttered under his breath:

"There's some things you're still on top form with, my friend!"

Sacha grabbed a towel and left the ring to go over to the newcomers. Antonia shamelessly ogled his body as he was drying his torso.

"Honoré takes me out at night when I can't sleep."

"His insomnia coincides with yours; how fantastic," said Sacha, staring at the giant.

A blank, distant look on a perfectly groomed face. The chauffeur's memory must be well worth a visit, thought Sacha. He didn't return Antonia's smile.

"You're not pleased to see me? Am I invading your rare moments of leisure? I can understand that. You must also be wondering how I located you. That's easy: Fabert. He often sees my husband. Richard knows so many people in so many sensitive areas. The two of them were talking about you yesterday. Fabert knows everything about you."

"And you listen at closed doors. Bravo!"

"Richard hides nothing from me. Fabert doesn't like you. He thinks you're dangerous. But I'll let you have your shower. I'll wait for you outside."

She turned towards the giant, who draped the fur jerkin round her shoulders. They sauntered out.

"Extremely hot stuff and dangerous," commented Rachid as he removed his shin-pads. "Am I right in thinking our session is over?"

"We'll continue on Saturday. I'll give you a call."

"Of course."

As the steaming hot water ran down his soothed body, Sacha thought of Antonia's calmness.

It was perfect. A luxury that those enjoying real power could offer themselves.

A short way down the street, he saw Honoré leaning against a Bentley with tinted windows. The chauffeur opened the door, and Sacha slipped in.

Lily of the valley, lilac, damp wood. Her perfume had invaded the whole interior, but Antonia seemed frailer now, languishing in the plush leather upholstery. She was drinking a glass of milk, with the fur jerkin rolled up behind her head. She put the glass of milk on a tray, and rested her hands on the silk of her suit.

"I could tell you a long story, but in some other way, because I'm too tired to talk for long. I wasn't lying when I said I had insomnia. Would you like a glass of milk, or something else?"

"No thanks. Doesn't your husband accompany you on your nocturnal ramblings?"

"Basically, I'm more of a daughter to him than a wife. I know that's odd."

"If you say so."

"It's true."

"Why did you tell me all that about Fabert just now?"

"Because you're someone I want to talk to. I saw that you have scars on your body. Your split eyebrow. A few others on your torso. You and I are similar. You'd never have thought that, would you?"

"What are you talking about?"

"Couldn't you treat me as a friend?"

"No."

"You see, I told you I wouldn't be able to tell you my story in words."

She was no longer smiling. Sitting upright in her seat, she slipped the sides of her top from her shoulders, revealing breasts as magnificent as Sacha had imagined. He managed to remain unmoved.

Antonia twisted until her suit was pulled down to the top of her pubis. Her stomach was slashed by a long horizontal scar. Sacha swallowed hard.

She put her free hand on her tortured stomach. The scar appeared in purple blotches between her ringed fingers.

Sacha took the jacket and unbuttoned it, then placed it over Antonia Gratien's naked body as best he could. She folded her legs up beneath her, and hugged the jacket.

"Three of them attacked me. With a machete. They tore out the child from my belly. Do you understand?"

She was chewing her lips, peering at him imploringly.

"Do you understand, Sacha?"

"I'm truly sorry."

"No, you don't understand. I feel eternally grateful to Gratien. He saved me. I was bleeding to death in the street, and he rescued me. I was hovering between life and death for weeks, and he watched over me. Don't hurt him."

"Who says I intend to?"

"Everything does. I like the way your body moves and is supple when you're boxing, but I can sense, or rather I'm sure, that you're implacable. You won't hesitate."

"Do you know who killed Vidal?"

"No, but it wasn't Gratien. Vidal was like a son to him. He sheds tears over him every night. He tries to hide it, but I can feel the old man's pain. You have to believe me, I never lie. Please go now. I'll come to see you again soon."

She had resumed her nonchalant position on the back seat. Her face was that of a child about to fall asleep. As he left the Bentley he and Honoré exchanged glances. Sacha thought the mute giant must have heard the most interesting conversations in all Paris at the wheel of his master's luxury limousine. He would have given a lot to hear his answer to any number of questions. Such as: what was Richard Gratien really like? Was he the bully hitting a woman already prostrate with grief? Or was he a saviour who plucked a young girl from certain death?

As he walked towards the metro, it was as if Antonia's perfume formed a halo around him.

*

The early hours, and it was still night. Terminal 2C was an enormous sleek conch-shell beneath the dark sky. A few desks were open, a cleaner pushing his trolley, passengers scattered here and there. The two women studied the board and saw the area where passengers and crew would arrive.

Twenty minutes after touchdown, they saw her coming in the midst of a group in the airline's uniforms.

"Gently, wait till I give the signal," Lola warned Ingrid.

A few friendly words, and the group began to split up. Isis Renta headed for the exit. Ingrid, Lola and Sigmund followed her. The young air hostess pulled her wheelie case to the shuttle bus-stop for Paris. Lola was pleased to see there were no other people in sight.

Isis lit a cigarette, and leaned back against the wall. She let out a cloud of smoke that seemed to do her the world of good.

"You're right to relax."

"I beg your pardon?"

Lola waved her out-of-date police credential under her nose.

"It'll help you cooperate with our interview."

"But I saw your colleagues yesterday! This is harassment."

"Commandant Duguin has his own agenda. I'm from the 6th arrondissement, where the deceased Florian Vidal was based."

"Well then, sort it out with Duguin. Besides, I've got nothing to say."

"That's for me to decide."

"You're a bit past it to be from the police. And the Dalmatian and your blonde friend here don't fit the part either . . . Stop bothering me or I'll call security."

Through the terminal windows, two men in bright orange jackets: maintenance men for the Air France buses. A scandal looming. Lola took a syringe from her pocket, jabbed Renta in the neck. The hostess' eyes rolled up, and she collapsed to the ground. Ingrid stifled a cry.

"You can have your breakdown when we have time. Grab her under the shoulders."

Ingrid stammered a few incomprehensible words.

"For heaven's sake, do as I say, or we're in real trouble."

A quick glance at the fluorescent workers, but they hadn't noticed a thing. Ingrid did as she was told. Lola pointed to a pillar. Her American friend laid the air hostess out behind the concrete column. Lola tied her up with extra-strong sticky tape.

"Can you explain what we're up to?"

"The best we can with what little we've got."

"Not that little: where did that syringe come from?"

"It's just something I asked Barthélemy for. Confiscated from raids on dealers. You've no idea what people get high on these days."

"A bit over the top as a method, isn't it?"

"That depends. It was this kind of stuff that Toussaint's killers used on him."

"And you're using the same methods as those bastards . . ."

"It was my plan B. If she had cooperated, it wouldn't have been necessary."

"If she's got nothing to hide, she'll sue your ass off."

"There you go again with your bottoms, Ingrid. You need to realise there are moments when you have to take risks."

"May I remind you that I'm a foreigner in France. One wrong move and I'll be deported."

"I understand, you don't want to get involved. That's your right. Take Sigmund back to Paris. Thanks for everything, and see you later."

"That's too easy!"

They went on bickering in similar vein until Isis Renta started to come round.

The Dalmatian sniffed at her hair as she began to groan and struggle. Ingrid ended up going off and sitting in a corner. Sigmund decided it would be better to bury his snout and his conscience in her lap. Lola fished a small tape recorder out of her raincoat and placed it close to her prisoner. She switched it on.

"Norbert Konata. Tell me all you know."

"Let me go at once, you old crone, or I'll call security!"

"Norbert. And quick about it. I'm getting seriously pissed off."

The young Congolese hostess began shouting at the top of her lungs. A Stanley knife appeared from the raincoat. Lola waved it in her victim's face. She immediately fell silent.

"Listen carefully, Renta. I may look past it but I've dealt with far tougher people than you. Either you answer my questions or I'll redesign your pretty mug."

Big drops of sweat appeared on the air hostess' face. Her eyes looked as if they were going to pop from her skull.

"You didn't go to your ex's funeral in Africa. Why?"

20

The divisionnaire stared at the newspapers his secretary had placed on his desk as if they were going to leap up and bite him in the face. The press was having a whale of a time with the Vidal affair, and this frenzy was upsetting his superiors.

"I could bear it if it were only these hacks breaking my balls," sighed Mars. "But I had lunch with Fabert's boss to try to get him to keep his bulldog on the leash. I don't know how long I'm going to be able to keep them back."

"So tell me all you know about Antonia Gratien," Sacha suggested.

He had given him a detailed description of the scene in the Bentley. Mars stretched out in his seat, but the gesture didn't seem to help him relax. Sacha knew the feeling.

"It's a true story. Raped as an adolescent, she became pregnant. And since ill-fortune never comes alone, she was set on by a militia. It happened during a riot, under Mobutu. Gratien found her by chance. And saved her *in extremis*. Later on, he made that superb but irreparably damaged woman his wife. It's said he keeps none of his business deals from her. Antonia has looked the devil in the eye. So whatever he does is unlikely to disturb her much . . ."

"I'd like to know what game she's playing when she warns me about Fabert."

"Don't worry, we'll find out."

"Vidal came out of nowhere; Antonia has been to hell and back. Gratien likes to adopt stray dogs."

"True enough."

"She said to me: *Basically, I'm more of a daughter to him than a wife.* Vidal was something similar."

"So according to you, the two of them had an affair? Gratien discovers that the only son fate has allowed him is humping his wife. He takes his revenge by grilling him like a sausage. We know he can be violent because he slapped Nadine Vidal, who's almost his daughter-in-law."

"It could be. There's a lot of passion in that murder."

"Gratien looks destroyed."

"Sertys claims he's an excellent actor."

"Your theory might work."

"Only *might*?"

"The secret service knew how to do its job before someone decided it should turn into the F.B.I. The Gratien couple have always been of great interest to them. Everyone knows that Antonia collects lovers. Preferably young. And good-looking. Believe me, if she had slept with Vidal, they would have known about it. In addition, it's always with her husband's blessing. Don't forget, we're not in some middle-class drama when it comes to the Gratiens."

"Another possibility. Simpler this time. Antonia is the young wife, and since there are no children, she's the heir. Unfortunately for her, *the old man* takes on a mongrel as his chauffeur. He discovers he has something in him, and pays for his studies. The kid does well. Gratien introduces him to his contacts, involves him in his deals. Antonia can't stomach this. She thought she was destined for a life of luxury, now she finds she has to share everything. So she gets rid of Vidal, with the help of the faithful Honoré. And disguises his death as an act of political revenge, taking inspiration from the death of a cop whose murderer is still at large."

"It's a more solid theory than your first one."

The two men stared at each other for a moment in silence.

"But there's one detail that doesn't fit," Duguin said finally.

"The way Fabert keeps going back to Gratien. Because you think he's on the scent of something more than a crime of passion."

"Exactly. And I say again: I don't understand why Antonia came to warn me about it."

"I'm working on the Fabert problem. Everything in its proper time."

"I know."

*

Lola pushed the blade out with her thumb. She heard Ingrid's muffled cry: *Lola, no!*

"Renta, look at me! Didn't you believe me when I said I'd go as far as it takes for his sake?"

The Congolese hostess' eyes were still wide with terror. Trembling moons.

"Don't do it, I beg you," sobbed Ingrid.

"We advance along the edge of the cliff to peer into the darkness of the sea, but the wave is interested in the way we're attracted by misfortune." The knife seemed to be welded onto her arm. It would only take the slightest of movements. "It likes us too much. The wave decides to sweep us away."

Lola plunged the blade into Isis Renta's neck. Ingrid shrieked. Her jeans and T-shirt were spattered with blood. She drew back in horror. A car was approaching. The squeal of tyres. Lola saw the silhouette of her friend trapped in the acid light of the headlamps. The driver began to sound the horn, sound the horn . . .

Lola woke up in a sweat. Raised herself on her elbow. Her radio-alarm was showing 4.17 a.m. She staggered out of bed, picked up the telephone.

"Hello, is that you, boss?"

"Bless you, Jérôme. You've saved me from a 3-D Technicolor night-mare. But you'd still better have a good excuse for waking me up at such an indecent hour . . ."

"It's Bangolé. At least I think it is."

Barthélemy was speaking softly, no doubt to avoid being over-heard by his colleagues.

"What's happened?"

"It's not a pretty sight. You must come. Right away."

He gave her the address of a museum being built between Rue Curial and Rue d'Aubervilliers. Then he hung up. Lola wiped the sweat from her brow and suppressed a shudder.

The taxi dropped her outside a big brick building with wide metallic bays. Lola had seen the photos of the façade in the press, and recalled a description something like: *Creation of a new space for culture where the dialogue between art, cultural practices and diverse communities will be ongoing.* As far as practices and communities went, she knew the area above all because of the high proportion of crack dealers operating there. The authorities in Paris were investing millions to recuperate old funeral parlours. They wanted to turn them into a variable geometry cultural gimmick crossed with an artists' residence. It seemed some people confused public money with manna from heaven.

A police car at an angle on the pedestrian crossing, its blue light still whirling on the roof. And a van from the scene of crime officers parked across the pavement.

She made her way into what looked like a gigantic market hall open to the winds, strewn with rubble and dimly lit by the misty moon. A flapping of wings made her raise her head towards a glass roof occupied by pigeons. She lit her path with a pocket torch until she reached a central staircase.

She stumbled over a cable, dropped her torch. The sound of hasty footsteps. Picking up her light, she turned quickly, and illuminated Barthélemy's face.

"You scared the living daylights out of me, you big dummy!"

"I wanted to catch you before the Garden Gnome did."

This was the nickname her former colleagues at the 10th arrondissement had given Jean-Pascal Grousset, her successor. Someone to be avoided like the plague.

"Is he here?"

"About to leave, thank heavens. Find a discreet corner where you can wait."

She waited for almost three-quarters of an hour before the Garden

Gnome passed by, flanked by a uniformed officer. His words echoed for a long while beneath the glass roof. The public prosecutor wasn't going to like this massacre. Nor was the mayor: especially as it had occurred in a place dedicated to culture for all. Blah-di-blah. The threat of a scandal. The last thing they needed! His voice drifted away down the street.

She ventured down the staircase, saw a dim light, heard voices. In the second basement she found Émilien, a competent lieutenant Barthélemy liked to team up with. With him were Ferrand and Baccari, two crime scene veterans, who greeted her respectfully.

A floor littered with rubbish. The characteristic smell of blood and excrement. In one corner, the remains of a fire with embers still burning, and Captain Métayer talking to a homeless guy who could be any age.

"He was the one who raised the alarm," explained Barthélemy. "He was sleeping it off under a pile of cardboard boxes when the killers arrived. A man and a woman."

"He saw them?"

"Métayer has been making him repeat his story for hours. No luck: he can't give any precise description."

"Their voices perhaps? He could at least give some idea of their age, geographical or social background . . ."

"Don't let's get carried away, boss. He was pretty far gone on booze. But not so stupid as to show himself when the massacre started. Then he can't remember for how long he kept his head down before rousing the caretaker, who was asleep in his hut. This site is enormous. The caretaker wouldn't have heard a thing."

The crime scene technicians had finished taking their samples. Barthélemy turned his torch on the body.

He was on his back, in his green track-suit. Lola recognised his basketball boots with their pink laces. That was all she could identify: his face was nothing more than a bloody pulp. Barthélemy lit up a plastic bag containing a messy hammer.

"Is it Aimé Bangolé, boss?"

"I'm afraid so."

She felt as though by tracking him down in Belleville she had sentenced him to death. Barthélemy didn't look very proud of himself either. Baccari announced that he had found a puncture mark in the victim's neck. Lola and Barthélemy exchanged sad, knowing glances.

He offered to take her home in the patrol car. She refused. He had a crime to solve; she could look after herself. After a muttered conversation, Barthélemy let her leave.

She walked in the direction of the Saint-Louis hospital, driven by an unhealthy energy. A jumble of words pinged along her synapses. She felt as though she could hear Toussaint's voice, his poem swelling to fill her brain:

Hear in the Wind / The Weeping Bush / It is the Breath of the Ancestors . . .

She had played with destiny, paid attention to the voice of a dead man begging her from the shadows to lend him a helping hand. She had chosen those shadows and put life at risk.

The walls of the hospital. She walked alongside them, heart heavy with regrets, then turned into Rue Alibert. The Saint-Martin Canal was nearby. She could already sniff its muddy smell, heightened by the recent rain. *They are in the running Water . . . They are in the sleeping water . . . They are . . . They are . . .*

A silhouette on the bridge. Tall, thin. Lola kept on walking. She felt that if she stopped, her heart would turn to ashes that would be scattered on the dark water. The silhouette was a tall, thin woman. The face of a grinning mummy, a rotten smile. Lola saw a bleeding neck, realised she was wearing a red scarf no wider than a snake.

Lola rummaged in her pocket, and took out some small change.

"Bah, not very generous are you, my plump princess?"

"You don't look as if you're lacking for anything though," she heard a man's voice say.

Lola had not spotted him, seated against the balustrade. Broken nose, tow-haired and ravaged-looking. Fifty-something, but still with strong arms and upper body. He stood up, brandishing a knife.

Lola took the Stanley knife out of her pocket:

"If it's blood you're after, come and get some."

The man's lips twisted in an uncertain smile. He turned to look towards the canal. A jogger in a light-coloured outfit was running alongside it with a dog. Lola held her knife braced in her arm.

The early morning runners were none other than Ingrid and Sigmund. A few metres from the bridge, Ingrid started to sprint, shouting out loud. She looked ridiculous: her outfit turned out to be a pair of green polka-dot pyjamas. Had she deliberately decided to copy the Dalmatian? Whatever: Sigmund was imitating her. He was barking furiously, and for the first time since Lola had met him, he looked threatening.

"Let's get out of here," the man said to the old woman. "We've run into a pair even crazier than us."

They fled in the direction of the Bastille.

"I told you it was dangerous to go wandering around here at night," panted Ingrid.

"I was taking control of the situation when you turned up."

"Yeah, with your blade, like at the airport."

Lola knew what her friend was thinking. You lied to me yesterday morning. You had everything ready to force the air hostess to talk.

"I never intended to use it."

"I never suggested otherwise."

"What then?"

"In the past, your natural authority was all you needed."

"That's possible. But it's not always possible to choose our weapons. What are you doing here anyway?"

"Barthélemy."

"Huh! He decided to wake up the whole neighbourhood, did he?"

"He didn't like the idea of you going off on your own. Especially in the state you were in. He told me about Bangolé. I'm so sorry, Lola!"

"It's Bangolé you should feel sorry for. As for me, I'm nothing more than an old hag, a female gorilla with winter coming on. The last caravan of the travelling circus has just gone by, but I didn't notice. Enough fooling around, it's time to go home, put on my slippers and my quilted dressing gown and forget the whole world. With a bit of luck, the whole world and its ills will forget me too. Although I'm not so sure about that."

"You weren't to know."

"Yes, Ingrid, I was."

"Let's go back, you'll see things more clearly in the morning."

No point insisting. Lola followed her American friend and the Dalmatian along the familiar streets. Her mind was made up in any case.

21

Sacha, Carle and Ménard had been trying for some time to fit Bangolé's death into the equation. At nine, the secretary interrupted them to say they had two visitors.

Carle bridled when she saw Ingrid and Lola enter the Duguin team's office, but she quickly recovered the impassive look of a diplomat from the Middle Empire. Ménard offered Ingrid a seat; Carle did the same for Lola. Sacha was expecting the worst. Bribing a witness, theft of documents, intimidation of a spook or a politician: the adjective "impossible" did not exist for the infernal duo from the Canal Saint-Martin. He observed the firebrands one by one. Done up like the ace of spades, gorgeous-looking but with an air of melancholy about her, Ingrid afforded him a quick glance, then studiously followed the progress of the clouds drifting southwards. Wearing a sack dress apparently fashioned out of a chubby monk's habit, and with a face to match, Lola was staring at him determinedly.

She explained that she had gone to Roissy to question Isis Renta. Then had been on a building site in Rue d'Aubervilliers to identify the body of Aimé Bangolé.

"Is that all?" Sacha said.

She raised a conciliatory hand.

"I don't intend to compete with you in the best sleuth's stakes.

Renta gave me new leads, but only because I used rather unorthodox methods."

Sacha intercepted a look from Ingrid to Lola that said a great deal. The young American did not approve of her old friend's methods, but had decided to remain loyal. That was just like her. A pure heart even if her hands were full of concerns. As she listened, she was vigorously folding an old metro ticket. Apart from that, she appeared completely calm.

Rather than make a long speech, Lola took a tape recorder out of her bag and pressed start. Sacha recognised her voice, then that of the Congolese air hostess, close to panic.

"Listen carefully, Renta. I may look past it but I've dealt with much tougher people than you. Either you answer my questions or I'll redesign your pretty mug. You didn't go to your ex's funeral in Africa. Why?"

"I wanted to cut all links with Norbert. I could have been spotted."

"Who by?"

"By the people following him at Kinshasa airport."

"You saw him before he died?"

"Yes."

"How was he?"

"Terrified."

"What did he want?"

"He wanted me to help him get out on a flight. I didn't have time to arrange it. Some militiamen turned up. Norbert slipped an envelope into my hand and told me to give it to Toussaint when I got to Paris. Then he ran off, with the militiamen after him."

"What were they like?"

"There were three of them in military fatigues with balaclavas."

"Africans?"

"Yes."

"*Are you sure?*"

"*I heard them talking.*"

"*What did they say?*"

"*They were wondering where to find Norbert.*"

"*And did you give that envelope to Toussaint?*"

"*No, I was far too scared. I didn't want anything to do with any of that. I posted it to him.*"

"*What was in it?*"

"*A key.*"

"*Did you look?*"

"*No, Toussaint told me.*"

"*Why was that?*"

"*He guessed Norbert had contacted me. He didn't trust many people: only his sister, Toussaint, and me. I told Toussaint what had happened at the airport. That was when he told me about the envelope. He said it contained a key and a scrap of paper with two words scrawled on it: 'Locker. Oregon.'*"

"*Did Toussaint know what that meant?*"

"*He thought it must be the left-luggage lockers at Kinshasa airport.*"

"*Did he check there?*"

"*I didn't ask him. I didn't want to know; I suspected it could be dangerous.*"

"*Do you know what Oregon means?*"

"*No.*"

"*Toussaint must have told you about it!*"

"*If he knew anything, he said nothing to me. I swear! After that visit to Paris, I never saw him again. Then I heard about his death . . .*"

Lola switched off the tape.

"After that there's nothing very interesting. I'll leave you the recording. You can listen at your leisure."

"You've changed your mind and decided to collaborate, Lola. Why's that?"

"If it weren't for me, that woman would never have said a word. She's been silent for five years. Like all the others, by the way. They're scared to death."

"But you aren't, apparently."

Sacha couldn't help turning towards Ingrid, indicating to Lola that she was dragging her friend, a civilian, into a perilous adventure.

"I know to stop when I come up against a brick wall, Sacha. *Oregon* is obviously a code word. You have more opportunities than me to uncover that kind of information. My illegal recording wouldn't please a judge, but it will be very useful for the police. I admit you were right. There always comes a time when you have to accept your limitations. Be kind: keep me informed of any progress you make."

Carle accompanied her to the exit, with Ménard looking daggers after them. He must be dreaming of throwing the ex-commissaire into the deepest dungeon.

"Can I talk to you for five minutes as an old friend?" asked Ingrid.

Ménard blinked furiously to make sure he hadn't misheard. Ingrid was an old friend of his boss.

"If you wish."

And his boss acknowledged it.

"Well then . . . I'll leave you to it. If you need any help from me, just ask . . ."

Neither of them deigned to respond. Ménard took his bemusement with him.

"I'm listening."

Ingrid had put the concertinaed metro ticket on his desk and was staring at it in silence. She finally raised her eyes to look at him. Blue eyes, with golden glints . . . and a determined look.

"If Renta makes a complaint, you'll need to be very proportionate."

"See things in proportion, you mean?"

"Lola only pretended to threaten her. She wouldn't have touched a hair on her head."

"Possibly."

"Definitely. And when she found Aimé Bangolé, she told him he should come to you for protection. He refused."

"You ought to be telling all this to Lola."

"I already have. But I think if it came from you it would have more impact."

"All cops together, you mean?"

"Pretty much."

"Tell me what Bangolé said."

Ingrid summarised what had happened in Belleville. The chase, the questioning. The discovery that Kidjo had grilled his informer about Konata and then Gratien. And Bangolé's fear. A tangible one. But what was done was done.

"You know nothing about yourself until you're in a fight. At least Lola isn't afraid of looking at herself in the mirror."

"I'm pleased to see you surrender your weapons in time, Ingrid. And reassured."

He wanted to tell her he had been scared for her, but she was already standing up. And said nothing more than "Good luck with Oregon" before she left the office.

He picked up the small folded metro ticket, stared at it for a moment, then slipped it into his pocket. He pulled out his mobile and found Antonia Gratien's number. She replied on the second ring.

"What can I do for you, Commandant dear?"

22

He was standing in front of the Jardin des Plantes railings, practising his swing without a club but with conviction. The Bentley was brazenly parked in a restricted zone.

"Has your boss initiated you into the joys of golf? Or did you learn carrying his clubs?"

The giant simply straightened his peaked cap. Perhaps he really was mute after all. Sacha crossed the street, entered the hammam, took a towel and left his clothes in the changing room.

I never lie, Commandant Duguin. He found Richard Gratien exactly where Antonia, always so eager to please, naked or dressed, on the telephone or in her Bentley, had said he would be. In an alcove perfumed with an Algerian essence. Alongside him, a stranger in his twenties who like him was wearing only a white towel. Whereas the lawyer's outline had nothing extraordinary about it, the same couldn't be said of his companion. Gratien was clasping his *misbaha* beads; the youngster was on the alert. The body and mind of a paid thug.

Gratien smiled at Sacha. The smile from the video. *Some of the biggest bastards I've known looked just the same.* The wounded beast was coming back to life. He signalled to his bodyguard to go and breathe some steam elsewhere.

"Thai boxing suits you, Commandant."

A complete resurrection. Strong voice, steady gaze.

"Fabert keeps you informed of everything. That's very kind of him."

"Lieutenant-Colonel Fabert isn't the kind sort. You've probably noticed that."

His fingers kneaded the amber beads. There was no apparent irony in his remark.

"Are you using Fabert to sabotage my investigation?"

"I assure you I'm not."

"That's hard to believe."

"Way back, I had nothing against manipulation. It was the only way to get on. But now it's different. I've become philosophical."

"Is that with the benefit of age?"

"No doubt."

"Does the question of Toussaint Kidjo inspire any philosophical reflexions in you?"

"I'm not sure I catch your drift, Duguin. But do go on. I'll give you five minutes, then I have a meeting."

"Kidjo was very interested in Vidal. He met his mother in Ménilmontant. Questioned her about you. But also about Norbert Konata, the assassinated journalist."

"I know who Konata was. I read the African press for my job. We even met on several occasions at cocktail parties and other social events. An intelligent young man. What happened to him is terrible. Our journalists in France don't realise how fortunate they are."

"Konata, Kidjo and Bangolé?"

"It's true they wouldn't win any bets on longevity, Duguin."

"Honoré seems very gifted with a golf club. It's easy to imagine him swinging a hammer."

"Are you joking?"

"Not really. We have the statement of a homeless guy. Bangolé was brought onto the building site by a man and a woman. And executed by the pair of them."

"Antonia and Honoré as the murderous couple: is that your trump card?"

Sacha perceived the relief beneath the feigned amusement. The lawyer shook his head incredulously, and let the *misbaha* dangle between his knees.

"And what could Bangolé have had to say that might have interested me?" he said.

"It's more what might have interested other people regarding you. Lieutenant Kidjo asked him what he knew about you."

"I was not unaware that Aimé Bangolé was an informer. And I'll even let you into a secret."

"Go on."

"I had given Antonia and Honoré the task of finding where he was living. Several years ago. One always needs to know where information comes from. I knew he had taken refuge in a religious community. And had changed his name. Show this homeless person my wife's photograph if you wish. No problem."

"I haven't waited for your authorisation."

"Mars told you I tried to get you removed from the case, didn't he?"

Sacha did not respond.

"You impress me more than you did the first time we met, Commandant Duguin. You're restless, that makes an excellent driving force. But what I like most of all is your calmness. I've met a few men like you, capable of reining in their anger. But they are rare. Florian was one of your kind."

"Whereas you aren't."

"What do you mean?"

"Nadine Vidal remembers your punchy conversation."

"What on earth are you talking about?"

Gratien had leant forward towards him. For a couple of seconds Sacha thought he was going to gouge his face with the heavy amber *misbaha*. He didn't budge an inch.

"No-one has ever spoken to me like that. Do you hear me?"

"I couldn't give a damn. You asked what I'm talking about. It's very simple or very complicated. I'm talking about Richard Gratien's true nature. Something that gives me pause for thought. I sense you're determined to carry out your own idea of justice. That's a big mistake."

"Let's not spoil things, Commandant. I've just admitted I misjudged you. Don't expect any more compliments, I'm very sparing with them. I'll see you soon. And keep me up to date with your progress, I think that will be useful for both of us."

"Your urbane veneer is cracking, Gratien."

"And your five minutes are up, my friend. It was a real pleasure."

Gratien called his bodyguard. The young man came trotting up, carrying a white dressing gown. He wrapped it round his boss. Sacha stared at them both for a moment.

"Why do you need this flunkey?"

"What's eating you now, Duguin?"

"Do you want me to get rid of this guy, Monsieur Gratien?"

"This guy is a policeman. Take it easy, David."

The young David chewed his lips, struggling with a strong desire to lash out. Sacha ignored him.

"I thought Honoré was your bodyguard."

"It's so kind of you to show such an interest in my domestic arrangements. Well, if you really want to know, Honoré has a problem with nudity."

"Does he have something to hide? A mangled body? Tortured perhaps?"

"Maître Gratien, cop or not, I think you should let me rearrange his ugly mug."

"I said no, David, and I hate having to repeat myself." He turned to Sacha: "This is a day for celebration, Duguin, because you've earned a second compliment. You possess another rare quality: prescience. If you're ever thrown out of the police force, get in touch: I might have something to offer you."

"I'm too good for you, Gratien. Remember that what you value is damaged goods."

Gratien's face showed he had touched a raw nerve. Sacha dedicated a broad smile to both silent men, left the hammam and got back into his car.

He had followed his instinct, and was almost sure he had done the right thing. Gratien had let him glimpse his anger. *If you're ever thrown out of the police force.* This veiled threat did not really worry him. Gratien had the best contacts in the Interior Ministry. That meant getting an ordinary policeman sacked presented no difficulty for him; but to attack a commandant in the B.C. backed by a divisionnaire with a past as a diplomat was another matter. His mobile rang as he was going past Place Maubert. Mars wanted him to join him at Tante Marguerite, a restaurant near the Assemblée Nationale that was the haunt of the Who's Who of politicians. Sacha headed for the quays bordering the Seine.

An atmosphere of light wooden panelling, immaculate white tablecloths, fake deer heads on the walls, Mozart in the background: the canteen where politicians and their friends lunched was bathed in a genteel atmosphere. Sacha recognised a Socialist M.P. seated with a famous television journalist.

Mars signalled to him. He was at table with a man with a growing bald patch that Sacha could see as he approached from behind. As he came closer, he realised it was Olivier Fabert, who looked startled to see him. The lieutenant-colonel had obviously not been told he was joining them.

"I was just recommending the celebrated 'Tante Marguerite snail ragout' to our friend," said Mars with a smile. "Are you tempted?"

"Why not?"

"Are you going to explain?" Fabert said between clenched teeth.

"The ragout recipe? I don't know it. How about you, Sacha?"

"Me neither."

"But I have an idea who *Oregon* is," said Mars quietly. "Nostalgia can be such a trap, Fabert. You were posted to the United States, and that left its mark. My friends in the diplomatic security service had some difficulty making the link with you, but they managed in the end. That's one advantage of having competing services. Besides, your enemies are well aware of your name. When you're on a mission, you always choose Yankee code names: *Dakota, Vermont, Idaho.* Strange for an Africa specialist."

Fabert tried to stand up, but Mars gripped his wrist.

"I could cause a scandal in front of all our charming companions," he said, making a sweeping gesture that included the entire room. "Or brief the journalist having lunch with the histrionic M.P. All's fair . . . Why do you think I didn't reserve a private room?"

"I'm not sure it's a good idea to play games with me, Mars."

The divisionnaire slid an envelope towards the man from the D.C.R.I., and suggested he take a look inside. Fabert discovered a key.

"The left-luggage lockers at Kinshasa."

"What's that got to do with me?"

"That's where Konata stashed the documents he couldn't pass to you. Thanks to a succession of coincidences the details of which I'll spare you, it was Lieutenant Kidjo who recovered the key. The message with it suggested it should be handed on to you, but Kidjo preferred to keep it. So really I have only one simple question for you: why?"

Fabert remained silent.

"I have an idea about how you persuaded Konata to work for you. The first attack on him was a fake."

"What attack?"

"Your playing the innocent is about as convincing as a garter-belt on a bishop. Konata was the victim of a first attempt to kill him in his own country. You orchestrated that, didn't you? From what I know, that's your way of doing things. After that, you promised you would protect Konata. Possibly get him a job on a newspaper in Paris. Am I wrong?"

"Can anyone back up this nonsense?"

"Of course."

"Who?"

"Do you think I've slaved in all those different embassies without making contacts? Fabert, I think I can put my finger on your problem."

"You're off your head."

"You're piss-poor at your job. It's quite simple. The result: Konata paid with his skin. And what was all that mess for?"

Arms folded across his blazer, Fabert was trying to look calm and dignified. For once, although Sacha was no great fan of going in for the kill, he felt no compassion.

"Let me guess. For Gratien's notebooks, wasn't it? The kickbacks Candichard got to finance his campaign are all written down in those precious books. Everyone knows he took the money, but nobody has ever had real proof. And then it's not only Candichard. There are people of all political stripes. All Paris has got the hots for those note-books. Especially Judge Sertys, who'd dearly love to claim the scalp of the former minister before he retires. You wanted those notebooks. Obviously. So you hit upon a scheme."

The waiter brought the wine and appetisers. Picking up on the tension at the table, he filled their glasses quickly and withdrew. Mars took the time to try the Bordeaux before continuing.

"Gratien has always taken a shine to lots of different people. Norbert Konata had recently become part of his circle in Kinshasa. Spurred on by your promises, Konata agreed to steal the notebooks from Gratien's villa one night when a reception was being held there. Unfortunately, things went wrong. Gratien set some militiamen on him. What was the risk? The murder of journalists is hardly a rarity in Africa. Who could accuse Gratien? Those bastards didn't even need to shoot him. Konata died in an accident trying to escape from them. The famous notebooks end up in the hands of a low-ranking cop of African origin in Paris. Konata's best friend. Why? Probably because for security reasons you hadn't given Konata your real name. The journalist thought that his policeman friend would be able to find Oregon."

"You must introduce me to your diplomat friend, Mars. He's phenomenal. He knows my C.V. better than I do."

"Did Toussaint Kidjo come to you?"

Fabert laid his hands flat on the table, and leaned forwards towards Mars.

"Naturally. And when he refused to give me the notebooks, I tortured him to death. Toss that to the journalists in here if you like. It's completely grotesque."

"You may be piss-poor, but you're not mad, Fabert. I've never imagined you with your hands covered in blood. I'd be more inclined to see Gratien's people behind it."

"Well then you're in deep shit, Mars! Gratien is untouchable."

Sacha could tell Fabert was regaining confidence. Now that he finally knew what he was being accused of, he seemed relieved.

"I'll leave you now," he said, standing up. "You've got your work cut out. How can two poor cops muzzled by their bosses lay their hands on the great Gratien? Don't miss the next thrilling episode . . ."

"That's right, Fabert, get lost. We don't need you anymore."

"Don't ask me to come and see you again, Mars; the answer's no. Too bad for you, I could have been useful. You're on your own now. Take care."

"You're desperate to have the last word. How pathetic. Why do you think anyone would want to save your tiny crushed ego? You're nothing more than a doormat."

Fabert turned green at this last insult, delivered in a neutral voice. He stormed out. Mars raised his glass.

"One should always toast when a stupid jerk leaves the stage. Besides, he gave me what I needed."

Sacha raised an inquisitive eyebrow.

"That cretin confirmed what I suspected."

"He did?"

"His expression said it all. He really did use Konata to steal the notebooks. And then messed up."

"So your diplomat-informer doesn't exist?"

"Yes, he does. But he could only pass on rumours. Now we know exactly what we're dealing with."

"Was the key a fake?"

"It's from an old cycle lock of my wife's."

"Are you convinced by the idea that Gratien had Konata killed?"

"Absolutely. My diplomat friend was at that reception in the Gratien villa. So was Konata. And that was the night before he died."

"Have you known that for long?"

"Only a few days. My friend's a ruminant. He always chews over any information a long time before he spits it out."

"O.K., let's say that Gratien had Konata killed. If it hadn't been an accident, it would have been a military-style killing. So why the burning tyre for Kidjo? That's not very discreet in the centre of Paris."

"The method was meant to suggest it was a political crime. Among Africans. And it worked. At the time, nobody knew Kidjo had Gratien's notebooks. Fabert has just confirmed that too. He's dying to get his hands on them."

Mars was scrutinising Sacha. He smiled briefly and tapped him on the arm.

"There's a certain logic to what Fabert said," he said. "He claims we're on our own, and he's not far wrong. And I know what you're thinking."

"What's that?"

"You think your career's at stake. But there's one thing I have in common with Judge Sertys. He wants to go out with a bang. So do I. I want to bring down Gratien before I take my final bow. If a fuse has to blow, it'll be me. You've nothing to fear."

"I trust you, boss. Otherwise I wouldn't have had my arm wrestle with Gratien."

"Tell me about it."

When Sacha had finished, Mars invited him to another toast.

"You raised his blood pressure. Perfect."

"None of this tells us who killed Vidal and Bangolé."

"That's true."

"If the accident hadn't happened, Konata would have been executed soon enough. Kidjo was tortured methodically. But Vidal's murder betrays the signs of passion. And so does Bangolé's. Yes, he put Kidjo on Gratien's trail, but from there to massacring him with a hammer . . ."

"Nadine Vidal told you that on the night her husband died, she was visited by Gratien. To recover important documents."

"The notebooks? I can't see Vidal just keeping them in his safe."

"Perhaps he had a copy of them that Gratien knew nothing about."

"Gratien knew the safe's combination."

"That's what Nadine claimed. But perhaps Gratien forced her to give it to him."

"The last time I saw her, she didn't seem to want to hide any secrets. She would have told me: she confessed that he had hit her, so she had nothing more to hide."

"O.K. Well, one more big push and we'll get there. Fabert will leave us in peace for a while. He realised I wasn't lying when I said I could spill the beans about him to the press. But time is pressing. Carle, Ménard and you need to bring all this out in the open before somebody comes and tries to tidy everything up."

"That's what we're doing, boss."

"Gratien has had his moment. Times change. You're broad-shouldered enough to take my place one day. No false modesty with me, Sacha. I chose you: don't forget that."

"About that . . . I suppose this isn't the right moment, but . . ."

"But what's your problem?"

"Basically, I don't know why you chose me."

"My goodness, because you're capable of asking a question like that! And also perhaps because there comes a time in one's life when one doesn't want to waste what there is left on people we don't get on with."

A waiter placed two steaming plates in front of them. His colleague hovered with Fabert's stew.

"Our friend didn't have the stomach for it. Offer this enchanting snail ragout to a deserving soul," Mars suggested.

The two waiters raised their four eyebrows like synchronised swimmers, then disappeared promptly back into the kitchen.

23

"Do you know Murphy's law, boss?"

Ménard was already in hyperactive mode, even before Sacha had finished giving his report. Carle was digesting the information in silence.

"Tell me anyway."

"*Never play leapfrog with a unicorn*. I think that's pretty good advice."

"In other words, you and your sphincter are shit scared of taking on Gratien," said Carle, to everyone's surprise. "And there I was thinking you had a backbone."

"And I always wondered what you had in your belly," retorted Ménard. "But it was nothing more than a superwoman complex. I'm sorry, but I'm not impressed."

"Give me a break, will you?"

"There's no way we can touch Gratien by the usual means, is there?" Ménard went on. "That guy has known all the high and lows. Right now, he's a bosom pal again with our politicians. He's untouchable. The same can't be said of Candichard."

"Carry on," Sacha said.

"I think the notebooks have already been put to use."

"Someone suggested to Gratien he should threaten Candichard in the run-up to the elections?"

"Exactly. Either the minister gave up on his presidential ambitions, or the methods used to finance his campaign would be revealed to the whole world. Ever since, Candichard has survived as a chairman of semi-public companies. They're regulated by laws that don't impose such tight budgetary constraints. Nice touch. Our council taxes don't only go to paying for rubbish collections. They also serve to support people like Candichard. It's a tidy sum, but compared to the coffers of the Republic, it's loose change. In short, apart from Sertys who thinks he's Joan of Arc, no-one is interested in Candichard any more. It's in Gratien's interest not to make waves. His notebooks must contain a few more bombshells, but he has to tread carefully."

"You can screw around with Power, but not for too long, and only so far: is that your idea?"

"That's right, boss. Gratien is smelling of roses again, and so it suits him to keep the info to himself."

"And by annoying him we'll only cause trouble for ourselves?"

"I don't agree," Carle said. "I may be naive but I can't accept that a guy like him can carry on just as if nothing had happened. If he was the one behind the deaths of Konata and Kidjo, he has to pay."

"So what are you suggesting?" Ménard said. "That we disguise ourselves as ninja turtles and jab him with our pointy steel stars until he begs for mercy?"

Mars' secretary poked her head round the door to say he wanted to see them.

The expression on Mars' face was that of his dark days. He motioned for them to sit down. Carle preferred to remain standing. Mars glanced at her briefly with a look that hinted at his exasperation, then rubbed his cheeks with both hands. Commandant Duguin was familiar with the gesture. Mars had reached a difficult decision, but one he would stick to.

"I've just come back from seeing Maxence. I got two judges for the price of one: his colleague Sertys was waiting for me, licking his lips. We've been handed down our verdict. We're not to touch Gratien."

Sacha stiffened in his chair. The divisionnaire's words were still fresh in his memory. *I want to bring down Gratien before I take my final bow. If a fuse has to blow, it'll be me. You've nothing to fear.* Now it seemed Gratien was protected not only by politicians but the justice system as well.

Mars went on to insist there was a weak link, and that was where "they had to direct their attack". Sacha relaxed and observed Carle. She was still in the same position: on the defensive.

"And that link is called Antonia Gratien," he guessed.

"The lady likes to confide in you. Gratien has lost his bearings ever since Vidal's death. If we can convince Antonia we've got enough to pin on Gratien, she'll do her calculations and jump ship before it sinks."

"Her loyalty might be unshakeable."

"Let's put it to the test. Antonia is looking for a way out from a marriage that's lasted too long. The string of lovers she's had must mean something, don't you think?"

"It may be that the arrangement satisfies them both. And let's not forget he saved her life."

"I'm not forgetting anything. But I don't have any other plan. We've nothing to lose, Sacha."

Honoré led them down to a basement gym. In a low-cut body-stocking, Antonia was going through a pilates session on luxury equipment. She straightened up with cat-like suppleness, and spoke to Sacha as though Carle was not even there.

"Where are you taking me, Commandant?"

"To our headquarters on Quai des Orfèvres. Just a few questions. Back to basics."

"I'd have preferred a weekend alone with you, no matter where. But I'll make do with what you're offering."

Sacha and Carle waited in the vestibule. Antonia reappeared in the same body-stocking, plus fur coat. She had put on some perfume, and was wearing very high-heeled sandals. Carle studied this dangerous footwear with a sneer. Antonia swept past her without apologising, Honoré in her wake.

"There's no point in him coming."

"I never go out without Honoré."

"Would he have gone along on your weekend with the boss then?" Carle said slyly.

Antonia ignored her jibe. Honoré opened the rear door of the patrol car for her, and she stepped in nonchalantly.

She was taken to the interview room. Honoré sat on the floor in a corner and seemed to doze off, head resting on his forearms. As Antonia replied to the questions, she regularly turned towards the two-way mirror and smiled. She knew perfectly well that Mars was observing her.

She stated that she knew of the existence of the notebooks. They contained confidential information concerning arms deals for which her husband had provided legal expertise. She affirmed that she had received Norbert Konata as a guest on several occasions in their Kinshasa villa. When Sacha mentioned the date of his death, she said it was possible she had held a reception that evening, but how could she remember with any precision something that had taken place five years earlier? She did however insist that her husband had been present throughout the evening. He always was whenever they held one: he owed it to his guests.

"A militia group was meant to kill Konata."

"I have never been present at any meeting between my husband and hired killers, Commandant. I'm sorry if that disappoints you."

Antonia Gratien had perfected an interesting technique. She replied to every question in the subtlest way possible, whilst remaining sufficiently evasive never to lie. *You have to believe me, I never lie. Please go now. I'll come to see you again soon . . .*

Five hours later, he released her and accompanied her to a taxi rank. She gestured for Honoré to get in before her.

"I was serious about that weekend, no matter where, with you."

"I know."

"Well then?"

"What interests me at the moment is to get you to understand that Gratien and his gold-plated den are not eternal. It may be time to protect your back."

"I understood that. But I can't."

"Why?"

"How could I possibly betray the man who saved my life? If I did so, I think it would destroy me. Can you understand that?"

"Gratien has blood on his hands, and you know it."

"He's not the only one. See you soon, Sacha. There are still a few things I want to do before I die. One of them concerns you."

"What could that involve?"

She pressed her first finger lightly on his lips.

"Enough questions. Just imagine, that's better."

Sacha ripped the tiny recorder from his torso.

"Well?" Carle said.

He said nothing, but rewound the tape, and played her the recording.

". . . *Just imagine, that's better.*"

He stopped the machine.

"Like eighty per cent of the female population, she seems to want to bed you. Apart from that, I'd say it was a waste of time."

"She did admit there was a potential reason to betray him. And that her husband was no more innocent than anyone else. It's a start."

"You'll have to sleep with her to get any further. If that's one of your methods."

"Carle, I preferred you in your Zen period."

"For a while now, I've had no idea what you're up to. Neither you nor Mars."

"Why only eighty per cent, Carle?" said a well-known voice. "I'd say it was more like ninety-eight per cent. In other words, all those fine ladies, apart from you and my wife."

Sacha and Carle turned and saw Mars standing behind them.

"I'm sorry, but I don't feel like apologising to you, *Monsieur le Divisionnaire.*"

With which she left the Duguin team's office, looking daggers at them.

"Finally," Mars said. "For a long time I thought Carle had no more feelings than a block of wood. But why that look, Sacha? Do you think she's right?"

"To some extent."

"Trust me. I like to keep in touch with my diplomatic past in Africa. I go to African embassy parties in Paris. Antonia never misses a single one. Believe me, I've seen her at work. She can't resist certain kinds of men. Excuse me for being so blunt, but you're her type. Does that shock you?"

"I didn't join the force to be some sort of sexual bait."

"You're smiling, but you're not happy. I'm getting to know you. Here's what I suggest. An outsider's view. Clémenti is having dinner at home tonight. Join us. You can both talk about your cases. He offers good advice . . ."

"I've got something on this evening."

"As you wish. I'm still convinced that of all of us, you're the one most likely to get somewhere with Antonia. The only one, in fact. Give yourself a break. We'll talk about it again tomorrow."

Sacha called Rachid and suggested they had a sparring match. Part of the tension knotting his shoulders loosened when his friend replied that he would leave his cousin in charge of the restaurant and come and meet him.

"Get ready for a thrashing, Sacha. I'm going to give you the hiding of your life."

"That's what I'm hoping."

"Still electric, the atmosphere at work?"

"Nuclear."

"Want to talk about it?"

"No."

"That's what I thought. See you soon."

24

Ingrid dropped her clothes on the chesterfield and slipped on the Calypso dressing gown. Marie had finished her costume and left it on the dummy. Paris was still being regularly flooded with rain, and she had created an outfit for a cloud fairy. Ingrid studied her face in the mirror, wondering what make-up would go best with her atmospheric disguise. Two heavy blows on the door made her turn her head.

"Yes?"

The door was flung open. Three armed goons burst into the dressing room.

"What the fuck!"

A survivor from the Cro-Magnon era threw her to the floor and handcuffed her. Ingrid's chest was crushed, and so she couldn't utter the stream of insults that flashed through her mind. Although her field of vision was restricted, she could see the two other motherfuckers ransacking her domain. They searched the wardrobe, destroyed all her pots of make-up, threw the contents of the drawers on to the floor. The ransacking seemed to go on for ever, punctuated by grunted comments. Ingrid was more angry than scared. They were looking for something precise. What could it be? And what the fuck had happened to Enrique? What did Timothy pay his security guard for?

"What do you want, for God's sake?" she bawled, trying to shake off her attacker. He was too heavy for that.

"Shut your mouth!" he said, punching her in the side.

The pain brought tears to her eyes. She had bitten her tongue, and the sour, metallic taste of blood filled her mouth.

One of them tore the cloud fairy's costume to shreds. Ingrid roared with indignation. The other, stockier guy tipped over the wooden and iron dummy and started rummaging inside it.

And pulled out a plastic bag full of crack crystals.

Ingrid struggled, protested. She had never seen that shit. Somebody must have hidden it there without her knowing it.

"That's it, make us laugh," said the oldest of the three. "It's the joke we hear every day."

"What's going on here?"

Timothy stood in the doorway with Enrique.

"Are you the boss of this joint?" asked the thug who had discovered the crack.

"Who are you to adopt that tone with me?"

"Drugs Squad," he replied, pulling a police armband out of his jerkin pocket and slipping it on. "The name's Marchal. And I'm inviting you to a private party at our place that'll blow your mind."

"She's in the lock-up," Captain Marchal said. "Follow me.'"

Sacha could sense his hostility. His Drugs Squad colleague had learned that his prisoner really did know a B.C. commandant, who was coming to get her out as soon as he heard of her arrest. He shot off down the stairs like a cannon-ball, his tight-fitting jeans showing off a backside and thighs worthy of an ox. Sacha followed him. Once they had reached the basement of the Palais de Justice, Marchal demanded an explanation. Sacha told him openly about his relationship with Ingrid. Just as well to avoid any confusion.

"Who tipped you off about the Calypso?"

"A smartass who preferred to stay anonymous. We seized a good kilo of *youka*."

"She has nothing to do with it, Marchal. I'll vouch for her."

"You seem very keen."

Sacha gripped his shoulder.

"What do you mean by that?"

"I made some enquiries with our Yankee colleagues. Your friend has already been arrested for possession."

"What are you talking about?"

"Ten years ago, in San Francisco."

"That's impossible."

"I don't know what it is that keeps you from seeing, but you ought to do something about it. Lucidity never killed anyone."

The unmistakable stench, the dim lighting, the complete lack of intimacy. Sacha had never been able to get used to the "five stars of hell" style of the police cells. A guard opened the door. Looking wan and exhausted, Ingrid was lying on one of the three bunk beds — nothing more than a wooden plank with no mattress. The sound of loud snoring. A woman with torn fishnet stockings was sleeping it off on the bunk above her. The smell of vomit competed with that of the toilet.

"Get me out of here, Sacha. I've done nothing."

"Marchal told me about your arrest in the United States."

"I was cleared."

"Tell me anyway."

"I was sixteen. Julian, my boyfriend, took a heroin overdose. They found some shit at my place. It had nothing to do with Julian's death:

it belonged to Jimmy, my younger brother. I told the police it was mine. There wasn't enough of it for them to charge me with trafficking. I was taken in for questioning. That's all it was: it's the truth, I swear."

"I believe you."

"They've closed down the Calypso. Timothy Harlen doesn't deserve that. He's always been straight. You know that."

"I'll see to it. Don't worry."

"Excuse me for butting in," Marchal said, 'but I need something more than sweet nothings if I'm to swallow your little floozie's story."

Sacha brought his face right up to his colleague's.

"Mars and I are working on the Vidal affair. Have you heard of that?"

"So? What's the link with this chick?"

"Nothing I can tell you about for the moment, but take my advice and stop playing the fool."

Marchal bawled for the guard to open the door. He charged through the deserted basement, then halted after ten metres.

"All this crap over a bitch who earns a living stripping off in Pigalle. Take care, Duguin, you're cracking up."

"I'm telling you, she has nothing to do with drug trafficking."

"Diesel may be your grass, or your bit on the side, I couldn't give a fuck. She's not getting out of here without a solid gold reason. That's clear enough, isn't it?"

Sacha imagined punching his lights out, but thought better of it and left the building.

When he entered Mars' office, he found him in the company of Lola Jost and Carle.

"How is she taking it?" Lola said.

"As well as can be expected, in the circumstances."

"I wouldn't have thought so, to look at you."

"There's a problem."

Sacha told them what Marchal had discovered in the States. Lola took it badly. As an ex-commissoire, she knew what was at stake. Ingrid not only ran the risk of being jailed, but could be extradited back there.

"If Gratien is behind this, he'll be sure to find some friendly immigration official who'll help him."

"And on the spot," Carle said.

For once, Mars had nothing to say. Sacha asked his opinion.

"This could have come from Gratien or from Fabert. Or even that asshole Sertys. Whoever it was, the aim is to get you off the Vidal case. They have nothing on me, so they attack my right-hand man. Clever move. A rock and a hard place, Sacha. But you're the one who has to choose."

"The important thing is the investigation and not the investigator, is that it?"

"That's right. I hand the controls over to Carle, and you stay on the sidelines for a while. Or you stay, and Mademoiselle Diesel returns to the States."

And gets to wear an orange jump suit for five years, thought Sacha. He turned towards Carle. She could hardly contain her desire to jump for joy, but managed to keep her monolith look. Wonderful. The day had begun stinking of white spirit. And was ending with the smell of disaster.

"I'm going home. Keep me up to date."

"No problem," Mars said, clapping him on the shoulder. "It's just for the moment, Sacha. Don't give up."

25

That idiot Arthur had forgotten yet again to lock the door. Sacha bolted it, then went to the bathroom to splash his face with water.

Antonia appeared behind him in the mirror. She was smiling. He suppressed a great desire to slap her.

"Make yourself at home."

"Your apartment will be interesting, once it's finished."

"What can I do for you? Screw you while Quasimodo films everything then puts it on the internet?"

"Honoré doesn't like the cinema."

"That doesn't stop you play-acting."

"Had a bad day at the office?"

He gestured for her to get out of the way. She stepped aside to let him out. He opened the window slightly, and saw the moon was in the first quarter. Antonia and her smile were reflected in the glass. She pressed herself against his back, then ran her hands over his chest and stomach.

"What are you doing exactly?"

"Checking for a microphone."

"What's the point? You never say anything interesting."

She went to curl up like a cat on the sofa, and struck a pose similar to the one in the Bentley.

"D'you know what would be good?"

He ran a weary hand through his hair.

"I love it when you do that, Sacha. It makes me feel like comforting you."

"Thanks, but I'll survive."

"What would be even better is if you were dropped from that stupid investigation. We could finally make love without any problems."

Mars had been right. Antonia, the weak link. But he would need to be cruel, and he had about as much desire to do that as to slit his stomach open with a butter knife. *I don't have any other plan. We've nothing to lose, Sacha.*

"Are you with him because you can't have any more children? Or because you came from nowhere? Will that rotten old man protect you until his dying day, is that it?"

She had blinked. At last. And Sacha knew that at that precise instant she would have killed him if she could. Her eyes flashed. Her bottom lip twisted.

"You're as beautiful as a sarcophagus, do you know that?"

"And you're an empty shell."

Her voice was pure hate. A voice like steel-tipped spears thrusting to the sky.

"Have fun, Antonia. Have fun with me if that's the only way you can get your kicks these days."

"You redecorate your place but there's nobody here."

"Perhaps that's because unlike you I don't like antique relics."

She leapt up off the sofa.

"Is there any music? Or are you one of those people who don't like it? Who only like their job."

She was in a fury. It was as if her hidden scars were climbing to her face like an army of brambles. He didn't like what he had provoked.

She grabbed a stack of C.D.s and flung them around. She finally found one she wanted, and inserted it in the sound system.

The voice of R. Kelly: pure sex.

Antonia was already dancing.

Kelly was inviting his girl to a session of uninterrupted sex. Her boss had been told she wouldn't be in for work that day. He told her to get over to his place as quickly as possible. She had to put on the underwear he had bought for her and join him in bed, where he'd been waiting for her for hours, just thinking about her.

Antonia was dancing ever more enticingly.

I want your echo, echo, echoooo . . .

The music suited her perfectly. She took off her pullover and threw it against the window. Sacha was about to grab her by the arm, tell her he already had one striptease artist in his life, and that was quite enough.

Sex in the morning, sex all day . . .

Pain. A jab in the neck. Crushing darkness. *Is this where it all ends? Why not . . . After all, I've already given enough . . . .*

He had been sleeping on his side in the same sarcophagus for five thousand years. Antonia had not taught him anything, he himself had discovered the secret of the embalming fluids of ancient Egypt. One part turpentine, two parts white spirit . . .

Sacha opened his eyes. He was staring at a patchy white ceiling. Someone had forgotten to do the second coat. A nervous buzzing was upsetting the whole world.

It took him several seconds to comprehend that he was lying flat on his bed, naked from the waist up, his brain full of colliding lead shot. He was shivering. The window was open wide on a dirty pink dawn. And still there was the buzzing sound, sawing at his neurons, a rusty saw. He lifted himself up on one elbow, had just enough time to lean over before he vomited onto the wooden floor. Saw a reddish trail on it.

His sheets were stained with blood.

His stomach and jeans were stained with blood.

He felt his body. No wound. His neck was swollen; he touched a puncture mark. He slipped backwards out of his bedroom. A quick look around his empty apartment. He put his jacket on without a shirt. Still the buzzing: the door downstairs. Could it be Arthur?

He opened the apartment door to a squad of police officers. He recognised Seguelas, a lieutenant on the night shift. Seguelas stared at his body and face covered in blood. His eyes widened.

"What's going on, Duguin?"

"You tell me, Seguelas."

"We got a call . . ."

"Who from?"

"An anonymous caller. Max is going to have to cuff you. That's the procedure, so don't be mad at me, eh?"

"Are you off your rocker?"

The said Max pushed him up against the wall and handcuffed him. He heard them prowling round the apartment. Before too long they would reach the bedroom and see the bloody sheets.

You trapped me like a rat, Antonia.

26

We're not to touch Gratien. It was night-time now, but no-one had broken the sacred rule. For the simple reason that the lawyer had come to police headquarters at his own insistence, driven by his chauffeur. Patience personified, Mars waited while the deaf and dumb Honoré, who turned out also to be illiterate, finished drawing his statement on A5 sheets of paper. The African was no Leonardo da Vinci, but there was no difficulty understanding what his clumsy fingers were trying to convey. The Bentley dropped Antonia off outside Sacha's apartment. Antonia ordered Honoré to leave. The chauffeur obeyed, and returned to his employers' residence to sleep.

"I have complete confidence in my employee," Gratien announced. "My wife spent part of the night at your officer's home. I demand to know where she is. And I hope for your sake that the blood isn't hers."

Sacha and Carle were alongside Mars, but Gratien ignored them. He was focused on the Big Chief.

"It's being analysed in the lab."

"When will you have the results, Mars?"

"I asked for them urgently. Just as I did for the drug used on my officer. He was assaulted in the presence of your wife. And something tells me your chauffeur knows more about this than he is admitting. Your wife herself says she never goes out without Honoré."

"How do you know your officer didn't inject himself?"

"Why would he do that?"

"To make it seem he had been attacked, when he was the aggressor."

"I repeat: why would he do that?"

"To push me to the limit, perhaps."

"That's ridiculous."

"I hope so for your sake, Mars. If the opposite turns out to be true, your reputation is done for."

"Is that what you're after?"

"For that you would have to worry me."

"And I don't worry you?"

"I find you pathetic."

Mars smiled to himself, then got up and stood beside the lawyer. He put a hand on his shoulder. Gratien didn't flinch. Mars leaned over and whispered in his ear:

"Did you know your wife intended to visit Commandant Duguin?"

"I know she would some day or other."

"Why?"

"Antonia is a free spirit."

"That's very broad-minded of you."

"I have no intention of discussing my married life with you. I demand to know where my wife is."

"Clear one thing up for me. Why did she want to compromise the officer who was in charge of the Vidal case? I've got my own idea about that, but I'd be interested to hear your version."

"Are you one of those people who believe in conspiracy theories? That's surprising, and sad."

Mars strode up and down the room, then turned back to Gratien and spoke more harshly.

"Was it you behind the crack planted at the Calypso?"

"Now you've really lost me. What on earth are you talking about?"

Sacha had carried out hundreds of interrogations. He also had a sixth sense for detecting lies, and was ready to wager that this was the only true answer to come from Gratien's mouth. Besides, why organise two attacks almost simultaneously? Antonia's spectacular performance was enough. Mars shook his head, as if he thought the same.

"I've got another story that might interest you, Gratien. It's a little old but still has its charm. It concerns an African journalist used by a lieutenant-colonel in the French secret service to steal incriminating notebooks from a lawyer who specialises in the arms trade. Pursued by a militia hired by the lawyer, the journalist misses his meeting with the lieutenant-colonel, but transfers the notebooks to his best friend, a lieutenant in a Paris neighbourhood police station. The lawyer has the young man tortured to recover his precious possession. Then organises a very special killing, a flaming necklace, to suggest it might have been an act of African political revenge. Five years pass. Until the day when the lawyer's right-hand man, an engaging young fellow, dies in the same way as the little Parisian cop. The lawyer isn't laughing anymore. In fact, he's lost the taste for life. He wants to take justice into his own hands, to punish whoever killed his adoptive son . . ."

Finally, Gratien had turned pale. He stared hard at the division-naire as if he was about to tear his eyes out. Honoré had turned towards his master with an expression that could have been pity beneath his expressionless features. But Gratien had already regained control of himself.

"For many years, the lawyer has been able to carry on his business just as he liked. But now the police are bothering him. What, these wretched little mosquitoes are stirring in the swamps? They have to be kept off. His wife can deploy her smoke screens. The only thing that counts now is to find the killer of his protégé. And to make him pay with his life, even if it's the last thing the lawyer does. It's no easy task. Who organised the show at the Colombes swimming pool? A spook? The lieutenant-colonel for example? Why? To recover his holy grail, those damned notebooks he's so obsessed with? The heir and his mentor work as one. There's a strong possibility this heir knows how and where to lay his hands on those books. All he had to do was torture him to make him talk. Or it could be a more classic story. Reprisals for an arms contract that wasn't to the liking of everyone in the upper echelons. It's possible. The lawyer will find out. Sooner or later."

"I'm beginning to find you tiresome, Mars."

"I have one more question. Do you really think you can be untouchable all your life?"

"I'll make sure your officer is arrested, Mars. And I hold you responsible for Antonia's disappearance."

Richard Gratien put on his cashmere coat and gloves in a leisurely fashion. He signalled to his chauffeur to follow him, and left the office, as calm as could be. Mars turned to Sacha.

"What do you reckon?"

"The best solution is to push him as hard as we can. He's recovered his energy, but it's all centred on one thing. It's obvious he's kept on his feet by the desire for revenge. And we're worrying him. I insulted him openly in the hammam, and that stuck in his craw. So he used his wife and chauffeur to undermine my reputation. And I bet he'll go running to the press."

"Me too. We'll just have to grit our teeth."

"But why did you single out Fabert? Because that provides you with a target where we can expect his riposte?"

"Exactly."

"Am I part of this?"

"No, I'm sorry. You're under arrest. Unofficially, go home and wait for me or Carle to phone you. Got that?"

Sacha nodded. But he had picked up on the note of dismay in his chief's voice. *No, I'm sorry* could be translated as: how could you have let yourself fall into a trap like that? Carle was trying to adopt the expression of a pillar of salt, but could not help looking like a Mcdonald's assistant who had just won the lottery. No point trying to justify himself to Mars with her in the room. Sacha swallowed his pride and took his leave.

"What on earth's happened to that blood analysis?" Mars asked angrily.

"Be patient a while longer, chief. The lab promised me the results by this evening."

"For heaven's sake, it's already six o'clock!"

"I'll give them another call. In the meantime, I've got something hot. Very hot."

"Cut the suspense crap."

Ménard shrugged as if to say "not in front of a civilian".

"You can talk freely. To me, Madame Jost is still one of us."

"Thank you, Arnaud," said Lola, quite pleased to see the young whippersnapper taken down a peg or two.

To her, people like Mars were an endangered species. They knew how to behave in almost all circumstances. Officers in nappies like Ménard seemed to find it hard to grasp this obvious point.

"The same stuff was injected in the necks of Kidjo, Vidal and . . . Bangolé, boss."

Lola studied Mars' face. The news obviously shook him, but he recovered quickly.

"Get it compared to what was injected into Sacha."

"That's already done. I went to the lab myself."

"And?"

"It doesn't coincide. The commandant was doped with a barbiturate: pentobarbital. In the other three cases it was benzodiazepine."

"That would have been too perfect," muttered Mars. "It would have established a link between the three murders and Sacha . . ."

"A link with the face of Antonia Gratien on it," Ménard took it upon himself to add. "But that fine lady is too clever for that."

Mars pointed at Carle and told her to keep Fabert under surveillance. She replied with a "Consider it done, boss" that left Lola with the feeling that she had filled Sacha's shoes with astonishing ease. Between the whippersnapper and the treacherous Jezebel, the commandant couldn't have had an easy time of it. And to think he had sacrificed Ingrid on the altar of his career. He'd live to regret it when he eventually grew up.

Mars invited Lola to join him in his office. Once they were installed, he offered her a whisky. She accepted gratefully.

"What are you going to do for Ingrid?"

By way of a reply, Mars beeped his secretary and asked her to call Lieutenant-Colonel Fabert for him. Thirty seconds later, his phone rang and the divisionnaire put it on speaker.

"Good old Mars, what a surprise! To what do I owe the honour?"

"Stop pretending you don't know what this is about, Fabert. With regard to the Calypso, what's the deal?"

"It's a real pleasure working with professionals; it avoids wasting so much time. I want Duguin off the Vidal case. Full stop."

"That's already been done, but I don't really see what you gain by it. If this is a contest to see who has the longest dick, I gave up that kind of game a long time ago."

"In a few months you'll be swapping your service revolver for a fishing rod, Mars. So it's more useful to fuck over your assistants in the meantime."

"No-one could ever accuse you of being a class act, could they? But I already knew that."

Mars put the phone down on him and smiled at Lola.

"I'm sorry about that little testosterone-filled interlude."

"No problem. I've heard worse."

"Mademoiselle Diesel is a free woman. Well, as good as. And I'm sorry for this annoying . . . setback."

"The fact is, Ingrid and I deserved it, for trampling all over your patch. Thank you anyway."

"Don't mention it."

"Will you be able to manage without Sacha?"

"He's my best officer. It's a low blow, but I have my methods. Prodding the crocodiles so that they devour each other."

He explained the plan he had in mind for Fabert and Gratien.

"Can you imagine a secret service officer murdering Vidal?" she objected. "Where would that get him?"

"No, I can't see it either, Lola. But that doesn't matter. What's important is that Gratien believes it, comes out of his hole, lowers his guard. And there's a good way to get him to swallow my line."

"What's that?"

"Rumours. I've contacted some well-placed friends. They'll find the right channels to make Gratien see Fabert as the killer."

"I heard you tell Carle to put Fabert under surveillance, but if Gratien is behind the deaths of Konata, Bangolé . . ."

"And Toussaint . . ."

"Yes. If that's the case, you're playing with fire."

"I've no intention of warning Fabert, if that's what you mean. He could screw up my whole plan. Gratien is growing old. He's hesitating, making mistakes. Otherwise, why send his wife to trap Sacha? He's thrashing about like a drowning man. If you like, you can have a ringside seat."

"Meaning?"

"Come back to Carle's team. Help them anticipate Gratien's attack. Or get directly on Antonia's trail."

"I'll think about it."

"A very diplomatic reply. Well, as you wish, Lola."

She left her empty glass on his desk, and Mars accompanied her to the door. She confessed she had long dreamt of the day when she could get her hands on the bastard who had tortured Toussaint. She had felt she would stop at nothing, even inventing a few special punishments of her own . . .

"But now you've changed your mind?"

"Jean Cocteau had lots of ideas about lots of things."

"I imagine he did."

"*The devil is pure because he can only do evil.*"

"So . . . ?"

"So, I don't believe in either the devil or in purity, but I do think one can become a terrifying creature if one forgets to look at oneself in the mirror regularly. I almost crossed to the far side, but I caught myself in time."

"So you believe in that *far side*?"

"I think that as long as one has the choice, it's better not to let yourself get carried away by hatred. Tornadoes only travel one way."

"Is that Cocteau?"

"No."

27

"Who's that?" she muttered, pointing to Arthur sprawled on the tarpaulin covering the sofa. He had a can of Kronenbourg in his hand and two empty ones by his feet.

"Ménard's cousin. Hard at work."

"Painting and decorating of all descriptions?"

"Painting at the speed of a cruise ship, and decorating through contemplation. Arthur has been studying the geography of a crack in the ceiling for forty-five minutes."

"Let's go and have a drink somewhere close. I don't feel like talking in front of him."

"I'm supposed to stay here, Lola. House arrest."

"Who cares, Sacha? Follow me."

They ended up in the square by the Marché-Sainte-Catherine, on the terrace of a nice-looking restaurant. The birds were whistling away in the trees, rocked by a breeze that was far from unpleasant. Sacha smiled and stretched his legs.

"I'm really pleased to see you, Lola."

"I believe you. Thanks for Ingrid. I have to admit you astounded me."

She studied him for a moment. A ray of sunshine was dancing on his brown, closely cropped hair. In spite of everything he had had to put up with, he was a picture of serenity.

"I'm angry with myself for sending you packing when you came to see me about Bangolé. If I had been more cooperative, he wouldn't be dead."

"There's no point blaming yourself. Whoever did for him must have had him in his sights for a long while. Gratien in particular had known for years where he was hiding. And Bangolé could have come to us for protection. He made the wrong choice."

"Even so, I should have trusted you. And talking of that, there's something I can't get out of my mind."

"Tell me."

"I think Mars used us."

His reply was a knowing smile. Which she found totally beguiling. Thank heavens the age of her arteries protected her from any great rush of emotion.

"Your boss played us off against each other. He knew I would do all I could to find Toussaint's murderer. And he was well aware that you'd refuse to let me invade your territory. By setting us both on the same trail, he knew we'd each pull out all the stops. Because we like to compete with each other."

"I agree completely. Mars is a first-class manipulator."

"Yes, credit where credit's due. So you came to the same conclusion as me?"

"I did."

"That's reassuring. I'm not completely senile."

"Far from it, Lola."

"What is he after, d'you think?"

"To get a result quickly. He thinks speed is of the essence."

Sacha explained the tussle with the D.C.R.I., and Mars' fear he might lose "his case to the spooks". And his wish to end his career on a high note.

"And to cock a snook at those who owe their loyalties to a system he's not wholehearted about," said Lola, shaking her head. "It's typical of his lone wolf attitude."

She understood Mars. She had never forgiven her superiors either for having drawn a line under the Kidjo affair.

"Since we've become accidental allies, I'd like your opinion about Antonia Gratien's dirty little trick. Did Mars tell you about it?"

"As if I were still on the force. Which is kind of him, but I'm not falling for it. He wants me around in case he needs me."

"I've been sidelined, so Mars reckons you could be useful?"

"I think that's a bit optimistic on his part. I can hardly see myself interrogating Gratien, for example. I've got no authority."

"Nor have I for the moment."

"Gratien has won the first round. He's managed to get you put on the bench. That was what he was after. But it also provides us with an essential bit of information."

"Gratien has regained all his ability to cause trouble. But he's using it badly."

"Exactly. And in that sense, I agree with Mars' analysis. By attacking you, Gratien is proving he's no longer thinking straight. It was a gut reaction."

"I have to admit I brought it on myself. The last time we met, he told me no-one had ever talked to him the way I did."

"And so he immediately thought of revenge. We're agreed on that. Vidal's death has wounded him more than he realises. Now that Antonia has disappeared, there's going to be a ruckus. You can be sure the media will give you a hard time. Especially if the lab confirms it was her blood. But you're a tough sort, Sacha – I know that from experience. Besides, Mars won't abandon you. He has the means to find Antonia, and he won't stint on them."

"I know."

"And yet there's something bothering you, isn't there?"

He didn't answer, but simply stared at a pretty young woman crossing the square. But this apparition was not enough to ease his concern. He turned back to Lola, and looked at her as though he was sure she could read his mind.

"You think Mars is angry with you for having let yourself get caught in a trap? That's probably true. But what can you do about it? Mars is a complex man."

"No doubt about that."

"So what's on your mind?"

He ordered another round of coffees before replying.

"The confrontation between Mars and Gratien in his office was like a duel of titans. For a second, I felt as though they were in the centre of an invisible circle . . ."

"And that you and your team were excluded?"

"To some extent. Have you already had that feeling too?"

"Yes."

"When?"

"Scarcely an hour ago. When Mars officially invited me to join his investigation. I'm under no illusions. He's encouraging me just in case I could play a role in a baroque strategy where every means is valid. Your boss has a real hatred of Gratien. Negative passions always lead to solitude."

"Mars is in love with Africa."

"I've heard he once lived there."

"For a few years. But they must have counted double in his life."

"So now Gratien is the symbol of the harm we're doing to the African continent?"

"That's the theory I can't get out of my head."

They finished their coffees in an easy silence. While waiting for the storm that was soon bound to burst over them, Lola enjoyed every minute of this calm, and sensed that Sacha felt the same way.

"Do you have any problem with me ordering you something more interesting than an espresso?"

He gave her a quizzical smile.

"I suggest we drink a nicely chilled white wine. This sunny square could almost be Italy. We ought to take advantage of that. And seeing that you're no longer on duty . . ."

Sacha called the waiter over, and ordered a bottle of Ribolla Gialla and some olives from him.

There were worse ways of killing time than sharing a southern wine with a good-looking young man with Mediterranean charm.

The American friend was set free around nine that night. She seemed so exhausted she hardly wanted to speak. Lola hailed a cab and during the ride brought her up to date on events. Learning that Sacha had sacrificed himself to get her out of jail jolted her like an electric shock.

"I have to go and thank him."

"I've already done that, spare yourself the trouble."

"It's only polite. I'm the main interesting person."

"*Interested*, you mean. I'll go with you."

Lola was worried. Sacha had been dealt a body blow, but that had only increased his charm. Ingrid was heading straight for the lion's den. Lola was about to tell the driver to change direction, but Ingrid stopped her: they had to continue on to Canal Saint-Martin. Lola studied her friend's anxious profile. What was simmering behind that stubborn forehead of hers? It was bound to be something dangerous.

When they reached Ingrid's place, she told Lola to pour herself a drink while she had a shower. Why not, agreed Lola. The Italian libations were nothing more than a fond memory by now. She opened the big silver refrigerator. A sad sight for any lover of earthly nourishment. It was as deserted as the tundra in December, apart from two bottles of Mexican beer and half a lime.

"Thank you, my boy," she said to the fridge. "You know how to preserve the essentials."

Ingrid had roamed almost everywhere on the planet, so Mexico and its customs were no stranger to her. She had learned there that a slice of lemon brought the flavour out in beer, and that a pinch of salt glorified it. Lola preferred to zap the condiment and only keep the citrus element. She cut a slice of lime and slipped it into the glass, then filled it with beer. She pressed the glass to the side of her head, and listened to the bubbles' little dance. These small pleasures were even more important when they accompanied major events. Like the freedom of a friend.

The friend in question came out of the bathroom in a cloud of steam and not much else. Lola followed her to her bedroom, where she saw her ransacking her wardrobe in search of a garment that was proving hard to locate.

Finally, after trying on lots of different outfits, Ingrid chose the same as she had just taken off. But a clean version. An old pair of jeans that had played host to an entire civilisation of moths. And a T-shirt with an aggressive slogan. *Tiger Lady is ready to bite* had been swapped for *Save the planet before it pisses on you.* She emphasised her Pacific blue eyes with a dab of grey kohl, and transformed her short blonde hair into a punk nightmare with the help of copious amounts of gel. Glamour is a relative concept.

"Do I look alright?"

"Yes, if you're a fan of roller coasters with no safety belt. Where are you going?"

"I told you: to thank Sacha."

"Don't forget that last week I could have scraped you up off the floor with a spoon. Sacha is drop dead sexy. But he's also to be dropped, quite simply. At least, as far as you're concerned. Do you follow me? But then again, I'm not your mother."

"I've no intention of retying a knot with him."

"Of renewing your affair with him, you mean?"

"Yes, that's what I mean. Exactly."

"Do you know what Eugène Labiche dared say once?"

"No idea."

"*Devotion is a woman's prettiest head-dress.* Well, I don't agree, and besides, I detest titfers."

"Tit for what?"

"Hats, if you prefer. Don't count on my devotion if he drops you a second time. Don't you think that with all the advantages Mother Nature has endowed you with, you could find someone to take Sacha's place?"

"I'll keep to my decision, I promise."

"Oh la la! We'll see about that, Ingrid."

"You French are always so funny with your 'oh la las' all over the place. Well, it's time to go. You can wait here if you like. I'll be back within the hour."

"Yes, yes, off you go. My Mexican friends and I wish you a good evening."

Ingrid put on a pair of silver-striped basketball boots and bounded out.

Lola finished her beer and decided to get some air over at the Belles restaurant. Maxime had been looking after Sigmund for far too long, and it was time to free the man from the dog, or vice versa. Besides, it would give her the chance to find out what the restaurant owner thought of Ingrid's latest recipe. A slab of disaster. A grimace soup. A guaranteed indigestion. Lola was pretty certain that Maxime would see Ingrid's romantic crisis in the same light.

She locked Ingrid's studio and walked up Passage du Désir to Rue du Faubourg-Saint-Denis.

"Don't come running to me when it all turns sour!" she muttered to herself, startling a passer-by.

28

Nessun dorma! Nessun dorma! Tu pure, o Principessa, nella tua fredda stanza, guardi le stelle che tremano d'amore e di speranza . . .

Arthur had plugged his MP3 into Sacha's sound system and was singing along vigorously to Pavarotti. "Turandot" repeatedly massacred. Sitting cross-legged on the wooden floor, Sacha was summoning up the strength to throw the artiste out.

When the doorbell rang, he thought that a gang from the Drugs Squad, a commando raid led by Antonia, or even a tribe of spooks might be an interesting diversion. Anything to avoid another minute in the company of Ménard's cousin.

Ingrid! What a heavenly surprise. Disguised as a hedgehog, but that didn't matter.

She came to a halt when she saw Arthur singing at the top of his lungs on his ladder. The idiot nodded at her, jaw somewhere round his ankles.

And stayed in that cataleptic state until Sacha told him to gather his things. He wouldn't be needed until further notice, thanks very much.

"I'll be back tomorrow morning. You're the boss, chief. But it's a shame. I'd got into my stride tonight. If you'd let me finish, I could have given the final coat to this damn room that's been resisting us so fiercely."

"Out."

"O.K., fine, just give me a moment to tidy up, boss."

"He can stay," Ingrid said. "I won't be long." She turned to Sacha: "Thanks for what you did for me. I suspect it can't have been easy. You've had to give up your investigation . . . I'm really sorry, you know."

"You shouldn't be. Don't worry. Would you like a glass of something?"

"No, thanks."

"We don't have to stay here. Lola introduced me to a place round the corner that's just like Italy . . ."

"No, that's O.K. I only wanted to tell you . . . what I've just told you. Hang on in there, Sacha. There'll be other investigations. Things will work out, won't they?"

"I suppose so. It's a matter of being patient."

A moment's silence, apart from Pavarotti booming out triumphantly, on his own this time:

Ma el mio mister è chiuso in me, il nome mio nessun saprà!

"I didn't know you liked opera."

"Nor did I. Ingrid . . ."

"No, don't say anything. It's better that way. You were right. It would never have worked. Goodnight."

She raced off down the stairs. Sacha leaned over the stairwell, in time to see her small hedgehog bristles disappear. He went back in, deep in thought.

Arthur had a brush in one hand, a pot of paint in the other.

"I'm going to tell you something, boss. In life there are only two things that make it worthwhile getting up in the morning or going to bed in the morning. Women and alcohol. And I know what I think about what you've just let escape. A really poxy idea. That girl is a prime cut. She's like a lifelong cruise on the Atlantic. You ought to be running after her instead of giving me that odd look."

Pavarotti on and on.

"My cousin told me you had a stunner in your paddock but that you preferred to let her go. I told him: your boss is off his head. It's true though, isn't it? What's your problem, eh?"

Ed il mio bacio sciogliera il silenzio che ti fa mia!

Sacha grabbed the paint pot and tipped it over the head of the Michelangelo of the Marais, then threw him out. He picked up the loudmouth's jacket and bag and flung them down the stairwell after him. Arthur dripped his way down the steps, muttering to himself that Sacha was inhuman and that "what had hit him – the house arrest and the American woman taking off like that – was no more than he deserved . . ." Sacha slammed the front door and went over to the balcony. Seven floors below, Ingrid's silhouette was swallowed up by the night.

He listened to Pavarotti. For a long time. Arthur had put "Nessun Dorma" on loop. For a while, the music took him to borderless lands where he didn't have to think about what had just happened, or what might have happened. The door bell rang. He opened. It was Mars.

"The analysis results have arrived. It's not looking good, Sacha."

"It's Antonia's blood?"

"Unfortunately."

"Understood. I'll be right with you."

Ménard was waiting in the Renault. They climbed into the back. Mars explained that Carle and her team were already outside Fabert's place. Another group was combing Paris in search of Antonia.

"The problem is she could have headed out for good, which would really land you in it, boss."

"Give yourself a break for five minutes, Ménard, will you?" Mars pleaded.

"She could be dead," Sacha said.

To judge by the look on Mars' face, the same thought had occurred to him.

"Whoever is playing games with us could well have killed her," Sacha said. "Vidal's murder is along similar lines."

"Yeah, that makes sense," Ménard couldn't help adding. "To create total panic, a complete shambles. The Americans have an expression for it: *When the shit—*"

"*—hits the fan,*" Mars finished for him. "Thank you, Ménard, we've heard that one before. In the meantime, Gratien has been working overtime. I've got the police internal investigations department on my back, the minister on the phone every five minutes, taking turns with the Prefect. Not to mention the media. I'm forced to arrest you properly this time. Like a common criminal. And that gets my goat."

"No point giving them that satisfaction, boss."

Sacha took his copy of *The Art of War* out of his jacket pocket.

"I brought it to have something to read if you had to keep me inside for a while."

"Is it your bible?"

"More or less. Have you read it?"

"A long time ago. You're right, best to take things philosophically. What would Sun Tzu have said about all this?"

"Nothing," said Ménard. "If not, the title of his book would have been *The Art of Dirty War*. Other days, other ways."

Mars gave him a thunderous look, then tapped Sacha on the forearm.

"Dirty or not, we'll survive."

29

More than ever, the Belles restaurant was like an oasis of calm in a world ruled by hysteria.

"It's 'Fantasia' every day," Lola said, folding up the newspaper.

A week had passed since her visit to Mars at police headquarters. Seven days of continuous revelations in the media. The Vidal affair was exploding all over the place. Especially since Antonia was nowhere to be found. "Where is the body of the international lawyer's wonderful wife?" "Who did away with the arms trade guru?"

The methods employed by the B.C. were pulled to pieces. Mars was under attack. Sacha Duguin was dragged through the mud. The most incredible rumours were circulating on the internet. Some smartass had made a secret recording of Ingrid at the Calypso, and the clip of "the former mistress of the rotten cop" went viral. Enrique the doorman had taken on two assistants. Excited crowds gathered every night outside the cabaret. Everybody wanted to see the show of Gabriella Tiger, a.k.a Ingrid Diesel, the "American bimbo who brought down a B.C. commandant". Timothy Harlen had mobilised his journalist friends for a counter-attack, but it was a real struggle. Whenever Ingrid went out she wore dark glasses and a brown wig.

"It's true," said Maxime. "Every commentator has his own opinion about it."

"What a circus! I miss the days of Léon Zitrone, when there were only three channels on T.V., and computers filled whole laboratories."

"Léon Zitrone wasn't bad at all," admitted Barthélemy, even though he was born in the years of cable T.V.

Leaning on the counter, Ingrid was absent-mindedly crushing the straw of her orange juice. Her melancholy face was an open book. In it Lola read of her compassion for Sacha. Not a day went by without her wondering if it was possible to do something to limit the damage. Apart from discovering who had bumped off Vidal, finding Antonia alive, understanding what sick games Fabert and Gratien were playing and blowing up all the internet servers on the planet at the same time, Lola couldn't see what to do.

Even Sigmund was aware of the electricity in the air. He brought Lola's boots for her, leaping up and down on the spot, or rubbed himself against Ingrid's legs, searching for attention rather than to be stroked, as if to say "For goodness' sake, why aren't you doing anything?"

The Dalmatian was going to find it hard to readapt to the quiet calm of his psychoanalyst master's consulting room.

Lola consulted her watch: eight minutes to twelve. No reason why just because the world was suffering a nervous breakdown they should forget to eat and drink. She turned to the slate above the coffee percolator: walnut and chicory salad, stuffed guinea fowl with cabbage, followed by a prune tart.

"I'll have the menu of the day," she said to Maxime, making her way towards her usual table. "And of course, a big pitcher of the house wine."

Ever since her neck-brace had been removed, she had felt like new. She still had a bandaged left arm, but at least she no longer looked like Eric von Stroheim in "La Grande Illusion". When she was seated and had spread her white napkin across her knees, she motioned for Ingrid and Barthélemy to join her. They seemed to her to be taking things in far too offhand way.

"Do me a favour and cheer up, will you? Just because the outlook is stormy there's no reason to wallow in gloom. One thing's for sure at least. It can't get any worse."

"That's easy to say," Ingrid said, nibbling at the end of her baguette.

Chloé came over with the pitcher and a bowl of big, shiny olives. The ex-commissaire's favourites. She filled their three glasses. Ingrid tried to refuse, but Lola insisted it was time for a toast.

"To what?"

"To Commandant Duguin's good health, my dear. Turn the situation upside down. A fresh way of looking at it. What do you see?"

"I can't see what you're getting at."

"The troubles pouring on him all the time are his big opportunity."

Even Barthélemy looked doubtful at this.

"Imagine if his arrival at the B.C. had gone smoothly," Lola went on, determined to convince the other two. "The lad would have seen everything rosy. There's nothing like a straight line to soften your brain. Anybody who arrives too quickly is an *arriviste*. But anyone who reaches the finishing line covered in bruises and foaming at the mouth is a hero. That's better, isn't it?"

"*What doesn't kill you makes you stronger*. Ah, I see what you mean, boss."

Barthélemy's renewed enthusiasm did not appear to have spread to Ingrid. The American friend was dismally twirling the foot of her glass. Have I lost the knack with words? wondered Lola.

Maxime pointed to the television recently installed next to the toaster.

"Watch this."

They gathered round the screen. A journalist was speaking from outside an elegant Parisian residence. He broke off to run towards a blue porch. A black giant in grey livery emerged, carrying an umbrella that he used to protect his dark-suited employer from a downpour that was as intrusive as the horde of photographers all around him. He pushed a reporter who had ventured further forward than the rest. A scuffle. Chauffeur and employer climbed into the Bentley, which glided off through the murk. In the background, a glimpse of the Musée d'Orsay and a small stretch of the Seine.

The journalist returned to the foreground:

A copy of Richard Gratien's famous notebooks was sent anonymously to our colleagues at the Canard Enchaîné *satirical magazine yesterday evening. Another has apparently been delivered to Judge Sertys, the prosecuting magistrate in the EuroSecurities case. The notebooks contain damaging evidence against Louis Candichard, who in the past was forced to abandon his presidential ambitions, and is still a central figure in the ongoing investigation. According to our colleagues at the* Canard, *the committee running M. Candichard's campaign received some fifteen million euros during the campaign. This amount apparently came from secret commissions paid in the context of the sale of combat helicopters to an African country. Richard Gratien himself has refused to comment. The man whom our Anglo-Saxon colleagues call "Mister Africa" has always shown absolute discretion when it comes to his links with African leaders and our own government. But will M. Gratien be able to continue to be so unforthcoming? We should recall that his right-hand man, the lawyer Florian Vidal, died recently in Colombes in the most atrocious circumstances, tortured and killed with a burning tyre. This murder is reminiscent of the one suffered five years ago by a French police officer of African origin, Lieutenant Kidjo. Could there be a connection between the two cases . . . ?*

"There's someone who's asking the right questions at least," Lola said, badly shaken by the news.

"And you said the worst was behind us?" Ingrid couldn't help remarking.

*

Mars visited Sacha that evening. The radio was constantly spitting out bad news: the main one was that the former presidential candidate Candichard was in the headlines once again.

"I met André Gustave, Fabert's superior. It's panic stations: no-one knows who leaked those damn notebooks to the press. But it's a splinter bomb. I've got bad news . . ."

"They found Antonia? And she's . . . ?"

"No, it's Candichard."

"What's happened?"

"He's blown his brains out, Sacha. The commissaire in his neighbourhood has just informed me."

"What are you going to do?"

"I'm going to Avenue Bosquet. You're coming with me."

"Perhaps that's not such a good idea, boss."

"To hell with it. I can think better when you're around. Carle is efficient, but she's a pain. She doesn't inspire me."

Hauled in to act as their driver, Ménard greeted his boss warmly. Sacha was taken aback at this show of sympathy. The young lieutenant stuck the siren on the Renault's streaming wet roof and enjoyed himself getting to the Invalides as fast as he could.

In the huge apartment full of bibelots and wall hangings – it was a residence lent to the former minister by well-wishing friends – Mathilde Candichard looked like a ghost come back to haunt the ancestral home. The family doctor had given her a sedative, which had allowed the widow to recover her spirits somewhat. Mars launched into a string of condolences.

"He liked you a lot, Arnaud. Do you remember the garden party at the Élysée? You two got on well."

"I remember, Mathilde. Can you tell me what happened?"

"When I came in, I found his dead body. In his study."

"Did he leave a note?"

"Yes. He asked me to forgive him."

She choked back another sob. Mars asked if there had been any warning signs.

"Louis took it very badly when his name was sullied in all the media this morning. He felt he had already paid a high enough price. He had lost everything. All he had left was his honour. Those notebooks robbed him even of that. It's disgusting. And pointless."

They went into the study. The forensic pathologist stood aside. Part of the top of the skull had been blown off. Blood and brain matter had spurted as far as the ceiling, and stained the imposing crystal chandelier.

To Franklin, there was no doubt it had been a suicide: Candichard had propped his hunting rifle between his knees and fired a bullet into his mouth; the time of death coincided with what his wife had stated.

"Why kill yourself if you've nothing left to lose?" Mars said.

"Except for his honour. That's the problem. Some people cannot bear losing face," Sacha said.

"So they do that literally, yeah, I can see that," Ménard said.

"Whoever released the notebooks to the media was probably expecting Candichard's reaction."

"Trust me, Sacha, we'll find out."

"You hadn't told me you knew the former minister."

"I know a lot of people. Far too many. Sometimes that prevents me thinking things over objectively enough. Thanks for agreeing to come . . ."

Sacha was back in Rue du Petit Musc in the Marais shortly before midnight. He had cleaned the paint stain off the floor, installed his books on the unpainted shelves, and bought some sticks of furniture. Even so, the apartment still felt as if it belonged to someone else. He undressed, and stood out on the balcony naked. Raising his head to the sky, he allowed the driving rain to stream down his face until his body began to shiver. His tension gradually dissolved. Then he gave himself a scalding shower. He lay on his bed and put Gerry Mulligan on: his West Coast jazz always soothed him. But this time, the charm didn't work.

Mars.

His mind was racing with the words Lola had spoken at their table in the momentary calm of that small, timeless square that evoked Italy. *He's encouraging me just in case I could play a role in a baroque strategy where every means is valid . . . Negative passions always lead to solitude.*

Her eyes adjusted to the darkness. She slid over to the bedroom, listening for the sleeping man's regular breathing. She pulled the knife from the strap round her ankle, tested the tough blade against the vinyl glove.

She switched on the bedside light, gently pulled back the sheets, sat astride the sleeping body. A muscular, interesting body. A shame. She pressed the knife against his throat.

He woke up with a start. Shrieked.

"You thought you could escape me? A big mistake."

One false movement, and the blade would pierce his flesh. She loved the feeling of power that came from the perfection of these final moments. She had always loved it. How strange are our souls . . .

Terrified, he begged her, moaned her name. His body gave off the unmistakable smell of fear.

She slit his throat from left to right.

Blood. A geyser of anger.

The anger that had never died in her heart.

30

It was 03.45. Carle decided to wake up Mars.

"Chief, the chauffeur has just turned up. He's going into the building."

"Are you set?"

"Everyone's in position."

"No sign of Antonia?"

"No."

"Well done, Carle. Keep me informed."

With that he hung up. Carle ordered her men to be ready. They had to catch Honoré *in flagrante*: at the moment he tried to break in to the apartment. The lift shook as it made its way up to the fifth floor, where Gratien's chauffeur got out. He kneeled down to pick the lock with a screwdriver.

"Don't move!" shouted Carle, switching on the light.

Honoré turned on his heel and raced towards the stairs. Carle and her colleagues threw themselves at him. The African had the strength of three men. Carle took a blow to the face that knocked her to the ground. Her mobile started vibrating in her jeans pocket.

It was an out-of-breath Ménard.

"I'm chasing after a cyclist . . . she came out of the building."

At three in the morning, in this dead neighbourhood.

"Intercept her."

"I'm running to the car . . ."

"Do whatever you need to, O.K., Ménard?"

She went back to the struggling mass of bodies, service revolver in hand. She snapped it against Honoré's head; promised to shoot unless he was quiet. He stopped wrestling and punching. Vautron had a broken nose, Marcadet could barely stand. Stefani, the only one still intact, cuffed the chauffeur and pushed him down the stairs. Honoré no longer offered any resistance.

Carle raced up the street. The patrol car was blocking the road, its doors wide open. Ménard had his gun trained on a young woman kneeling beside a crashed bicycle. Her hands were folded behind her head. Docilely.

Ménard did something strange: he grabbed the woman's hair.

A wig. And the face of a ghost. Features still twisted with rage. Antonia Gratien on her way back from a country full of bad memories.

Carle ran back along the street, ordering Marcadet to follow her. They leapt up the stairs. The door to the apartment wasn't locked. They checked all the rooms, guns in hand. Noticed a strong smell of burnt plastic.

When they found him, his throat was nothing more than a gaping wound. The blood had spurted like a fountain, and converted the bedroom into a butcher's stall. Marcadet swore. Carle fought to stop herself being sick. And couldn't help thinking that her career was over.

Sacha studied her from behind the two-way mirror. The harsh light on her calm face. The rest of the room in darkness. Who would have thought she had just slit a man's throat? Ménard had been grilling her for an hour. All she did was smile.

"She's yours," Mars said.

There was an edge to his voice that Sacha did not recognise.

"That's illegal. I'm officially off the case."

"We'll ignore that. I'll get Ménard to sign the statement. The two of you can question her."

"It'll be used against us when it comes to trial, chief. Send Carle instead."

"Carle's done enough damage for one night. You're the one I want in there."

Sacha peered at Antonia Gratien again, noting her arrogant attitude towards the young lieutenant, who more than ever looked like a grown-up kid. The dressing on her right wrist: the one she must have slashed to stain his bed with blood.

"You can't let us down, Sacha. Not now. The prosecutor Maxence is stuck. Despite his good friend Sertys' protests, he's going to have to let us charge Antonia Gratien. We've got the upper hand."

"Chief . . ."

"It's an order."

The two men stared at each other.

Sacha went into the interview room. Antonia's face lit up. Ménard instinctively withdrew, and went to sit on a chair in the corner. Sacha sat across the table from her.

"I was beginning to think you'd never come."

"Why him?"

"What are you talking about?"

"Don't play the fool. It doesn't suit you."

"Thank you."

"I'm talking about the murder of Olivier Fabert, whose throat was cut with a knife found beside his bed. Why Fabert?"

"I don't know."

"Was it you who killed him?"

"You're so good-looking, Sacha, that I always end up forgetting you're a cop."

"We found a burnt overall in the bathroom. You put it on to avoid being splashed by any blood."

"It's impossible to find any D.N.A. traces on a pair of burnt overalls, isn't it, Sacha?"

"Did you burn it to get rid of any D.N.A. traces?"

"You won't find any D.N.A. traces on those overalls. Not mine or anyone else's."

"What were you doing in the building?"

"I knew your colleagues had it under surveillance. I was hoping to see you – you know I suffer from insomnia. And I enjoy your company. I seek you out. Don't pretend you don't know that."

"Was it Gratien who asked you to kill him?"

"Now you mention him, where is my husband?"

"He's using you. Can't you see that he deliberately sent you to the slaughter? There was no way you could escape."

"Has he been told? He'll get me out of here."

"Not this time, Antonia. The prosecutor is going to charge you."

"The old man always finds a way."

"You played a dirty trick on us. You'd been hiding in his apartment for a good while. You waited for night, so that you could attack him in his sleep. I've an idea as to how you got the keys."

"I love hearing you think out loud."

"Fabert came to your residence. Nothing easier than making a copy of the keys he left in his coat. You knew his place was under surveillance – you've just told me so. You needed to be able to escape, so you brought in Honoré to distract our attention. A very risky plan. But Gratien had ordered you to kill Fabert, and you never disobey him. Ever. Isn't that right?"

"The old man can be tough, but not that tough, don't you think?"

"You surpassed yourself. You took incredible risks so as not to disappoint him."

"My husband doesn't want anything bad to happen to me, I mean everything to him."

"Possibly."

"Definitely."

"You're the one who's going crazy then. You think you're invincible. You think you've tamed Death. She came very close to you. Now you think you've got your own back."

"I don't think anything. There are mysteries I don't understand, Sacha."

"You've been doing his dirty work for a long time, is that it? And you've always got away with it. But not this time. Your only hope is to tell us everything."

"But I'm talking to you, Sacha. That's what I'm doing. I love to hear your voice."

"Either that, or Gratien has lost it. Vidal's death has deranged him. He's no longer capable of judging the risks he makes you run."

"How exhausting it must be for you to try to get inside other people's minds, eh, Sacha?"

"You're done for, Antonia. Because of him. What do you gain by protecting him? You don't owe him anything."

Their duel went on for some time. Sacha tried to pierce her defences, Antonia juggled with words, and succeeded yet again in not openly lying. Gratien had shaped her like clay. And like clay, she slipped through Sacha's fingers.

"Do you really think he saved your life?"

"Of course."

"He used your suffering as a weapon. How did you kill Bangolé? Were there two of you?"

"Two of us?"

"With Honoré? Who smashed his face in with a hammer? Was that you, Antonia?"

"I didn't kill Bangolé."

"It was Honoré then."

"Honoré didn't kill Bangolé."

Her first two affirmations. Clear and concise. After two hours of evasions. Sacha was inclined to believe her.

Antonia had demanded to see a doctor. She had the legal right to do so. One had been sent for. Ménard stayed in the room with them.

Richard Gratien was pacing up and down the corridor, like any ordinary member of the public. He was accompanied by Maître Joseph Robillard, a famous criminal lawyer. Mars intended to keep them waiting before he saw them. Antonia was under arrest. Legally she only had the right to see a lawyer when she was officially charged.

"She's ripe, Sacha. The doc's a diversionary tactic. She's exhausted, but clinging on with all her heart. Keep going and you'll get her."

Sacha liked nothing better than the day-to-day work of tracking down criminals. His colleagues, with Mars foremost among them, told him how good he was at obtaining confessions. He knew they were right, but it gave him no pleasure to strip souls bare.

He got a lousy coffee from the machine, and thought about Antonia's weak point. It was only just beneath the surface, but how could he expose it?

He was heading back to the interview room when he noticed the smell of tobacco smoke coming from the women's toilet. He heard a muffled sob. He knocked on the door, pushed the cubicle open. Carle was slumped against the tiles, her eyes haggard and red, a lighted cigarette between her fingers. His hand brushed her shoulder. She jumped as though an electric current had gone through her.

"Don't touch me! You're to blame for this shambles!"

"What are you talking about? We're in the same boat!"

"My career is fucked. That's what you and Mars wanted, wasn't it?"

"This is no time to have a paranoid crisis, Carle. Who knows, in your place I could have been taken in as well. Who would have dreamt that Antonia would have made such a kamikaze plan with her chauffeur?

She crushed the cigarette out spitefully against the tiles. He held out his hand.

"I don't need your sympathy. I'll manage."

"As you wish."

He left her to it, took a deep breath, straightened his tie, and went back into the interview room. Antonia Gratien was stretching on her chair, hands in her bronze hair, perverse smile on her lips. Ménard was explaining to her that he saw himself as a cast-iron witness. A witness Judge Maxence would find irresistible. He had seen her leaving the building just minutes after Olivier Fabert had been murdered. They would find the copy she had made of the keys. They would search dustbins, sewers, gutters, everywhere. The same went for the clothes she must have put on to avoid getting any bloodstains on her. They must be somewhere. And how was she going to explain the mark on her ankle? Could it have been a strip of Velcro used to hold the knife?

Sacha took his seat opposite her again. Ménard moved back to a corner.

"I missed you," Antonia said with a smile. "This wasn't how I imagined our first night together . . ."

31

At around five in the morning there was a call on his mobile. Luce Chéreau. She had "struck gold". He had to come and see her at the Finance Squad.

He asked Ménard to take over and left, despite Antonia's protestations. Even though she was worn out, she was having the time of her life leading two cops a merry dance for the price of one.

"You're going to love me," Luce said, handing him a document signed by a public notary. "I used a totally illegal method to get it. Just for you."

Sacha read the document carefully. He gave his colleague a beaming smile.

"And I guarantee that Antonia Gratien knows nothing about it. I grilled the notary, used the worst kinds of pressure the Finance Squad has at its disposal. I wheedled and cajoled him so much he'll never forget me. Your intuition was a stroke of genius, Sacha. Go and show them what you can do."

"I will."

"You know, I pulled out all the stops for you when I heard what shit those Gratien people had tried to land you in."

"Thanks, Luce."

"Think nothing of it. I'll make do with an invitation to dinner followed by a session of rolling in the hay. Or two consecutive sessions. I'm not a complicated sort."

"And you like running jokes. You've already told me that."

"At least that shows you listen. That's something gained from all this."

She gave him a thumbs-up, and he copied her. As he was returning to B.C. headquarters, he thought over what Mars had said about Carle. The veteran wasn't wrong. Carle would never have been able to influence Luce Chéreau the way he had to get her to uncover key documents like this one using doubtful methods. *Carle, or the love of straight lines and complete respect for the rules.* And what did Mars say to the others about him? *Duguin, or all's fair in love and war?*

He entered the interview room and laid the document in front of Antonia.

"This was signed by a public notary two months ago. Drawn up by Maître Garnier for your husband. It's a gift. The donor is Richard Gratien, and the beneficiary is one Florian Vidal, and consequently now his heir. The gift, which cannot be legally revoked, is for seventy per cent of your husband's wealth."

Antonia's body became taut as a bow.

"Nadine Vidal had been hammering away at her husband for years to get him to leave Gratien and finally escape abroad to live his life with her. In recent months, Florian Vidal had begun to listen to her. Gratien felt the wind changing direction, and so he decided to show Vidal he really did see him as his heir."

"It's a lie . . ."

"You weren't aware of it? Well, now you know what to think of your *old man*. He saved your life, he promised to protect you as long as he lived. But it was Florian Vidal he loved. Like a son. That's to say, unconditionally. And he proved it to him. You were nothing more than a tool he could use. Do you understand the situation at last, Antonia?"

Her face had been transformed. A woman alone, a woman scorned. Her eyes were dry, but her mouth was trembling.

Sacha called his lieutenant forward. He didn't intend to leave the room, but didn't have the heart to put Antonia through the inevitable humiliation on his own.

"How did you get into Fabert's apartment?" asked Ménard.

Antonia stared from one to the other. Her eyes seemed drained of colour. She stayed silent for a long time. The two men waited.

"I made a copy of the keys," she said, her voice expressionless.

"Where is that copy?"

"Inside the cycle frame."

"When did you get in?"

"That morning, dressed as a delivery person. I waited for night. I attacked Fabert while he was sleeping."

"Did you wear an overall to prevent getting any bloodstains on you?"

"The polypropylene one."

"Was it you who burned it?"

"Yes."

"To avoid us finding your D.N.A.?"

"Yes, that's right."

"Who gave you the order to commit this murder?" asked Sacha.

"Gratien."

"For what reason?"

"He thought Fabert had killed Vidal."

"How did he know that?"

"Thanks to well-informed friends."

Sacha felt an electric shock go through him. Mars' tactic had worked. All too well. *"Why did you single out Fabert? Because that provides you with a target where we can expect his riposte?" "Exactly."*

"Why would Fabert have killed Vidal?"

"To recover Gratien's notebooks."

"Did Vidal have access to them?"

"No. Gratien thought Fabert had killed Vidal for nothing."

"And yet there is a copy of those notebooks going around."

"Obviously; extracts have been in the press."

"Who leaked them?"

"I've no idea."

Sacha glanced at Ménard, who had of course imagined that it was Gratien or Fabert who was responsible for exposing Candichard to the media. A misdiagnosis.

"Did someone steal the notebooks from your husband the first time, five years ago?"

"Yes."

"Where did that happen?"

"In our Kinshasa house."

"Who was it?"

"Norbert Konata."

"Who killed Konata?"

"A group of militiamen hired by my husband."

"Did your husband recover the notebooks?"

"No, Konata had handed them on to a policeman."

"Who?"

"Lieutenant Toussaint Kidjo."

"Was it you who killed him?"

"I lured him into a trap. Honoré tortured him, until Kidjo told him where the books were hidden. I lit the tyre round his neck."

With empty eyes and talking in a dull monotone, Antonia seemed to be telling a story that had nothing to do with her. Sacha no longer understood who he was dealing with, although he had thought he knew. He motioned to Ménard to take over:

"Why was he tortured with the burning necklace?"

"That was Gratien's idea."

"For what reason?"

"To lead people to think it was an act of political revenge between Africans. No-one would ever have suspected Gratien of doing anything like that."

"Where did you find the notebooks?"

"In the left-luggage office at Gare du Nord."

"What did you do with them?"

"I gave them back to my husband."

"Was it you who killed Vidal?"

"I don't know who killed Vidal."

"Bangolé, was it you?"

"No."

"Honoré?"

"Honoré and I have nothing to do with his death."

"But Gratien asked you to lay a trap for Commandant Duguin, didn't he?"

Antonia turned towards Sacha.

"I didn't want to," she said, her eyes fixed on his face. "Richard ordered me to, and I had to give in."

"Why?" asked Sacha.

"Because I owe my life to him. At least, that's how I saw things."

"What did Gratien hope to achieve by tarnishing my boss' reputation?" said Ménard.

"Gratien doesn't like people poking their noses into his business. And he felt that Sacha didn't show him enough respect."

"In my opinion, it was more because he was frightened the commandant would discover he was behind the murders of Vidal and Bangolé. Isn't that the truth?"

"Gratien has nothing to do with any of that."

"Give us a name."

"I never had one, little man, and it's not my problem anymore . . ."

32

Towards seven in the morning, Maître Robillard protested and demanded to see his client. Mars received him and listened with Olympian calm, but Sacha knew that at that very moment he was rejoicing inside and wouldn't have changed places with anybody. When Robillard repeated his demand, Mars told him that his client would be charged with murder as soon as Judge Maxence arrived, and that anyway she was enjoying the privilege of being held in the VIP single cell, with its own toilet and shower, "a treatment befitting her position". He also announced that he intended to place Richard Gratien under arrest.

Ménard accompanied Robillard to the lock-up. Antonia Gratien did not wish to make any statement. The lawyer insisted and demanded that Ménard let him talk to his client in private. When he refused, all the lawyer could do was to inform her of her rights, and warn her to be careful about anything she said from then on.

Mars' secretary passed him a call from Judge Sertys. The divisionnaire put him on speaker.

"Maître Robillard has just called me. You want to arrest Gratien! On the basis of his wife's testimony. Antonia Gratien is obviously deranged. You're sending six years' of my work down the drain, Mars!"

"Bah, you're exaggerating, Sertys."

"I want to be able to negotiate with Gratien over the EuroSecurities affair. I *have to have* those notebooks. We're not going to get our hands on them if we treat him so brutally. Gratien will close up like a clam."

"Candichard is dead. Time to move on, Sertys."

"But there are all the others. Candichard wasn't the only one to line his pockets."

"Play Mr Clean with whoever you like, my dear friend. I've got a cop killer to put inside at last. Each to his own."

"Mars, I solemnly swear that I'll make your life hell."

"All this stress isn't good for you at your age . . . if I were you, I'd try to avoid it."

He hung up with a smile that was close to a snarl, then looked at them both in turn.

"Where's Carle?"

"At home, trying to get over an acute migraine," said Ménard.

"Tell her to come here *illico presto*. Three of you won't be too many to corner Gratien."

"You're not staying?" asked Sacha in astonishment.

"I haven't slept for two nights, lads. It's up to you now. Ménard, you're the most ambitious of all the little bastards I've known, but be careful. As for you, Sacha, your holiday's over. Get back to work. And Carle has to stop breaking our balls with her existential crises. The Duguin team is rising from the ashes."

After months dreaming of nailing Gratien, Mars was bailing out. Sacha insisted, but the divisionnaire wouldn't change his mind.

"While you wait, you need to call Lola Jost. Five years of uncertainty and anguish is a long time. Will you do that?"

As soon as Mars had left, Sacha called the ex-commissaire. He told her about Antonia Gratien's testimony. Explained that she had killed Toussaint with Honoré's help, on Gratien's orders.

"Thanks for telling me, Sacha."

"It's the least I could do."

"Forgive me, but I'm going to hang up now . . . I have to . . . to take all this in . . ."

"Of course. See you soon, Lola. Without you it would have taken us much longer."

He called Carle, and put her on speaker. She was to come back to headquarters. They were counting on her to question Gratien. Any past slip-ups were forgotten. Mars had wiped the slate clean.

"Besides, I think you'll be ideal as the one who breaks Mister Africa."

"What makes you think that?"

"*Move quickly where the enemy least expects. Go round his defences. Attack him where he is least expecting it.* That's exactly you, Carle."

"You know you're beginning to get on my nerves with your *Art of War*, boss?"

"Come back, Carle. Ménard and I are languishing here without you."

She gave a big sigh, and hung up. Sacha smiled at Ménard, who gave the victory sign. They headed for the interview room, where Gratien was kicking his heels in the company of Stefani.

"I feel like a G.I. about to step into a minefield," declared the lieutenant.

"Maybe that's why you chose this stupid job."

"I chose this stupid job because I didn't want to get bored."

"Well, you got what you were after!"

At about eleven, Sacha left Gratien and Honoré to Ménard, Carle, and two uniforms, and went out to stretch his legs. Gratien had considered himself above the law. Tormented by seeing his wife in jail, Mister Africa was starting to crumble. It had begun with the death of Vidal, whom he loved like a son. Now it was simply a matter of time.

Some seagulls were squabbling above a barge as it glided slowly down towards Pont Neuf. The rain had signed an armistice. Sacha stretched, considering how he could catch Gratien out.

He heard shouts, people running, and turned back. Two uniformed guards were in the corridor, panic-stricken. The head of the lock-up, Major Attal, was with them.

"It's Antonia Gratien. She's been shot."

Sacha's heart felt as if it was gripped in a vice. He got his breath back, tried to look calm, and followed the three men. In the lock-up the guard seemed to have been scorched by the devil. It was the same man who had opened the door to the shared cell where Ingrid had been kept. Now he unlocked the grille of the individual cell Mars had reserved for Antonia.

She was flat on her back on the bed, arms spreadeagled. A star of blood on her forehead.

Attal held her face in the bright glare of a torch. There was a visible mark. Whoever had done it had pressed the gun barrel hard against her brow before firing. To create fear. A gesture of hatred. So that he would get the taste of death, eye to eye, before he brought it to her.

"What happened?"

"I didn't see a thing. I got my head bashed in. By the time I came round, she was dead. Fuck it, I don't understand. I've been in this business for twenty years, Commandant . . ."

"Show me the video surveillance footage."

"No point," said Major Attal. "It's been disconnected."

By someone who knew the computer system and its passwords. By someone who could get this far without being noticed. And who had the keys.

"But there must be a witness, dammit!"

The poor guards simply shook their heads helplessly. The major confirmed that *a priori* nobody had "a suspicious presence to report".

Sacha rushed back into the interview room. He grabbed Gratien by the collar.

"You complete bastard, was it you who had her killed?"

"Let go of me, Duguin! Have you lost your mind?"

Sacha dreamt of pushing his gun into this monster's throat, to make him suffer as she had suffered. Ménard and Carle managed to separate them.

"Antonia has been shot. A bullet to the head. Nobody saw a thing."

Gratien's chair went spinning. He leapt to his feet. Honoré gave a strangled cry, and banged his head against the wall. Twice. Carle ordered the uniforms to control him. The deaf-mute started to struggle. Ménard called for reinforcements.

"Is this your way of trying to get me to crack, you scum?" howled Gratien. "That's sickening!"

"Who do you take me for, Gratien?"

The two men squared up to each other. Sacha didn't blink. Gratien read in his eyes that he wasn't bluffing. He fell to his knees and burst out sobbing.

Commandant Duguin had come up against many sons of bitches in his life, artists in lying who could mimic hurt to perfection. But unless the lawyer was a total psychopath, his pain was utterly authentic.

"You have reached Karen and Arnaud Mars. Please leave your message, and we *will* get back to you." Sacha's brain was disintegrating; even Karen's gentle voice grated on his nerves. He hung up, dialled the mobile number. It rang six times, until finally the divisionnaire answered. A sleepy voice. Sacha told him straight out what had happened. Mars swore, then fell silent. Sacha could hear his laboured breathing.

"Chief?"

"I took sleeping pills. I need to come round properly. But I'll be there. I'll be there right away. Count on me."

He hung up.

Sacha turned to his colleagues. Like Mars, he had to get a grip.

Carle was shaking the doctor they had called to attend Gratien. His hysterics had paralysed the young medic. Ménard and two uniforms were trying to control him.

"You're all responsible, you miserable pigs! I'll get the lot of you! I'll take everything you hold most dear from you!"

Honoré's eyes were rolling madly. His huge body was shaking as if he had a fever. A uniformed officer led him away *manu militari*. He gave Sacha a look of pure hatred, but allowed himself to be dragged out of the room.

Clémenti's bottle of gin. He kept it in a drawer. Sacha went into his colleague's office. The drawer was locked, but Sacha forced it open with the edge of an iron ruler, unscrewed the bottle top, took a mouthful.

There was a movement behind him. Instinctively, he dropped to the floor. Saw a meteorite flash over his head. A computer that smashed against the wall. Sacha was crushed against the floor, then flipped over like a pancake, and saw a contorted face an inch from his own. Honoré was grappling with his holster. Sacha had an image of him blowing his brains out. But the African threw the Smith & Wesson away, and instead began to strangle him.

He wants to kill me with his bare hands, so that he can feel his vengeance.

He could sense his eyes bulging from their sockets. He groped blindly in the air. The gin bottle. He smashed it on the madman's ear. Blood. The vice-like grip eased a little. He gulped down air. It was as if he were swallowing acid. Honoré was on all fours, groggy from the blow.

Sacha looked round for his gun. Nowhere to be seen. He rushed out into the corridor, which was empty but for two press photographers who were snapping away for all they were worth. The only sounds were their flashbulbs and Gratien's shouts.

He was thrown to the floor. He rolled over, got to his feet. He thought of Rachid and their frenetic sparring bouts. The strength he was able to find within himself. Without it, he was sure to die. Honoré charged at him. Sacha launched an uppercut, kneed him in the groin. He took a blow directly in the stomach which cut him in two. He retched up bile.

"Don't move, Honoré, or I'll blast your head off."

Ménard's gun a few inches from his face. The giant turned, weighed up the lieutenant's determination, and fell to his knees, head down. Then he started to weep like a huge, hundred-kilo baby.

The photographers were still snapping away.

"Who are those assholes?" Ménard wanted to know.

"Some guys who understand the times we live in only too well," Sacha said, his voice mangled.

"You're wrong there. Failure to assist someone in danger is a criminal offence, for fuck's sake."

"Thank you, by the way."

"It was nothing."

The photographers raced off. Sacha went to pick up his revolver, then telephoned to have the fleeing paparazzi intercepted and their rolls of film confiscated. He returned to Ménard. The officer who had been escorting Honoré had come round, his mouth bleeding, and was helping the lieutenant to cuff the African. Sacha felt his own neck. Death had left him a passionate love bite. And had possibly stolen his voice while she was about it.

Mars appeared at the end of the corridor. Unkempt, his hair a mess, whey-faced, staggering as he walked.

"Don't tell me that those two idiots I just ran into are photographers! I bet that's a ruse by Gratien's lawyer."

"Ruse or not, all this is worthy of 'Pulp Fiction', chief," said Ménard. "It's weird. We've lost the remote control to be able to zap chaos."

"What exactly did they take pictures of?"

Gratien's threats were redoubled. "I'll massacre all your families, you bastards!"

"I've had him up to here," said Ménard. "Let's agree we use a hypodermic syringe on Gratien."

The divisionnaire looked daggers at him, suppressed a fresh curse, and walked unsteadily over to the drinks machine. "There's no damned coffee in this fucking machine!"

"As I was saying, we've lost the remote control for everything," retorted Ménard. "But no-one listens to me."

33

Maxime was at the stove. Cheerful sounds of pots and pans and enticing smells wafted from the kitchen. An unexpected ray of sunshine was caressing the décor of Belles. Sigmund had discovered the warmest spot for a short siesta. The atmosphere in the restaurant was calm. Outside, the storm had swept in again with a vengeance.

"Barthélemy just called. Sacha is in deep trouble. Up to his neck."

Ingrid wanted to hear the latest. She already knew part of the story: Antonia's arrest. Her confession. The lawyer Richard Gratien questioned by the Duguin team.

Lola explained what had happened to the lawyer's wife.

With Mars absent, Sacha was at the helm when it happened. He would be held responsible.

"I've tried ringing Mars to find out more. I haven't been able to reach him for two days now."

"That's normal, Lola. He must have his superiors and the media on his back."

"Possibly, but his colleagues are also trying to get in touch with him. They've had no luck either."

"I think we should try to help Sacha," Ingrid said.

"I agree, but how?"

"You're always saying we ought to read and reread the files. Because it often happens that we've missed a chunk."

"A *detail*, you mean?"

"Yes, if you prefer."

They finished their coffees, woke up Sigmund, and made for Rue de l'Échiquier. The ex-commissaire fished out her old files, as well as the book where she had jotted down the results of their joint investigation. She plonked it all on the dining-room table.

"Here are several kilos of details, Ingrid. I propose we both read everything. We're quite different, so two heads looking at it could be fructiferous."

"*Fructiferous*. What kind of a word is that?"

"It evokes harvesting fruit."

"O.K., in that case let's play at being harvesters!"

"Combine harvesters, if you'll allow me. And if you want to."

"Doesn't *combine* in French mean a trick?"

"Yes, but not in this case."

"French is far too complicated."

"No, it's not."

"Yes it is."

"No."

"Yes."

Big sighs, and the two friends plunged into their careful reading.

After several hours of concentrated effort, the ex-commissaire had to admit she couldn't see anything emerging. The combine harvesters had gleaned poor results.

"I'm hungry," she said. "Let's go back to Belles for some sustenance. Truth doesn't sit well an empty stomach. Especially not mine."

They reinstalled themselves at their regular table, and Sigmund in his ray of sunshine. Lola devoured a pork steak with mushrooms, Ingrid nibbled on a ham sandwich.

After coffee and a liqueur, Lola received a call from Jean Texier. As usual, he wanted news. She told him about the latest disasters to have hit the B.C.

"That murder in the police headquarters isn't clear."

"That's an understatement, Jean."

"You need the means to carry out something like that. Connections."

"Duguin thought at first that Gratien had ordered his wife killed because she had spilled the beans, but that proved wrong. That bastard may have cellars full of corpses, but he's no Bluebeard. He used her to do his bidding, but he was also attached to her. As for his factotum, he almost annihilated Sacha when he thought it was he who was responsible for Antonia's death."

She could understand what Texier was going through. You spend years searching for the truth, and the day it bursts upon you, you're scared of how quickly it does so, you want a little more time. So that you don't lose your mind in all the torrents of mud . . .

"I would have liked her to stand trial. I would have liked . . . to understand."

"Me too, Jean. But Antonia Gratien took her secrets with her."

"She was beautiful. I saw her photo in the papers. I suppose she didn't find it very hard to lure Toussaint into her trap . . . don't you think?"

"Toussaint was careful. But it's true, Antonia was a beauty. She looked a bit like Isis Renta. Toussaint had been in love with Isis. Maybe that's why he lowered his guard."

"No, you're wrong there."

"What d'you mean?"

"Toussaint was never in love with Isis."

"I thought there was rivalry between him and Konata over Isis?"

"No, he would never have risked his friendship with Norbert over a girl. I'm sure of that."

"Alright, if you say so."

She responded as best she could to Texier's questions. She was as bitterly disappointed as he was. Of course, there was still Gratien's trial. But according to Sacha, he was nothing more now than a wreck, crushed by the loss of the only two people he loved. Had Toussaint's life ever meant more to him than that of a mosquito? She had her doubts.

Lola promised to call him and ordered another liqueur, despite her friend's disapproving look. She couldn't get the conversation with Texier out of her head. Ingrid would have said that a *chunk* of it was floating just below the surface of her consciousness. Shapeless, colourless, and tasteless. But present all the same, a disturbing ectoplasm, a mystifying medusa.

She sat bolt upright in her chair, and seized Ingrid's forearm.

"What the fuck, Lola! You frightened me. Aren't you feeling well?"

"Never better. Give me a moment to get my things."

Lola rummaged in her coat pockets and pulled out her precious notepad. She pointed excitedly at a certain passage.

"Adeline's statement," said her American friend, recognising it.

Lola stood up, and began to reconstruct her talk with the young wine merchant.

One day I surprised Toussaint on the phone to a woman I didn't know. I was listening behind his back, so he couldn't see me. He was begging her to meet him, for old times' sake. I made a scene. Toussaint told me it was all above board, he simply wanted to see her to talk about his friend. Norbert and he had both been in love with her as boys. She had preferred Norbert.

"That girl lied to us, Ingrid. Jean Texier's just shown me she did."

"Alright," said Ingrid, also rising to her feet. "The grape harvesters are off to the Vignes d'Oberkampf."

The wine cellar was attracting far too many customers for Lola's liking. Leaflets announced a wine tasting "to discover the slopes of the Lubéron". The joys of that Provence *terroir* had attracted a noisy crowd. She could hardly hear herself think. The owner came over, bottle in hand and salesman's smile on his lips. He asked if "they would be so kind as to show him their invitations to tonight's event".

"We don't have any," Lola said.

"Oh, dear lady, it's going to be difficult without invitations and with a dog . . ."

"What I'm interested in is having a few words with your employee."

"Adeline?"

"That's the one."

"If you have news of her, I'll buy," he replied, suddenly irritated. "She left me stranded like an idiot. Impossible to find her. And no chance of getting hold of a competent replacement at such short notice."

"Have you tried her home number?"

"Of course. And not once but twenty times."

"And what does her husband say?"

"What husband? Adeline has been divorced for three years."

Lola seized the bottle out of the wine merchant's hands and took a long swig before handing it back.

"Things are going from bad to worse. But I don't mean your wine. That's not bad at all. Good luck."

The wine merchant stood there bewildered. Lola patted him on the shoulder, took a leaflet on which was a photograph of Adeline wearing a big black apron, and left the cellar.

"My encephalogram is showing no vital signs," Lola moaned. "I should have taken the bottle." She pointed to the photo of Adeline. "Unbelievable. She looks as if butter wouldn't melt . . . I'm growing old. I'm a hundred and fifty years old."

"How about going to see the ex-husband?"

Simple ideas are the best. Lola had attended her wedding. The dinner had taken place in the restaurant on Boulevard Voltaire where Hubert Malick the wine waiter worked. The Bacchantes de Bacchus – an unforgettable name. The Twingo was soon parked not far from the restaurant.

The owner had a formidable waxed moustache and an equally unlikely first name: Hyppolite. The busy period was over, there were only a few stragglers left. Lola accepted the balloon glass the owner offered her and asked where she could find Hubert Malick.

"In Tokyo," Hyppolite replied.

"Oh no," moaned Lola, clinging on to the counter.

"Yes I know, I miss Hubert too. Adeline's departure was a tough blow for him. He met a Japanese girl, and decided to start a new life over there. As good a choice as any. Besides, it appears they've started to really appreciate wine there."

"Have you kept in contact?"

"I've got his phone number. But wait a bit before you get him out of bed. There's eight hours' time difference."

"That's the problem," muttered Lola as she polished off her drink.

34

He got the keys from the concierge, rapped on the door just in case. No reply. The apartment looked tidy: nothing to suggest any struggle or hasty departure. In the little girl's bedroom, the schoolbooks were lined up on her desk, her satchel was hanging from the chair. But there wasn't a single item of clothing on the wardrobe hangers.

The study was in darkness. He pulled the blind up, and the rays of the sun picked out the contents of the room. Family photos in their place, bottle of scotch and two cut-glass tumblers on the copper tray purchased in Morocco. The 1930s dancer striking her pose on the light-coloured Swedish wood.

He could still see Mars stroking her translucent body as he conversed with him.

So we have to be beyond reproach . . .

You're the one who got the job . . . I'll never regret my choice . . .

He started to go through Mars' personal papers, all carefully filed in individual folders. He couldn't find any trace of public notaries' documents, family book, or identity cards. The gas and electricity bills were all there; so too were the school lunch vouchers, the telephone and other bills. He looked in the "miscellaneous" file.

He found the receipt for the glass dancer. *I bought it for a disgusting amount of money, especially for a cop.* That was the least one could say.

The price was absurdly high. It had been sold by auction at Drouot's on February 22 two years earlier.

Sacha bit his lip when he saw the name of the auctioneer on the receipt. He slipped it into his inside jacket pocket, and returned to the living room.

A man was sitting on the sofa, gun trained on him. About thirty, military haircut, leather jacket, jeans. Totally relaxed.

"Who are you?"

"Duguin, B.C."

"Oh yes, the divisionnaire's deputy. Sorry, but you can never be too careful," he said, replacing his gun in its holster.

"And you are?"

"Darnaudet, D.C.R.I."

"Was it you lot who sidelined Mars?"

"You're joking."

"Not really."

"Did you find anything interesting among your chief's papers?"

"No, because you got there before me."

"What makes you think that?"

"The fact that you didn't stop me in his study. You must know exactly what's in his files."

"I think my boss would like to meet you, Duguin."

With that, Darnaudet sauntered out of the apartment.

Sacha waited a few minutes, then left as well. Heading for headquarters on Quai des Orfèvres.

He handed him the receipt he had found at Mars' apartment.

Clémenti read the name of the auctioneer in charge of the sale. Doris Nungesser.

"There wasn't a copy of this at her place, I'm sure of that."

"Which makes me think somebody told Nungesser to get rid of it."

"Who? Arnaud?"

"Who else?"

Clémenti found it hard to accept the evidence. Among the B.C. officers, he and Sacha were the ones most affected by the way the divisionnaire and his family had disappeared.

"The D.C.R.I. had been there before me. Do you know someone called Darnaudet?"

Sacha described him. Clémenti confirmed he was a colleague of Fabert's. He worked for André Gustave, someone Mars knew well. They had assumed that the divisionnaire had made his exit with the blessing or even at the suggestion of the secret service. Darnaudet's reaction had scuppered that theory.

"I don't think they've made the connection between the Vidal and Nungesser cases," said Sacha. "Darnaudet didn't know I'd dug up that receipt. The statuette is still on his desk, but nobody will link the two."

"Why would Arnaud have left such a valuable object behind?"

"To avoid problems at the Customs."

For the past two days, a general alert had been put out to locate Mars. The border police, Interpol, the airport authorities had all been told to keep a lookout. Arnaud, Karen and Aurélie Mars were nowhere to be found.

Clémenti laid the receipt on his desk. He stared at it.

"Arnaud is very meticulous."

"That's true. He took all his important documents with him. But not this receipt, which shows that he knew Nungesser, whereas he had always claimed the opposite."

"He left it so that someone would find it."

"A message?"

"That's the least he could do."

"It's not enough for me."

"I know. But Arnaud must have had his reasons."

"I certainly hope so."

35

It had taken them two whole days to find the wine waiter, who had moved and changed telephone number. On Tuesday at eight o'clock in the morning Tokyo time, Lola finally got him on the other end of the line. She introduced herself as Toussaint Kidjo's former boss.

"Yeah, I saw on the internet that the case had been reopened," said Hubert Malick.

She explained that Adeline had lied to her. And that her lie had confused matters.

"It looks as if Adeline lied to everyone! You know, I don't really want to talk about her."

"This is very important, Monsieur Malick. I'm sorry to dig into your private life, but I need to know what happened between her and you."

"Is that all?"

"Toussaint Kidjo is dead. So is a young lawyer and the wife of his employer. An informer has been bludgeoned to death. A politician has committed suicide. A police divisionnaire and his family have vanished."

"You don't say!"

"It's a disaster. Your evidence is vital. I beg you."

"I left because I couldn't stand sharing her with a ghost any longer. Adeline had never forgotten Kidjo, if you must know. She was obsessed with his death. Our relationship never had a chance."

"She's disappeared."

"I can't help you there. I've no idea where she might be. Sorry."

Lola thanked Malick, ended the call, and sat thinking for a moment. Adeline had lied about Isis Renta and about her relationship with Toussaint. She had kept quiet about her divorce. And above all, the fact that Toussaint's death had affected her so badly she had been unable to make a new life for herself. When Lola had interviewed her at the Vignes d'Oberkampf, she had learned from Adeline that Toussaint was investigating Konata's murder. *Why didn't you mention this at the time?* The young woman had seemed sincere. *I was convinced you knew about it.* Lola shuddered. Adeline had been concealing the truth for years.

And without her lies, several lives could have been spared.

She dialled Jean Texier's number.

*

Sacha left the car in a car park on Boulevard Haussmann and walked back up Rue de Courcelles to level with the Hilton. The café was on the corner with Rue de Monceau. Tiny and decorated in bright colours, it looked more like an American bar in miniature than a traditional Parisian café. The sound of jazz music. Sacha recognised the inimitable style of Marcus Miller. A follower of Miles Davis.

André Gustave raised a rolled-up newspaper in his direction. Darnaudet's and Fabert's boss was a stern-looking man in his sixties, wearing an English trench-coat and a smart grey suit with a black roll-neck. His tweed cap was lying on the table next to his mobile and a half of beer. They shook hands.

"What will you have?"

A kind invitation not backed up by anything friendly in his tone of voice.

"The same as you."

He motioned to the waiter, who served a half of draught lager.

Gustave unfolded his newspaper. The front page of *Le Monde* was devoted to the Vidal affair and the fall-out from it. There was a sketch of Mars which captured his ironic smile rather well.

"Was it you who leaked the notebooks, Duguin?"

Sacha was caught unawares by this direct approach.

"I assure you it wasn't."

"The interesting pages were scanned and sent by email to Sertys and the media from an address the D.C.R.I. has identified. It's in your offices."

"Not mine, I repeat."

"And yet your mug fits. An ambitious young officer who falls flat on his face thanks to several low blows. The last of them quite spectacular."

"Antonia Gratien was my responsibility. I won't deny that. But I have nothing to do with those notebooks, so don't try to pin that on me."

"Who then? Mars?"

Gustave had just put into words a suspicion that had been gnawing at Sacha but that he had not dared express openly.

"Why would he do that?"

"That's what I'm asking you, Duguin. Mars had it in for Fabert."

"What are you talking about?"

"Don't play the innocent. It doesn't suit you."

"And you, stop playing tricks."

"I beg your pardon?"

"Fabert came to headquarters to insult me. He wouldn't let go: he was furious that we were trespassing on his private territory: Gratien."

"You're off your head."

"I am?"

"It was Mars who contacted Fabert."

The tone of the D.C.R.I. chief's voice was unambiguous.

"Fabert came to our headquarters to get me sacked," Sacha said.

"Wrong, Duguin. Mars was the one who asked him to come, to shake you up a bit. He said he didn't like the way you were approaching the case."

"He had lunch with you to limit the damage, and calm Fabert down . . ."

"I haven't seen Mars in over six months."

In his mind's eye, Sacha saw Mars in his office during their first meeting with Fabert. The angry lieutenant-colonel. His accusations, his scornful attitude. Could Mars have orchestrated all that? *I'm sorry, Sacha. He caught me like a greenhorn . . . He claimed he wanted to meet you to put a face to a name . . .* And later, when he had asked for information about Antonia. *I had lunch with Fabert's boss to try to get him to keep his bull-dog on the leash . . .*

Mars had given the impression he was simply defending him against Fabert.

"I'd say you have a serious problem, don't you, Duguin?"

The D.C.R.I. bigwig's voice brought Sacha back to the present. Gustave had put his cap on and stuffed the mobile in his pocket.

"Gratien is a sad case since the death of Vidal. He's not even interested in writing his memoirs. We thought we could recover his notebooks without any fuss. But one of you lot preferred to stir things up. Candichard took the full force of it. But he wasn't the only one with his snout in the trough. We've only been given a very targeted sample. Others are bound to be involved. It's a huge mess. And let me tell you, the Élysée Palace is very upset."

For once, Gustave overlooked the ritual handshake and strode off. Sacha watched him cross the street and get into one of the taxis drawn up outside the Hilton.

The scene was still vivid in his mind. The décor in Tante Marguerite. The show Mars put on for Fabert. A balancing act. And those little remarks that Sacha had not picked up on then.

That's right, Fabert, get lost. We don't need you anymore.

Don't ask me to come and see you again, Mars; the answer's no. Too bad for you, I could have been useful . . .

Don't ask me to come and see you again. How had Sacha missed that? He'd been blinded by friendship and admiration. And had let himself be led by the nose.

It's madness, Sacha. No-one knows where the blow is coming from.

He had the choice: he could either bemoan his fate and draw a line under it. Or try to clean out the stables.

Gustave had paid the bill. Sacha left the café and found his car in the car park. He stayed motionless behind the wheel for a moment without switching on the engine. Mars had given him a detailed description of the way the secret services were being restructured. He knew that if he took on a case involving Richard Gratien he would have all the different departments on his back, and that people as senior as Gustave would be watching his every move. Conclusion: the game he had played was not some sudden improvisation.

Mars had set all this up. And a long while in advance.

36

Lola shivered as she clambered out of the Twingo: the cold air nibbled at her shoulder blades. She turned to look at Ingrid. It was true she was wearing a pair of garish woollen leggings, but on top of that was only a pair of denim shorts. She was taking deep breaths of the Pré-Saint-Gervais air. Her American friend and champion's metabolism never ceased to amaze Lola.

Texier was waiting for them in a quiet café on Rue Danton. Lola ordered four hot toddies; one for Sigmund despite Ingrid's disapproving look. The Dalmatian didn't seem to mind.

Texier was looking upset.

"I didn't know Adeline had divorced. And yet we were on good terms. Why didn't she tell me anything?"

He took copies of *Le Parisien* and *Libération* out of his bag. A photograph of Mars was spread across both front pages. By now the whole of France was aware of his existence and appearance.

"He's the person I wanted to talk to you about, Lola."

"Do you know him?"

"No, but I think I saw Toussaint and Adeline with him one day."

"With Mars? Are you sure?"

"It may have been someone who looked very like him. I must be wrong."

"Where was this?"

"Rue Montorgueil. Early one Sunday afternoon. Toussaint, Adeline and I were meant to be going to the cinema. We had arranged to meet by the market. I saw them coming out of a restaurant with this man, or someone very like him. Then they saw me. He kissed them good-bye, and hurried off. I didn't ask who he was."

"Do you remember the name of the restaurant?"

"I'm afraid not."

"Think hard."

"No, I'm sorry but I can't remember it."

"Any little detail could be important. What did you feel at the time?"

"Now I come to think of it . . . Toussaint seemed a bit embarrassed. But that was common with him: I've already told you he was as secret-ive as his mother. Back then I didn't attach any importance to it. I was early for our meeting, and shouldn't have seen them with their friend. I don't understand why Toussaint didn't introduce me to him."

"He should have done so out of politeness, is that it?"

"He was the same age as me . . . I read in the newspaper this morn-ing that he had worked for several years in Africa, so we had things in common. It would have been only logical for Toussaint to suggest I had lunch with them."

He shook his head, unable to make anything of it all. Lola tried to cheer him up, and promised to keep him informed if she had any news.

She and Ingrid headed back to the centre of Paris. Since the Rue Montorgueil was full of restaurants, they shared the task out between them. It was Ingrid who hit the jackpot. She called Lola and asked her to join her at Chez Malaïka, an African restaurant.

The owner, a friendly, smiling fifty-something, had recognised Mars at once.

"You've got a hell of a memory," Lola said to test him. "I've been told this man came here more than five years ago."

"Oh, you're wrong there, madame. If I can remember him so clearly, it's because he's a regular. And I've seen his photograph in the newspaper. He's disappeared with his family. A real drama. What on earth can have happened to them?"

"That's what I'm here to find out. Tell me about him."

"He was a nice man, and an expert on African cuisine. I come from Gabon, but he knew the traditional dishes from there as well as I do! Almost as well as my grandmother."

"Did he come alone?"

"No, always with the same young woman."

"For a long time?"

"For years."

"Meaning?"

"Four or five. They have, or I should say *had* their regular table."

Lola showed him the picture of a smiling Adeline Ernaux on the Vignes d'Oberkampf brochure. He confirmed she was the friend who always came with Mars.

"What did they talk about?"

"He was the one who did most of the talking. This photograph isn't telling the truth."

"In what way?"

"That young lady was melancholy. It was obvious he was trying to take her out of herself. In the end, he usually managed to get her to smile at his stories."

"What stories?"

"All kinds. The gentleman talked a lot about Africa. And knew what he was talking about. He had lived there."

"In which country especially?"

"I couldn't tell you. A few words reached my ears, but I never tried to follow what they were saying."

"But he must have told you things?"

"No, our conversations were always about recipes, spices, market smells. That gave us enough to talk about. Besides, I never asked him anything. There was a special link between those two. I didn't want to spoil it by poking my nose in where it wasn't wanted."

"I find it hard to believe you never asked him anything in all those five years. There can't be that many customers with a passion for Africa."

"Madame, I can see you don't easily change course once you've fixed your sights on a destination. I suppose that's the rule in your line of work. But in my country we say: *gèbo sa ngà, wà yirèyà!* 'Someone else's animal. Attention! They want you dead!'"

"*Beware of other people's business or you might run into problems*, is that the idea?"

"You would have made an excellent ethnologist, madame . . ."

"But who says that asking that man questions could have been dangerous, when you just said he was nice?"

". . . but you make an even better policewoman."

"I'm sure you must be able to remember at least one interesting detail."

"Human beings are like those statues with many faces. It's best to speak to their good ear, and only listen to replies from the good mouth. He was a nice man, but he gave off a heat that was more like that of a white-hot piece of metal than a kettle. My memory is careful, it only retains what suits it. As you see, there's nothing more I can tell you."

"D'you think this is a good idea?" whispered Ingrid, casting worried glances all round her.

Lola knew what she was thinking. If I'm caught breaking into somebody's flat, it will be the second time I've been arrested in a few days, and the police will be less lenient. Ingrid could already see herself on a plane bound for the United States.

"Don't worry. In my time I've got the better of far sturdier locks than this one."

A click confirmed her words. She put her Swiss Army knife back in her pocket, entered the studio with a beaming smile, and invited Ingrid and Sigmund to follow her.

Adeline Ernaux's domain was a complete mess.

"It reminds me of my son's room when he was an adolescent. Every time I ventured in there, I thought I'd arrived just after a terrorist attack."

"Do you think someone's been here searching before us?"

"Possibly not. Otherwise the mattress would have been slashed, the drawers would have vomited their contents, and those of the jars in the kitchen would be all over the floor tiles. I think this chaos reflects its owner's state of mind."

The wardrobe was three-quarters empty. A lonely sock sat limply in one corner. Lola concluded that Adeline Ernaux had taken flight in a hurry.

"And at almost the same time as Mars," Ingrid said.

"A man she already knew, but was careful not to tell us she did."

"Were you aware that Toussaint knew Mars?"

"No more than I was aware that Mars knew Toussaint. Alright, that's enough gossip. Let's go through this molehill with a toothcomb."

They started to sift conscientiously through the debris.

Sigmund wanted to join in, and stuck his snout in every nook and cranny. His detective impulse vanished once he discovered a bit of old dry sausage he immediately leapt on. Then he took a siesta on a thick fluffy rug that seemed to have been made especially for him. An hour later, he was awakened with a start.

Lola had given a cry of joy.

37

Luce Chéreau announced that on the eve of his disappearance Mars had emptied his bank accounts at the Société Générale. Current and stocks and shares accounts. His wife Karen, a customer at the same bank, had done the same. The couple had transferred the entirety of their joint savings, the sum of 450,000 euros, to the account of a broker, one Philippe Melun. When arrested and questioned, he admitted everything. Mars had paid him a fat commission for him to transfer the money discreetly to a bank based in Nassau.

"I can try to dig some more in the Bahamas if you wish. But don't get your hopes up. I reckon the dough has already bounced from bank to bank. It would take months to track it down. If we're lucky."

"Well then, do it."

He had not been able to disguise the anger in his voice. He apologised at once.

"I promise to do the best I can. Don't give up, O.K.?"

"Thanks, Luce."

Sacha rejoined Clémenti in his office. The commissaire was in a meeting with Captains N'Diop and Argenson. Sacha told them what the Finance Squad had discovered. Argenson announced that he had found a taxi driver who had picked Mars up just after Antonia had been murdered.

"I don't understand a thing anymore," Lola said.

The documents had come from Namur in Belgium. From the firm *SearchDNA*. They concerned a paternity test.

"In France this kind of test can only be done with legal authority. After his death, the investigators put Toussaint's life under the microscope, starting with me. If any such procedure had been started, they would have known it."

"That might be so in France, but in the United States the tests are available to anyone, and are confidential," Ingrid said.

She looked up the *SearchDNA* site on her iPhone. Based in Florida, the firm had a laboratory that specialised in DNA testing, and had eighteen subsidiaries throughout the world, from Europe to Africa, and including India. French clients were asked to get in touch with their Belgian associates. The method was simple: *SearchDNA* provided a DNA kit with cotton buds to take samples of saliva. From the child and the supposed father. For 220 euros, the results – accurate to 99.9 per cent for the father to be included, and 100 per cent to exclude him – were sent by post. Discretion guaranteed.

"I don't feel well."

"Why not, Lola?"

"Because we're going to have to have another discussion with Jean Texier, but a very uncomfortable one this time."

Sacha was going over everything that had happened that day as he wolfed down a frozen meal he had reheated in his microwave. All the information pointed in one direction: Mars had made complete fools of them.

With his body aching and his mind at half-mast, he decided to relax with some music. He had been listening to the same Gerry Mulligan album for years; a change would do him good. The tape sealing the box of jazz C.D.s had been undone then stuck down again. Had Arthur been rummaging through his things? *A priori*, nothing was missing. He found "Kind of Blue" and once again saw himself in Mars' apartment.

If I had to classify the all-time greats of jazz, I'd put "Kind of Blue" on top of the pile. Wouldn't you?

He opened the box. A plastic sachet lay on top of the C.D. In it was a S.I.M. card for a mobile phone.

Colombes. The swimming pool.

Could Mars have left him a message? He called for a taxi and was driven to police headquarters.

The desk officer downstairs brought him the documents for the Vidal case. He found the BlackBerry, inserted the S.I.M. card. It fitted, but the mobile screen didn't light up. The battery was flat.

Clémenti had a BlackBerry. With a bit of luck Sacha would find a charger amongst his things.

He went back upstairs and into his colleague's office. He found the charger in a drawer, plugged the phone in. The screen lit up, and an icon showed it was charging. But the BlackBerry wanted to know the password.

Who would know it apart from Vidal? His wife, of course. It was a quarter past two in the morning. In his own office, Sacha found the telephone number of the clinic where Nadine Vidal was taking her rest cure.

An unreal, airport voice answered. He said who he was, and

explained what he needed. They would not listen. Sacha argued for a few moments, then put the phone down on the receptionist. He commandeered a patrol car in the police car park and headed for Neuilly.

The clinic was a luxury building opposite the Bois de Boulogne. The wind brought the smell of damp vegetation with it.

Sacha showed his police credential to a sleepy security guard, who led him to reception. A tall blonde woman was playing a video game on her computer.

"What can I do for you?"

"I called you just now," he said, flashing his I.D.

"There are legal visiting hours, Commandant. And you're way outside them."

"Do you really want me to explain yet again that this is an emergency?"

"In order to regain their inner peace, our patients need to sleep, whatever the emergency. I'm going to have to ask you to come back."

Sacha knew the number of the room. He strode off towards the corridor despite the yelps of protest from the receptionist.

He greeted young Garcia who was on guard outside, and told him to keep the clinic employees at bay. He entered the room, switched on the bedside lamp, and woke up Nadine Vidal.

"Don't be afraid, it's me, Duguin. I need your husband's password."

Bleary from the sedatives, it took her some time to come round. Out in the corridor, Garcia was managing to ward the others off. As Nadine's mind cleared, she remembered the six-figure password for the BlackBerry. Sacha pressed Received Calls, and listened to the last few messages. The first was from Vidal's secretary. From Thursday at a quarter to seven in the evening. Alice Bernier was reminding her boss that he had a meeting the next morning with Richard Gratien and provided him with some information about it. The second message had come at seven minutes past seven.

Let's meet on Boulevard Ney as soon as possible. I'm waiting there already. I've some urgent information for you. Come alone.

That neutral tone. That voice.

Sacha felt as if his saliva had turned to acid. *Do you really think you can be untouchable all your life?* He had difficulty swallowing.

"What's wrong, Commandant? You don't look well."

Nadine Vidal's anxious face brought him back to reality.

Inner peace? Some other time perhaps.

38

He left the clinic. Installed in the car, he recalled his talk with Clémenti about the statuette.

He left it so that someone would find it – A message? – That's the least he could do.

Each time Mars passed him information, he claimed he had got it from a highly placed source. Had he invented those contacts? It didn't seem likely. He was always far too well-informed for his tip-offs not to come from real, solid connections.

Sacha rolled the window down and let the night breeze refresh him. Mars talking to him about Fabert in Tante Marguerite. His precious contact knew the dubious methods employed by the D.C.R.I. man, and his taste for "Yankee code names". Mars couldn't have invented that piece of information. Only a spy or diplomat could have known something like that.

He thought hard. The flat, white idea was hovering close by. All it needed was a little push to release it.

Ménard.

Mars did not really appreciate Ménard, and yet he often had discussions with him. If his highly placed informer was a diplomat, perhaps he had given some hint to the young lieutenant. After all, he had recently graduated in politics, and was one of the few people in the B.C. who could argue with him on political topics.

The lieutenant's muffled voice came on the line after six rings.

"Yeah, who's this?"

"Stir yourself, Ménard, and quickly. For once we need your insights . . . Did Mars ever talk to you about his contacts in the ministries? A diplomat, someone from your university, a high-flying civil servant, somebody in the secret service?"

"Oh, it's you, boss . . ."

"Rouse yourself, it's important."

"Wait a moment while I think . . . I have to say that the big chief was never short of a story to tell. You know, I reckon he had a high opinion of me. Such a shame . . ."

"Ménard!"

"Yeah, O.K. I remember that Mars once talked about a good friend, from the same university as us. A diplomatic career, a high-flyer. The chief had never been so talkative. Actually, I even found it a bit odd . . ."

"His name?"

"Esterel, Esteran . . . Oh, wait: Estéban. Yes, that's it, Estéban."

"Do you have an address, a contact number?"

"No, I'd never heard of the guy before Mars started going on about him. The university old boys' network is huge, and . . ."

Sacha ended the call, switched on the ignition and drove to Mars' apartment.

He let himself in with the set of keys he had kept, went into the study and switched on the computer. Mars had obligingly revealed that the password was his wife's first name. Thanks for the paper trail, boss. But why all this nonsense? He found what he was looking for in the electronic address book, and wrote it all down.

He got back in the car and sped over to the 16th arrondissement. He parked on Avenue Marceau, gained access to the building. In the vestibule, he found an intercom with a list of names beside it. He pressed the buzzer. For a long while. Finally an exasperated man's voice cut him off. He gave his name and rank. The door opened.

"Fifth floor," crackled the intercom.

In pyjamas and a claret-coloured silk dressing gown, a man of about Mars' age was waiting on the landing. Dishevelled hair, a day's growth of grey stubble, and the puffy eyes of someone woken up in the middle of the night.

"Michael Estéban?"

"The same. Come in. Coffee?"

"Willingly."

A corridor lined with full bookshelves led them to a kitchen equally crammed with books. A good sign. Book lovers usually also had a yen for conversation. Estéban put on a family-sized coffee pot. Another excellent sign.

"Mars told me you would be coming some day or other."

"Where is he?"

"I've no idea. You'll have to ask me a more intelligent question."

"Does this amuse you?"

"All these dead bodies strewn along the way? And Mars taking his final bow? No, I don't like it any more than you do. But apparently he's left clues so that you and I could meet. And for us to try to see clearly."

"You were his star contact."

"You think so?"

"I'm listening."

"What would you like to know?"

"How you met him: that would be a good place to start."

Estéban told him of a friendship that had started at the Jeanson-de-Sailly College in Paris. And of how life separated the two young men. One joins the police force, the other chooses a diplomatic career. One day Arnaud Mars, by now a commissaire in the Finance Squad, runs into Michael Estéban, a diplomat in Africa. The diplomat suggests to the police officer that he come to join him in the Democratic Republic of Congo. The post of head of security for the embassy is up for grabs. Mars accepts.

"That was the beginning of a distinguished career in the diplomatic service. Following Africa, Arnaud spent some time in Mexico, then Scandinavia, Finland and Sweden, where he met Karen. After their marriage, he rejoined the police back in Paris. I was back with the Foreign Ministry on Quai d'Orsay. We met again."

"Was it you who told him about Fabert's methods?"

"Yes, I gave him details about the lieutenant-colonel's inimitable technique for taking on people. Fabert got Konata to work for him by first scaring the life out of him. Nothing like a fake attack to soften you up and make you malleable. Then Fabert appeared on the scene as his saviour. Unfortunately, the journalist fell for it. Of course, some ready money may have changed hands as well. Who knows?"

"Did you know Toussaint Kidjo?"

"Not personally."

"Meaning?"

"Arnaud told me that Lieutenant Kidjo was searching for information about the death of his friend Konata. I knew that journalist."

"When did you last see Konata?"

"At a reception organised by the Gratiens in Kinshasa. In the meantime I had learned that Fabert had taken him on board to steal Gratien's notebooks. Something that had little chance of succeeding, as we saw later on."

"So Toussaint Kidjo went to see Arnaud Mars to find out more about Konata's death?"

"That's right."

"How did Kidjo meet Mars?"

"Probably when Mars was working in Kinshasa."

"Why did he hide the fact that he knew Kidjo?"

"This may surprise you, but I know absolutely nothing about that. And I'd give a lot for someone to tell me where the hell Arnaud has got to, and if he and his family are safe."

"Was it Mars who had Gratien's notebooks?"

That seemed unlikely to Sacha: hadn't Antonia stated that her husband had recovered them?

"Not the originals, but a copy," Estéban confirmed.

This information hit Sacha like a blow to the solar plexus. He took a deep breath and he regained control.

"Who gave it to him?"

"Kidjo."

Sacha thought this over. *All Paris has got the hots for those notebooks.* Had Mars' intention been to finish off Candichard? Once and for all? Had he been completely hypocritical then, pretending to detest Sertys and his knight-in-shining-armour role?

"Was it him who leaked them to the press?"

"I suppose so, unless there's another copy doing the rounds."

"Why would he do that?"

"Arnaud didn't tell me everything. He thought it was less dangerous for me that way."

"Did you trust him?"

"Yes. Arnaud is a loyal sort. As far as friendship goes at least. He has always been honest with me, and if he lied, it was by omission."

And if he had disappeared, it was because he had no other choice?

"Will you keep me informed?"

"I beg your pardon?"

"About Mars. You'll tell me when you know anything?"

The picture of innocence. *The advantage is, they cancel each other out. I know two or three people who can get us out of this. You just have to know the score.* And you were the one talking about intelligent questions, Estéban? He stared hard at the diplomat for a second or two, shook his head and left without another word.

39

He reached his office around six. He called Ménard at home and ordered him to come in immediately.

He told him part of what he had found out that night. Estéban was indeed Mars' star contact. The diplomat knew that Fabert had manipulated Konata to get him to steal Gratien's notebooks. After the journalist's death, it was to Mars that Kidjo had turned to ask for help to uncover his best friend's killers. Kidjo had the notebooks. He had given a copy to Mars.

"Mars knew Kidjo? And he was the one who leaked the note-books? I can't get over it."

"Make sure you do, Ménard, and go through all your notes. You're our reporter, remember?"

"Don't worry, boss, I'll get on to it straight away."

"There must be a link between them somewhere. Bring all your stuff, and we can share the files out."

Ménard ran to get his paperwork, and flung it on Sacha's desk. The two men knuckled down to the task. At around eight, Ménard shouted "Goal!" triumphantly and punched the air.

"It's written here in black and white, boss! Calixte Kidjo, Toussaint's mother, was employed at the French Embassy in Kinshasa. She worked as a secretary at the consulate."

"And Mars was working at the embassy at the same time, is that it?"

"Exactly. Kidjo must have gone to the embassy, and his mother introduced him to Mars . . ."

"That makes sense."

Sacha felt like adding: but that doesn't explain why Mars would set fire to Vidal and probably eliminate Antonia. No doubt all that would be revealed in good time. For now he had to try to assimilate everything that had happened.

And part of me doesn't understand, or doesn't want to understand.

Gratien has had his moment. Times change. You're broad-shouldered enough to take my place one day. No false modesty with me, Sacha. I chose you: don't forget that.

It was late morning. A white sun shone high in the sky. He had abandoned everything to come here: it wasn't like him at all.

A jab, hook, kick to the shoulder. Hook, roundhouse kick, reverse foot thrust. Agility, power, speed. He was a picture of vigilance: his adversary's blows rained down on him.

She had arrived early for their meeting, and slipped into the gym to see what he was like in the ring. Facing a tough opponent, his sweaty body glistening under the neon lights, ripped muscles, his desire bursting to the surface, he was fighting as if his life depended on it. It was a miracle his partner was still standing. He took a step back to give himself room to unleash a jump kick. Unbeatable. Followed immediately by a jab, hook, jab, hook. He was going to win. His bigger, heavier opponent did not want it as much as he did. Knee strikes, jab, uppercut. And a shin rebounding from a shoulder. A second uppercut. His adversary staggered like a stunned animal being led to the slaughter. Lola was on the verge of praying for him. The trainer blew for the end of the round. The winner: Sacha Duguin.

Lola felt relieved. The trainer whistled with astonishment.

"You've been eating lion raised on amphetamines, my son!"

"Yeah, especially for someone who hasn't slept a wink all night," his partner gasped.

"Shame you're a cop, Sacha. If not, we could sign you up for illegal fights. We'd make a load of dough!"

The two sparring partners and the trainer exchanged a few friendly slaps. Sacha finally noticed Lola. He picked up a towel, sponged his streaming torso and his unshaven cheeks, then climbed out of the ring. Smiled his beguiling smile at her. But Lola detected something new in his eyes. The look of someone whose trust has been shattered. It wasn't hard to guess the reason behind the ferocity of his attacks: Arnaud Mars.

The only positive aspect: Sacha wouldn't say anything about her break-in. He was beyond that kind of detail now. They agreed to meet at the Marquis, the café on the corner. Despite the leaden sky,

Lola decided to sit out on the terrace, which took up most of the narrow pavement. The hurrying passers-by brushed against her chair. Absorbed in their own worlds, several of them only avoided a collision at the last moment. Gone was the gentle transalpine atmosphere of the Place du Marché-Sainte-Catherine: by definition moments of grace are rare and fleeting.

When Sacha arrived, apparently relaxed but still with that haunted look in his eyes, Lola immediately told him what she had discovered. Adeline's lies. The fact that Toussaint and the young woman knew Arnaud Mars, and that after Toussaint's death, Adeline regularly met the divisionnaire at an African restaurant in the Montorgueil neighbourhood. Sacha almost interrupted her, but the words got stuck in his throat. Instead, he rubbed a nervous hand across cheeks that were as rough as his state of mind. Lola paused to let him digest what he had heard so far. He motioned for her to continue. She added that Adeline was nowhere to be found, but that a search of her studio had revealed a paternity test Toussaint had asked for.

"He wanted to know who his father was."

She handed him the letter from *SearchDNA*. As she had hoped, he read it without commenting on how it might have come into her possession.

"It's from seven years ago," she said.

"The time when Toussaint lost his mother, is that it?"

"That's right. Adeline took care not to mention it five years ago."

"The test is positive."

"Jean Texier knows nothing about it."

"Really?"

"I called and went to see him yesterday evening. Impossible for Toussaint to take a sample of his saliva without him being aware of it."

"Texier could be lying. He wouldn't be the first . . ."

"No, Jean is distraught. You don't invent that kind of emotion."

"You could be right."

"Besides that, he says Calixte asked to speak alone with her son before she died. Toussaint loved Jean. Knowing him as I did, I'm sure he didn't want to make him suffer from Calixte's revelations."

"So she told him that Jean wasn't his father?"

"I think that's more than likely."

"And Toussaint verified it with this test. Unfortunately the document doesn't tell us who the father was."

"It seems that whoever he was, he didn't want it to get out. And Toussaint kept the secret."

A landslide behind his sombre eyes. Commandant Duguin was digesting an unpalatable truth.

"When you said Mars was in love with Africa, it was a euphemism, Sacha."

He was still thinking it over. Lola watched him in silence.

"Calixte Kidjo was a secretary at the French consulate in Kinshasa," he said.

"And Mars was head of security at the same embassy? At the same time."

"Exactly."

"So Mars had an affair with Calixte, just before she married Jean Texier. Now I come to think of it . . . there was something about their manner . . . a tiny something . . ."

Lola had an image of Toussaint telling a story. His way of laughing, hands folded across his stomach, mouth tight shut just before he let loose a joyous whoop, his shoulders shaking. Mars did the same. And their way of walking. Similar. An echo rather than a direct resemblance, it was true, but it was possible.

Arnaud Mars, Toussaint Kidjo's father.

Mars a few years before Scandinavia, a few years before Karen. Mars meets Calixte Kidjo. Was she already engaged to Jean Texier? Whatever the case, Arnaud and Calixte have an affair. He gets her pregnant. She hides her pregnancy from him, or perhaps life separates them before Calixte has time to realise the state she's in. Some time later, she marries Texier when she is already pregnant by Mars. And decides to keep the truth from her husband. That truth remains hidden until Calixte's final illness. On her death-bed, she confesses to her son that his biological father is definitely Mars.

The rest is easy to imagine: Toussaint contacts Mars, who agrees to take the paternity test. The result is positive. The two men go further than simply discovering their genetic link. They *recognise* each other. And adopt one another. Toussaint abandons his law studies to enter the police, following his real father. Drops the surname Texier in favour of his mother's. But they both agree to keep their relationship a secret. Toussaint doesn't want to cause any pain to Jean Texier, who has always been good to him, and brought him up.

"Only Adeline knew," Lola said.

"And possibly Karen."

"Did you know Mars' wife well?"

"I knew the whole family well."

He might have added: *At least I thought I did.* Lola could sense his resentment. Mars had left him and his colleagues in the dark. He had drip-fed them information. Carefully, steering them in exactly the direction he wanted.

"Lola, what you've just told me . . ."

"What about it?"

"It's what was missing."

"Meaning?"

"The motive. Now I know it's him . . ."

Now it was Lola's turn to be left speechless. Sacha explained how he had resuscitated Vidal's BlackBerry, and what he had discovered in its memory.

"Are you sure it's Mars' voice?"

"Absolutely sure. Just as I'm sure now that he was the one who leaked the notebooks to the media."

The disparate pieces were falling into place and creating a coherent picture. The ex-commissaire could imagine Toussaint's last years. Years of intense emotions. He discovers his real father is Arnaud Mars. He decides to settle in France, joins the force, meets Adeline. Just after learning about the murder of his best friend, he receives a message in the post from Norbert Konata, which includes a key to an airport left-luggage locker. He goes to his friend's funeral in Africa, starts an unsuccessful inquiry there, and discovers what the locker contains.

"It was Richard Gratien's secret notebooks that he found in that locker in Kinshasa, wasn't it, Sacha?"

"Yes, I came to the same conclusion."

Back in France and in possession of the notebooks, he has no idea what to make of or what to do with them, except that they must be behind his friend's death. Toussaint searches for the truth. He realises that the only person connecting his lives in Africa and France is his childhood friend Isis Renta, the one-time great love of Norbert's life. The air hostess was mysteriously absent from the burial. Toussaint meets up with her in Paris. She admits she posted the letter. He forces her to tell him what she saw. Norbert pursued by the militiamen, with just enough time to give her the key and a code name before he dies in a desperate chase. Toussaint no longer believes his friend was killed because of his political investigations in his native country. The reason for his death lies elsewhere. It's somehow related to the code name he has to decipher: *Oregon*.

"Naturally, Toussaint goes to see Mars," Sacha said. "Because he trusts him. And because Mars knows not only Africa but the diplomatic and intelligence worlds."

"So Mars discovers who Oregon is."

"Yes, he identifies Olivier Fabert. Who is obsessed with recovering Gratien's black books. Someone for whom all means are valid. Mars understands that Fabert manipulated Konata into stealing the notebooks. And then logically enough Gratien has Konata killed to try to get them back."

They sat lost in their own thoughts for a long while. Sacha had not touched his coffee.

"The B.C. is not going to come out of this unscathed."

"That's for sure."

"If it's any consolation, you're not the only one he fooled. He took his time to avenge his son's death."

"Yes, and he chose each of us like little pawns for his game. Carefully, methodically."

"Don't forget he had a family to protect. If he had attacked Gratien head on . . ."

"Gratien would have gone for Karen and Aurélie. That's true, but . . ."

"But?"

"So many deaths, Lola. And the way they were killed. *An eye for an eye, a tooth for a tooth.*"

"He wanted Gratien to suffer what he had suffered. The loss of a loved one. The loss of a son. An only son whom he had found late on, but had learned to love. Toussaint was very appealing."

"Vidal was only guilty of being Gratien's assistant. If you set about getting rid of all the intermediaries in the international arms trade, you'd never finish . . . especially doing it that way. Disgusting. Inhuman."

Without realising it, Sacha was clenching his fists. Lola knew it would take session after session of Thai boxing to cleanse Mars and his dirty tricks out of his system. If it were ever possible.

"Vidal was Gratien's substitute son, the being he apparently loved most in the world. *But if the person dies, then thou shalt give life for life, tooth for tooth, hand for hand, foot for foot, burning for burning, wound for wound, stripe for stripe.* You yourself just said that the law of retaliation is alive and kicking."

"Mars didn't stop there. He killed Antonia. A bullet between the eyes. He made her feel what death tasted like, and then executed her. She was going to be put on trial . . ."

What if he hadn't stopped at Antonia? Lola had learned of the regular meetings between Adeline and Mars after Toussaint's death, and a nauseous idea began to take shape in her mind. She read in Sacha's eyes that he had just reached the same conclusion.

"That homeless guy spoke about a couple attacking Bangolé," she said. "And if it wasn't Antonia and Honoré . . ."

"Antonia had her own way of concealing the truth. But in fact she never lied to me. Gratien had known where Bangolé was hiding for years. He could easily have got rid of him. At any time. Long before you caught up with him at any rate."

For Mars it was a question of timing.

Lola had just put her finger on a detail he had not noticed before. Bangolé must have known that Toussaint was Mars' son. He was terrified of Gratien. But he was wrong: he wasn't afraid of the right person. Adeline must have approached him without arousing his suspicions. Bangolé had no reason to fear a high-ranking policeman and a young woman.

"Sacha?"

"Yes?"

"I reckon they killed Bangolé because they wanted at all odds to avoid the police or Gratien finding out that Toussaint was Mars' son. And that therefore Mars might want to avenge his death."

"I agree. And I suppose they killed him in that horrible way to deflect suspicion onto Antonia and Honoré."

"And injecting an anaesthetic into Bangolé's neck was a good way to make us think there was a connection to the other murders. Toussaint had been abducted by Antonia and Honoré employing the same tactic. Then Mars copied them with Vidal. The similarity was bound to disturb Gratien, and lead him to make a mistake. It was a master stroke to confuse the police in their investigation."

Lola could see it all clearly now. Mars had plotted his revenge for years, but in recent months his careful planning had accelerated. One false move and everything would have come to naught.

He was using Fabert to manipulate Sacha. And he had used her by inviting her to join the investigation, and by apparently taking her into his confidence. *If you like, you can have a ringside seat.* A magnificent operation, judged to the millimetre. Even Gratien had been fooled. Mars did everything he could to encourage him to come out of his hole. He needed Gratien to order Antonia to kill Fabert. *I've contacted some well-placed friends. They'll find the right channels to make Gratien see Fabert as Vidal's killer.* And Mars' strategy had worked to perfection. *He's hesitating, making mistakes. Otherwise, why send his wife to trap Sacha? He's thrashing about like a drowning man.*

"Mars chose us to pursue Antonia."

"He wanted me to arrest her. And to keep off Honoré, her faithful bodyguard."

"So that he could kill Antonia without problems after her arrest."

"This goes far beyond any law of retaliation, Lola. His main goal was to take the only two people Gratien loved from him. And to leave him alive so that he would be destroyed by pain. Mission accomplished: Gratien is no more than a human wreck."

Lola could fully understand what Sacha concluded from this. Mars had insisted on having Sacha in his team. There were hundreds of young police officers who dreamed of being part of the B.C. Mars must have spun him a line. Explained that he had chosen him for his particular talents. Stubbornness. Leadership qualities. Self-control. All things he did possess. But he wasn't the only one. Mars' reasons for choosing his new recruit were of a different order.

He was well aware of Sacha's driving ambition. It was a good lever to make someone strive their utmost.

He knew Sacha had been involved with Ingrid, a striptease artist in a Pigalle nightclub. This was a black mark in the career of a policeman, one that offered a weapon for anyone who knew how to use it. Mars had set Fabert against Sacha. He had stirred up their animosity so that Sacha would be even more determined. And so that the man from the D.C.R.I. would lose control, make mistakes, reveal himself to Gratien. Fabert had tried to get his revenge on Sacha by having Ingrid arrested. He had broken cover too soon and in too much of a rush.

Mars' strategy. A tight-rope walker defying death a hundred metres above the void. Nobody had escaped unharmed. Not even Candichard, whom Mars must have condemned because he profited from the system that had killed his son. By leaking the notebooks to the media and the judges, Mars had made Candichard lose face. He had stripped him of his last few shreds of honour.

"Those notebooks could give us more trouble yet. Candichard has been through the shredder, but there are more names of prominent people who profited from kickbacks in arms sales. Mars could blow the whole thing sky-high."

"Do you know something? I couldn't give a damn."

Sadness and rancour flickered beneath the surface of Sacha's skin, making his appearance even more disturbing. Mars had also seen how he controlled himself. And last but not least, he had chosen Sacha for his physique. *Antonia, the weak link.* Mars had repeated that time and again. It was his obsession. And a justified one. Antonia had obeyed her husband. She owed him an almost robotic loyalty after all those years when her *saviour* had patiently moulded her to become such a formidable weapon. But Antonia had really felt something for Sacha.

Mars had even foreseen that.

The ideal candidate.

Right now, thought Lola, the ideal candidate is weighing up all the implications of what he has just learned after matching his information with mine. He'll have a long grieving process to go through. And nobody can do it for him.

"I'm sorry, Sacha. Truly sorry."

"I know, Lola."

"If it's any consolation, I think anybody would have been taken in. Mars knew how to appeal to our emotions. We didn't stand a chance. And he had years to perfect his revenge. Sacha?"

"Yes."

"A penny for your thoughts."

"I was thinking of a precise detail. Of the moment I asked Luce Chéreau of the Finance Squad to use every trick in the book to put pressure on a public notary. It was thanks to her that I was able to get Antonia to talk. And Mars had counted on that."

"On your talent for getting the rules bent. It's a real talent, you know."

"I always asked myself why he chose me rather than Carle. Now I know."

She could have found other consoling phrases. She could have. But beneath the lowering clouds and so close to passers-by wrapped in their everyday indifference, she was only too aware of how alone he was, of how powerless she was to offer him any real comfort. Of course you learn from your mistakes. But what do you learn from betrayal?

"And the *funniest* thing about all this, Lola . . ."

"What's that?"

She studied his strained silhouette. He was staring at the façade of the boxing club. She saw the trainer emerge. He waved to Sacha, but her companion appeared not to notice, did not react in any way.

"The funniest thing is that he left me clues."

"What were they?"

"The receipt for a statuette he bought from Doris Nungesser, the S.I.M. card from Vidal's mobile in a box of C.D.s, the name of the diplomat contact he had casually mentioned to Ménard . . ."

"Why would he do that?"

"Probably so that I wouldn't die ignorant."

He turned towards her. His eyes were dry, but were spilling over with hatred. Lola saw herself back in Mars' office. She was talking to him about Cocteau. About how afraid she had been at going over to the far side, at being swallowed by a wave of hatred. So you believe in "the far side", he had commented. He was playing the saint, and lying to perfection.

For once, Lola Jost couldn't find anything useful to say.

40

"I've got a new word ending in '-ion' for you, Ingrid. It's very fashionable and very ugly. *Instrumentalisation*."

"You're right, it's really ugly, Lola."

"And even more so when it happens to us."

An anvil of silence hung over Belles. Beneath this looming weight, Maxime served Barthélemy a coffee with the look of someone who had discovered a new kind of perversion. Barthélemy accepted the cup as if he doubted he would be able to digest it. Sigmund insisted on being stroked by Ingrid. And Ingrid shed a few invisible tears on behalf of the most present absent friend there could be, Commandant Sacha Duguin.

Lola had just told her friends what she knew. Someone had to be the bearer of the bad news. She herself felt as though she had the energy of a marshmallow put through a blender. Five years of questions. Five years of sadness, guilt, regrets. And finally, the truth. The whole, bitter, ugly truth.

She asked Maxime to fill their glasses. She wanted to propose a toast. Nobody dared contradict her. They drank to the memory of Toussaint Kidjo. Lola gave a short speech in his honour, and succeeded in controlling her voice.

That was the moment a ghost chose to reappear. English raincoat over a tweed jacket and corduroy trousers. The unchanging chic of the best psychoanalyst of Faubourg Saint-Denis. Antoine Léger as he lived and breathed. Beaming face, deep tan, his hair bleached by a tropical sun. Sigmund rubbed himself against his master's legs.

"Good afternoon, friends. I see I've arrived in time for the aperitif."

When he saw their downcast faces, he made a rapid re-adjustment.

"Or perhaps I've arrived too late. What's going on?"

Too exhausted to begin all over again, Lola confided the task to Barthélemy, while the small group sat down to the day's menu and the house wine. Even though for years he had been constantly dealing with his contemporaries' most outlandish phantoms, Antoine was taken aback by what he heard. This story of vengeance touched him to the quick, and he asked a lot of questions.

In order to lighten the atmosphere, when they reached the coffee he wanted to know if Sigmund had behaved himself.

"Like an angel," replied Ingrid. "And he was very virtual, believe me."

"Very *virtuous*, do you mean?"

"Yes, Sigmund was very virtuous. That's what I mean."

"Why?"

"Well, he almost . . ."

Despite her tiredness, Lola aimed a kick at Ingrid's shin, and connected. She had to be stopped before she launched into a fateful list along the lines of:

"Your dog almost became an alcoholic, almost went under the wheels of a metro train, became a happy-clappy, bit a haggard old crone ill met by moonlight, lost his waterproofing in a deluge, died of hunger, got arrested for breaking and entering, had an acute nervous breakdown . . ."

But Ingrid would not be thrown off course, and a second well-aimed kick could not deter her.

"As I was saying, Sigmund almost . . . talked."

"What!" exclaimed Antoine, Barthélemy, Maxime and Lola in a barbershop harmony.

"Yes, I saw it. Sigmund was dying to express his thoughts, to help us reflect. And I have a question."

"*Woof?*"

"Do I.Q. tests exist for dogs? I'm sure Sigmund is exceptional."

"Do I.Q. tests exist for naked dancers?" Lola asked. "If they don't, let's invent one right now. I know a good guinea pig . . ."

Ingrid gulped down her coffee and stood up.

"I was only joking, Ingrid . . ."

"Don't worry, Lola, I'm not angry," her American friend said with her disarming smile. "I love it when you make fun of me, but there's someone I have to meet."

With that she strode out of Belles. Noticing that Lola was concerned at her mysterious departure, Barthélemy offered a round of liqueurs that she was the only one to accept.

"If it's Commandant Duguin she's looking for, good luck to her."

"I have to say that he's been tremendous," Lola said, pointing to the newspaper. "That kid has class."

The headlines in the *Métro* were all about the Mars affair. A senior police officer suspected of triple murder. A sordid story of revenge skilfully masterminded. The journalist spoke of a "huge scandal we still haven't got to the bottom of", and he was right. For a while, Lola had wondered if her ex-colleagues, led by Sacha, would stifle or at least minimise the affair. But no, it was exploding in the face of the public in all its grim horror. And was growing bigger and bigger because Mars and family were nowhere to be found. Not to mention Adeline Ernaux.

"But there's one detail the public still doesn't know about," Barthélemy muttered for Lola's benefit.

"I'm listening, my lad."

"People are whispering at Headquarters that Mars helped a woman escape. False papers and the whole works. She's wanted for murder. Shooting the paedophile who killed her son."

"There's a word that comes to mind. I can't help it."

"What's that, Lola?"

"Solidarity."

"Don't tell me you approve, boss."

"Of course not. But I understand. Mars is a whole lot of things, but he's not crazy."

"O.K., alright, solidarity if you like. But misplaced solidarity. We're cops, for God's sake."

For some of us it's more like: *we were cops*, thought Lola. And the club is getting bigger all the time.

Ingrid asked to speak to Lieutenant Ménard. It wasn't long before he appeared, grinning madly.

"Come and have a coffee, Diesel. You'd better not refuse, or I'll plant some crack in your dressing room. I know how it's done."

"Very funny. Where shall we go?"

They sat out on a café terrace on Boulevard Saint-Michel. In radiant sunshine.

"Where is Sacha?" she asked straight out.

"He doesn't deserve you. You know that, don't you?"

"That's not what I'm talking about."

"You mean it's finished between the two of you?"

"Yes."

"Well and truly?"

"I'm just worried how he is."

"Hallelujah! There is hope then. The beautiful Ingrid has come to her senses. By the way, my first name is Sébastien."

"I can't reach Sacha on the phone."

"Nobody at Headquarters knows where he is. Nor do I. He's taken unpaid leave. If you ask me, that's a strategic error. Carle hasn't been wasting time. She acted like a general and got her job back. It's as if she has speed-read the whole of *The Art of War*."

"No-one knows anything? But you're cops, aren't you?"

"Nobody, not even Clémenti. Although he's an ace."

"How was Sacha when you last saw him?"

"Bad, obviously. He needs time to swallow the pill. It's such a shame, because he's a good cop."

A gaggle of school kids was strolling along the pavement. One of them came up and asked Ingrid if she was Gabriella Tiger. He'd seen the video clip on the net. It was wicked. He wanted her autograph.

"Get going," said Ménard, flashing his police credential.

The boy shrugged and went off with his friends. Ingrid put on her dark glasses.

"The whole world knows you strip nude to earn a living, but that doesn't bother me . . ."

"It's not just to earn my living. *I don't strip nude*, as you call it. I dance."

"I didn't mean to offend you. I don't care. I like you from top to toe. I worship all your faults, even the ones I don't know about yet. Are you free for dinner tonight?"

"I'm free, but I intend to dine alone."

"How about tomorrow?"

"The same."

"And in six months?"

"Same thing."

"I'm patient. And I still love your accent."

She shook her head in despair and turned towards the Seine. She realised for the first time that the police headquarters building opposite looked like a cardboard castle.

"Very patient," Ménard stressed. "And I toured your beautiful big country in the footsteps of de Tocqueville. That must win me some points, doesn't it?"

Ingrid searched for a reply that would calm his libido without offending him. She needed his inside information. The lieutenant was curiosity personified: it was hard to believe him when he claimed not to know where his boss was.

She felt him put his hand on hers. This fan of de Tocqueville was very sure of himself. She gave him a hard look, ready to give him a blunt reply. She heard the sound of a motorbike, so loud she was going to have to shout to put Ménard in his place. He was smiling, his left hand cupping Ingrid's, the right one on his tomato juice. He raised the glass to his lips, inviting her to toast. To what, to his brazen cheek? What a jerk!

A detonation. Ménard flew from his chair. The tomato juice flew from his glass. Blood spouting from Ménard's skull. She screamed. Other throats screamed.

The passenger on the motorbike. His gun pointing at her. She threw herself to the ground. Shards of glass everywhere.

Nose to nose with Sébastien. His face covered in blood. His empty eyes. Another detonation. The clients on the terrace running for their lives. Chairs and tables soaring through the air. People shrieking.

She plunged inside the café, collided with a bewildered waiter, tray in hand, the only one standing among the flock of humans sprawled on the floor. The café had another entrance. She came out onto the quay by the Seine. Her only hope: to run through the traffic coming the other way. Perhaps that would make the motorbike rider hesitate.

She ran as fast as she could. Another detonation. A second-hand bookseller clutched his bleeding shoulder, collapsed onto his stall. Ingrid looked back: the motorbike was zigzagging through the cars.

The rider. He hadn't hesitated.

She ran even faster. All she had to do was to punch a hole in the world, and she would emerge into a landscape of peace. She ran and ran. Teeth clenched. All she had to do was to want it enough. To want to see his face again. One day. *Sacha.*

The motorbike was chasing her along the pavement. The roar of its engine grew louder. Notre Dame growing larger in front of her. The sky stained red from her bloodshot eyes. She ran.

The biker overtook her, braked, blocked her path.

Why have you abandoned me? No, I won't end with a reproach. It's your radiant face that I'll take with me, Sacha.

On the Quai de Montebello, Ingrid came to a halt and faced her two pursuers. The armed passenger raised the visor of his helmet, then raised his weapon.

"This is for Antonia Gratien, you bitch!"

He fired.

The train pulls into the station. Each of my travelling companions picks up a bundle, a battered suitcase. The stern-looking mother with the ritually scarred face tells her children to hurry up. Before leaving the carriage, the eldest of her girls smiles at me behind her mother's back. I smile in return, recover my bag, leave the train.

The platform baking under the white sun. The sky a blue cruelty. Another station, another town. The impatience of the first days has evaporated, I've adapted to this country's rhythm. Not many days ago, tons of water pummelled the red earth here and threatened to wipe out the hills. That liquid anger has been absorbed. The world is as fresh as the smile of that eldest girl.

Three young kids are lined up at the exit barrier. They stare at the new arrivals, but no-one seems to interest them. They're just watching the trains go by. Out in the street, my shoes immediately dusty, a pause at the store for my water supplies. The owner tells me how to get to the market. Women are heading for the square, carrying on their heads a basket or bowl full of fruit, vegetables, bars of soap. Babies are swaying on their backs. Music is pouring out of every house, a different tune from each one. The rhythms mingle with the scooter horns, the children's cries.

You explained to me there was no such thing as a cacophony in certain places.

The crowd grows denser. I've become accustomed to the colours and smells. I've breathed in a thousand places, heard so many voices, thrown your name into the air like a toss of the dice.

People no longer move away from me, my face has merged into their world. I think you'd be proud if you could see me.

You're broad-shouldered enough to take my place . . .

A band playing on a small platform. Musicians, a woman in spotless African robe and turban singing in a beautiful low voice. I don't understand the words of the song of course, but I suspect they're full of melancholy. The singer knows all about deceit and lies.

I chose you . . .

A shady corner. I wait.

The morning goes by, the market grows and grows. I occasionally leave my post, criss-cross the market from one side to the other. I plough my way through, a man among men. Sweat, voices, silence, nothing. Nobody is bothered about me being there, and I don't bother anyone.

There comes a time in one's life when one doesn't want to waste what there is left on people we don't get on with.

The singer, the market sellers, the passers-by all have their lives in front of them. It's only later, much later . . .

Much later, a silhouette in the market. A blonde presence. Graceful. Light-coloured dress. My heartbeat quickens. Then returns to normal. I recognise this woman who has no reason to fear me because she doesn't know me. I make sure I don't lose sight of her. She's doing her shopping, so she must live here. And you can guess what's going on, can't you?

Yes, my journey is at an end.

She escapes with astonishing ease. But how is all this possible if she had no idea when he was getting out?

Let her take her time. Mine is endless.

I think somebody helped her. At the last moment, and doubtless partly against her will.

My time is only worth the price of a watermelon, a small blood orange, a plantain. It has become elastic, it could fit inside my pocket, and that's fine. When the woman finishes her purchases, I follow her. We walk for a long while at a steady pace. She already knows the landmarks, has no need to slow up in familiar streets. She knows where she's headed. She is going back to you and yours.

The house.

Perched on top of a hill. Similar to how I had imagined it. It has high light-coloured walls, and the only tin roof in the neighbourhood that isn't rusty. The woman speeds up, quickens her pace in order to climb the incline as quickly as possible, get out of the sun that must be melting her. Her dress like a white flame in the light-soaked air.

It happens once or twice in a cop's lifetime. One feels an irresistible empathy for a murderer.

The roadside, a good place to wait for night. I'm sure you'd approve my choice. We two have a meeting. You don't know it, you think an escape is always possible, that fleeing is as simple as a straight line. Your lack of knowledge doesn't bother me. It doesn't please me either: I'm indifferent to it.

Some ties never die.

If I'm here, it's because of your ravaged face.

The crickets have been scratching the skin of the night for so long I didn't hear your door opening. But, accustomed to the darkness, my eyes do not miss your silhouette at the top of the hill. Moonbeams and a damp mist envelop you, offering false protection. You start down towards the town.

Cutting a swathe through the crickets' song.

You walk towards me, my leader, my liar.

You are wrong.

THE END

TRANSLATOR'S ACKNOWLEDGEMENTS

The translator gratefully acknowledges help from the author
and Amanda Hopkinson.

DOMINIQUE SYLVAIN worked as a journalist in Paris before relocating to Asia, where she lived for spells in Japan and Singapore. She is the author of a distinguished body of crime fiction. She lives again in Paris, where she writes full-time. *Dirty War* was announced as the best crime novel of 2011 by *Lire* magazine.

NICK CAISTOR has translated more than forty books from Spanish, Portuguese and French, including novels by Paulo Coelho and Eduardo Mendoza. He has thrice been awarded the Premio Valle-Inclán for translation from the Spanish.

Dominique Sylvain

THE DARK ANGEL

Translated from the French by Nick Caistor

Lola: A cantankerous ex-policewoman with two great loves: jigsaw puzzles and vin rouge.

Ingrid: An American in Paris, with a rather exotic after-hours alter ego.

They have only one thing in common: Maxime. He has endless charm, a beautiful restaurant – and a recently murdered neighbour. There are plenty of skeletons in his closet, and he's the prime suspect. If he's staying out of jail, it's all down to the most unlikely detective duo.

But a cell might just be the safest place for him. The victim's jilted lover is on the loose, an avenging angel with a dark past of his own . . .

MACLEHOSE PRESS

www.maclehosepress.com

Subscribe to our newsletter

Dominique Sylvain

SHADOWS AND SUN

Translated from the French by Nick Caistor

Lola Jost is busy fending off boredom with a jigsaw puzzle when she hears the news. Arnaud Mars – a disgraced police divisionnaire on the run after a seismic defence contracts scandal – has been found dead in Abidjan in the Ivory Coast. The gun that killed him belongs to Commandant Sacha Duguin, a former colleague of Lola's.

Convinced of Duguin's innocence, Lola throws off her torpor. Together with her occasional partner in crime fighting Ingrid Diesel, she embarks on a quest to clear her old friend's name.

Faced by a shadowy adversary determined to keep its past crimes under wraps, Lola and Ingrid must travel as far as Abidjan and Hong Kong to uncover the truth behind their most dangerous case to date.

MACLEHOSE PRESS

www.maclehosepress.com

Subscribe to our newsletter